A NEW LIGHT

A NEW LIGHT
THE ASTRAL WANDERER™ BOOK ONE

D'ARTAGNAN REY

MICHAEL ANDERLE

DISRUPTIVE IMAGINATION®

This book is a work of fiction. All of the characters, organizations, and events portrayed in this novel are either products of the author's imagination or are used fictitiously. Sometimes both.

Copyright © 2021 LMBPN Publishing
Cover copyright © LMBPN Publishing

LMBPN Publishing supports the right to free expression and the value of copyright. The purpose of copyright is to encourage writers and artists to produce the creative works that enrich our culture.

The distribution of this book without permission is a theft of the author's intellectual property. If you would like permission to use material from the book (other than for review purposes), please contact support@lmbpn.com. Thank you for your support of the author's rights.

LMBPN Publishing
PMB 196, 2540 South Maryland Pkwy
Las Vegas, NV 89109

Version 1.01, September 2021
eBook ISBN: 978-1-64971-645-3
Print ISBN: 978-1-64971-646-0

THE A NEW LIGHT TEAM

Thanks to our Beta Team:
Rachel Beckford, James Caplan, John Ashmore, Mary Morris, Kelly O'Donnell

Thanks to our JIT Team:
Dave Hicks
Dorothy Lloyd
Wendy Bonell
Deb Mader
Diane L. Smith
Jeff Goode
Angel LaVey
Kelly O'Donnell
Peter Manis

If we've missed anyone, please let us know!

Editor
SkyHunter Editing Team

PROLOGUE

"Devol!" Lilli Alouest called and her white dress flowed behind her as she hurried down the carved stone steps two at a time. "Devol, what did I say about running off?"

She reached the well-maintained path of stones and dirt that ran through Emerald Forest—the wooded area outside the kingdom of Monleans—from one side to the other.

The mother's gaze darted warily from left to right and she dragged in a nervous breath as she reminded herself of the old wives' tale. *As long as you stay along the path, you are safe.*

The Emerald Forest was not home to an abundance of carnivorous creatures, but it was not unusual to encounter animals there now and then, and some of those could be quite fearsome.

"Mother, come and have a look at this!" Her head jerked to the right as a boy's voice carried between the limbs and through the brush to her ears. "I've found an oasis."

She blew a sharp breath of relief and a little of her

tension released. "Those aren't found in a forest, Devol," she stated and allowed herself a small giggle, her humor somewhat restored by the fact that she could at least hear her son.

Curious as to what held his attention so completely that he didn't run to her as he usually did, she followed the direction of his voice and stepped off the path. Ignoring her nervousness, she pushed through the shimmering green leaves that gave the forest its name and into its depths. Finally, she found him walking around a large pond while he stared at his reflection in the glittering waters.

"You think this is on the map?" he asked, retrieved a scroll, and opened it. "We could be the first to mark it." His eyes narrowed before he flipped it right-side up.

"I'm fairly sure this is Franco's Pond, Devol," his mother answered and rested a hand on his shoulder. "You know, one of the original explorers of the forest?"

The young boy's gaze darted around the map until he tapped the location with a finger and sighed. "Yeah, I see." He rolled the scroll again and placed it in his back pocket. With a disappointed expression, he looked around at the trees surrounding the pond. "I suppose it is too close to the road for it to be undiscovered."

"I'm not sure there are many places here that haven't been explored by now," she agreed as she glanced at three azure-colored birds that soared skyward. "This forest has stood alongside the city since its founding. Many explorers and hunters have come through here for over a thousand years."

Devol sighed, removed his jacket, and dropped it

beside him as he crossed his legs and sat beside the water. "That's true," he said as he eased his arms back and leaned on his hands. "Guess I'll have to wait a little longer before I can think about finding anything new, huh?"

"Well," Lilli responded, "this is new to you, isn't it?" She laughed, hoping to comfort him with a fresh way to look at the experience. "You did not know some of the details I told you so in a way, you *are* making discoveries."

He shrugged and grinned wistfully as he stretched on his back on the forest floor with his hands behind his head. "You are technically right, Mother. But you know what I am talking about, don't you?"

"Of course I do," she replied and moved a small rock out of the way with her foot before she lowered herself to sit beside him. "And that day will come for you, Devol. I know you wish for adventure and despite my requests to your father for him to not hurry your training along so much, you will be more than ready when you apply for the guards."

The boy's smile widened. "I'm already better at swordplay than almost any recruit. I'll probably rank highly during the entrance trials and get to skip the beginner training and start with more advanced swordsmanship." He looked at his mother. "Father says the survey team could always use more members. I think I may join them when the time comes."

His mother looked at him with a smile to hide the trace of sadness stirred by the thought of him leaving. "If that is your choice. But that is a couple of years away." She stroked his auburn hair as she focused on their reflections in the water. "And until then, try to enjoy yourself as much as you can, all right?"

"Of course, Mother." Devol closed his eyes. "But you don't need to be anxious about anything. Your son will be one of the best swordsmen in the kingdom. You shouldn't worry about anything bad happening as long as—"

He was interrupted by the panicked cries of birds and deer behind them. His mother looked over her shoulder and he casually did the same. Animals fled in various directions as something approached them. "What is that?" he asked as a large, dark shape slunk forward.

Lilli turned pale. "Devol, we need to go," she ordered, scrambled to her feet, and yanked the boy up. "Now!"

The shadow launched forward with a ferocious howl and covered an unbelievable distance in one stride. It landed several yards from them and they gaped in horror at a large wolf with deep black fur and large fangs. The beast's gaze seemed to burrow into theirs with a blank, feral white stare.

"A dire wolf?" Devol gasped and reached for the short sword on his belt. "In the Emerald Forest?"

"Devol!" Lilli whispered, her tone quiet but urgent. "Get behind me."

By the time the boy glanced at her, she had already drawn his sword. The beast snarled and snapped its teeth together ravenously before it growled and lunged at him. She ran between it and her son and held a hand up.

"Shield!" She shouted the cantrip command and a yellow light sparked from her hand, flared into purple light directly ahead of her, and created the shape of a circular shield made of Mana, the magical energy of the realm. The dire wolf powered into it and hurled her back into her son, and both fell awkwardly.

She pushed quickly to her feet and pointed at the wolf. "Missile!" Three orbs of yellow light streaked away from her and all curved around the wolf. The animal began to run back to evade the attack before it darted quickly to the side. Two of the magical projectiles careened into the base of trees and left large indentations.

The beast skidded to a halt, turned to face the last missile, and ducked quickly as the orb sailed overhead and into the pond where it erupted. Water sprayed in a vertical column, reached an impressive height, and rained on the mother, son, and wolf.

"It is fast," she noted and prepared another spell. "*And intelligent.*"

A vicious snarl preceded a loud, ear-piercing howl. The humans covered their ears involuntarily to shield them against the painful noise. The wolf surged toward the mother, whose eyes widened as it attacked.

The onslaught flung her on the forest floor with a painful thud as her attacker uttered another cry, this one of surprise. She looked hastily at her son, who scrambled quickly to his feet and held his blade up, which was now smeared with a splash of blood. She promptly checked him for wounds but found none. The wolf, however, had a long gash along its left side.

"It's all right, Mother," he assured her, and although he did look slightly rattled, he wore a confident smirk. "What use is all that boasting if I cannot back it up?"

Lilli knew his confidence was misplaced. The wolf had been feral and hungry before and his strike had now made it angry as well. Dire wolves were known for their ferocity. Even if they now managed to escape, it would pursue them like the relentless hunter it was until it was able to tear them apart.

As it took a few steps closer to the boy, Devol raised his blade to defend himself. Lilli stood hastily and held a hand out. "Flash!"

A bright sphere of white light formed in her hand before it exploded and covered the area around them in a blinding light. The beast snarled as Devol shielded his eyes. She ran to him, caught his arm, and dragged him away.

They sprinted through the dense growth and onto the path and quickly ascended the stone steps that led to the edge of the greenery. She knew they wouldn't make it before the dire wolf caught up, however, and her mind raced. They would need to find the forest rangers to help them fell the beast.

Her heart sank when she realized they wouldn't have the chance for even that. Massive paws thudded on the forest floor behind them. Lilli looked over her shoulder and gasped.

The animal was already in pursuit. Its eyes still blinked rapidly, likely from the blaze of light, and it must have followed them using smell and sound. It was only a short distance away from them now, and from the jump she had seen it make earlier, it was an easy distance to cover.

She released her son and shoved him forward into a run as she spun and shouted the incantation to summon another shield. Before it could fully form, the wolf swiped a large, clawed paw at her. The incomplete shield protected her from the attack but was destroyed and released a small blast of Magic that knocked her off her feet but barely disturbed the beast's fur.

"Mother!" Devol shouted and raced back as the wolf attempted a killing strike. He vaulted high and swung his sword, to slice cleanly into the dire wolf's face and blind one of its eyes.

It uttered another angry, pained howl and lashed wildly at her with its claws. The boy attempted to pull his mother away but a warning from her made him turn and he attempted to parry or block the uncoordinated strikes from his adversary.

His short sword was eventually knocked out of his hands, and it spun blade over hilt, deep into the forest. The next attack hurled him away and lacerated his chest. Unable to slow his momentum, he collided painfully with a tree.

"Devol!" Lilli shrieked as the wolf regained at least some of its senses. Its front paws thumped into the dirt and it hovered over her. One eye stared relentlessly at her while the other dripped blood from its wound.

The boy forced himself up when he realized their attacker was about to kill his mother. He felt a fear he never had before—that he was about to see the death of a loved one. Desperate, he ran forward and extended his hand with no plan of what to do. He might have been a Magi like his mother and father, but he was a swordsman and not particularly gifted in cantrips like she was. His blade was now lost in the forest and he had no time to search for it. He did not know what he would do, only that he would not let her die.

The dire wolf turned toward him and opened its jaws

to bare its fangs. Saliva dripped to the dirt in anticipation of a kill. Lilli's cry registered vaguely but he could not hear the words. Instead, he lunged forward to attack the beast with whatever he had left.

As the animal left his mother and turned to meet his feeble assault, another blinding flash gave both adversaries pause. Was it his mother's cantrip again? He could see, even with the bright light, and frowned when he realized it had come from his hand. Something solid settled in his palm—the hilt of a weapon, as impossible as it seemed—and he grasped it instinctively in both hands.

Without looking to see what he held, he arced it to deliver as powerful a blow as he could. The beast was in the middle of its lunge and unable to break away. Devol slid along the dirt, breathing heavily, and grimaced when he felt something warm along his neck, hands, and face. Blood? He felt no pain, though, so he checked himself quickly and looked at his hand. It was indeed blood, but it appeared to not be his.

The dire wolf sprawled in a crumpled heap a few yards away, the front half of its body cut in half. His eyes widened as he checked his other hand, which still clutched the weapon that had appeared so suddenly.

Not unsurprisingly, it proved to be a long, ornate sword, but he could not discern the details as it glowed far too brightly. This was no ordinary blade, he could tell that much, but the way it looked, encased in the celestial light, he couldn't make out the finer features. Still, it felt right in his hand and although it seemed strange, it filled him with a sense of warmth and comfort.

Devol snapped to his senses and glanced at his mother

to check on her. He wondered if he wore a similar shocked expression as she did when she looked at the blade and then at him. Something appeared in her eyes—a similar look of concern bordering on sorrow to the one she'd had when he had discussed his future.

She stood with a grimace, walked closer, and hugged him before she drew back and placed her hands on his shoulders. "Thank you, Devol," she said and looked at the blade. "We will…need to talk to your father about what is to come."

CHAPTER ONE

"Hey, mister, can I have seconds?" a boy shouted above the loud chatter of the Hearthfire Inn. It was barely morning, but many men and women crowded the tables and ate their fill at the start of their early day.

"Aye, boy," the innkeeper nodded, took the empty plate with large, plump hands, and stroked his beard to the side. "As long as you got the cobalt for it, of course." The child offered a bright smile, slid his hand to his belt and into his purse, and withdrew a small piece of a blue metallic material in the shape of a jagged line. With an arched eyebrow, the proprietor asked, "A whole splinter? You only need a few bits for one plate, my friend."

His young patron nodded and placed it on the table. "Well, I might order more. Plus it's my attempt at recompense after I kept your kids awake far later than intended."

The man chuckled although the boy was fair and had the right of it. He had spent the previous evening regaling his children with tales of his old man, who was a captain of the guard in the capital city of Monleans. When the innkeeper had tried to shoo his brood away and stop them from disturbing the customer, the boy quickly defended his temporary playmates and continued, and his stories had eventually delayed the children's bedtime by a good hour.

"You did keep my children entertained, for sure, if a little too long." He placed the empty bowl on the bar and nodded to the chef, his chipper wife, through the window to the kitchen to let her know to prepare a second omelet and toast as he turned to the boy again. "You would think I had forced them to do hard labor with the way they whined getting out of bed this morning."

With a rather sheepish frown, the youngster pushed the splinter toward him. "Guess I did stretch it too long. Take it, please."

A little hesitantly, the innkeeper picked it up and examined it. The inert piece of cobalt would be far more valuable if it was charged, but even a splint like this was far more than was necessary. His young patron would have to stay another day and enjoy a couple of large meals to come even close to the value held in his hand. "Oh, not now," he retorted with a smirk as he sat across from the youngster and put the splint on the table. "I should be thankful. If the truth be told, I haven't seen my kiddies sit in one place for that long in many days. I was able to finish my list of chores for once instead of chasing them around."

The boy shrugged and smiled again as he gestured at the splint. "Well, I'll leave this here," he stated quietly and took a sip of water from his white clay cup. "I should be thankful as, well…you're the first innkeeper who welcomed me without a barrage of questions. I didn't mind answering them, but they hardly made me feel welcome in an inn." He pursed his lips to the side and looked up as a question seemed to form in his mind. "It seems counter-productive now that I think about it."

"There's an art to every job, my boy," the man reasoned as he set his massive arm on the surface elbow-first and rested his chin on his palm. "Some people have the skills but not the knowledge, you know?"

"My mother says something similar," the youngster responded and swirled the liquid in his cup. "She usually says, 'There is a difference between doing something and doing it well, and only those smart enough will know the difference.'"

"Smart woman," the innkeeper declared with a loud laugh. He leaned back in the chair and folded his arms. "At the risk of sounding like one of those idiot innkeepers you've run into, I must admit I am curious as to how you came this way on your own—if you don't mind me prying."

"Oh, it's not a problem." The boy fumbled beside his chair and lifted a dark-brown satchel that he dug through quickly. He brought a map out—mostly white but some areas darker than others—that suggested both use and age. "I won't bore you with all the details, but I'm heading to the bay town on the coast—Fairwind."

"All the way from Monleans?" The man didn't hide his understandable shock as that was almost three hundred miles away. "Whatever for, boy? You must have been making this trek for weeks!"

"Only about nine days, actually," he said and unrolled the map on the table. "My father had business in Warpaw. I traveled there with him and left a couple of days after." He traced his finger over the parchment to show his companion his route. "Went through Tuffles, then Leyoville, then Filo." He pointed to the village he was now in—Bluebell. "Before I arrived here at your inn."

"Truly now?" The innkeeper stroked his red beard. "Still, even starting in Warpaw, that's some distance to travel on foot."

"I got some rides from other travelers," he explained and glanced at a candle on the side of the table. "But I'm also a fairly fast walker." With a small smile, he pointed to the candle, pressed his thumb and middle finger together, and snapped them, and the wick lit itself.

"Ah, a little Magi, I see." His companion nodded. "My eldest daughter and son have something of a knack for that, although the most they use it for is getting the brooms to clean things themselves and anything else they can do to get out of doing their chores."

The boy's eyes lit up. "Does that mean you practice the Mana arts too?"

A noise that was a mixture between a grunt and a light laugh from his large companion made the boy grin. "Hardly, and no more than the average man. I use some of my Mana to help with heavy lifting." He stretched his already large arm and flexed. It increased slightly in size and a white light shimmered very briefly under the skin. "Nothing much more than that. They get it from their mother mainly. She doesn't use it much herself but there is a reason she can run the kitchen almost on her lonesome. Many of the dishes take care of themselves."

"So, you can use Vis, then?" A waitress arrived with his second breakfast. He thanked her quickly before he tucked into the meal with enthusiasm.

"Vis?" the Innkeeper asked before he nodded. "Right, that's the term for Mana enhancement—less wordy, though. I can but barely. Me forgetting the word should tell you how little mind I pay to it."

"It's not a problem," the boy assured him. "In all honesty, I only practiced it as much as I did thanks to my mother. Her mother used to teach at one of the academies and she taught me. And I can only use Mana in practical ways—the disciplines and all that. I can't do many of the fancy stuff like cantrips. Lighting that candle is basically my only trick."

"You didn't go to the academy yourself?" the innkeeper asked.

He wiped his mouth with his napkin and shook his head. "No, my parents tutored me—well, my mother mostly. I learned a few things on my own as well." He finished a piece of toast and leaned back "Thanks for the meal."

The innkeeper looked down and his eyes almost bulged. The plate was clean, and he realized the youngster had eaten it all in a little over a minute. He could eat like a likan.

"Hey, Devol!" a young voice called. The boy and innkeeper turned to see a young red-haired girl run toward them, followed by a boy with brown hair and another young girl with red hair. They dragged chairs closer and gathered around the table. "Hey, Devol, do you think you can play with us today? We'll have our chores done by noon."

Devol ran his hands through his long auburn hair. "Sorry, I'll be gone by then."

"Oh, boo." The girl in the pink dress sighed and her father darted her a disapproving look.

"If I come back, we can play then, okay?" he promised, and although the children nodded, they still pouted to reveal their disappointment.

"You should probably get those chores finished instead of spending your time sulking," their father said sternly. "Help your mother in the kitchen and tell her I'll be there shortly."

"Yes, Father," the children replied in unison, stood quickly, and raced away. Devol waved at them as they left.

"You have spirited kids," he noted as they disappeared behind a door that led to the kitchen.

"Aye." The innkeeper nodded and rubbed the bridge of his nose before he smiled affectionately. "They can try my sanity sometimes but they fill my heart."

Devol laughed and bumped the sword that leaned on his chair, which fell with a thud. He picked it up and placed it on the side of the table. The innkeeper studied it with open curiosity. It was sheathed in a scabbard of darkened leather but the hilt was silver and wrapped in a similar black leather binding. The handguard had a pointed tip, but only one way. In fact, despite its size and shape, it looked almost like it was half of a larger blade, even in the sheath.

"Boy, that sword…" he began, and the boy glanced at his weapon. "That's a unique weapon you have there."

"I know, right?" He grinned and gestured at it with his thumb. "It's the reason I'm out here. It's a magical sword."

"That so?" The man chuckled. "An exotic weapon? Those can be quite pricey."

"I don't think it's an exotic," the boy admitted. "Or at least not a typical one. It merely…appeared one day."

"Merely appeared?" he asked and stroked his chin in thought. "I've heard of warriors getting runes on their exotics that allow them to teleport the blade to their hands. Is it something like that?"

"No. Up until about a month ago, I'd never seen it before." The youngster shrugged and finished his drink. "I'm going to meet someone who can hopefully explain what it is."

The proprietor nodded and peered at the map again. "I see. About that…" He placed his finger on the dot marking Bluebell. "From what I've seen of your current path, you're not heading west, are you?"

Devol frowned a little in confusion and focused on the map. "Unless I read it wrong, that is the quickest path, right?"

"In distance, sure, but also to an early grave," the innkeeper warned and folded his arms. "That leads to the Wailing Woods. As you can probably guess by the name, it's not a great place to take a stroll through."

"Huh." The boy moved the map closer to the lit candle and studied it carefully. "You'd think they'd mention that here."

"It's more of a local name but one well earned."

After a moment, Devol looked away and out one of the inn's windows "I thought I saw a road in that direction."

"It splits and heads down another path around the woods," the innkeeper clarified. "They tried to make a road through it but the crew sent to chop it down only got part of the way in."

"They get scared off by something?" the boy asked as he tapped his fork on his plate.

"Some did and got right the hell out," his companion said with a grim nod "Others… Well, they didn't make it out. The 'wailing' part of the name comes from those who have been lost within or left to die or be killed by the beasties there. There is something off about those woods and the beasties are a big threat—snakes, giant rodents, flesh-eating insects, and even flayers. Some people have claimed even imps and likan roam the forest. Can't say I've seen them myself, but if it were true, this village sure as hell isn't far enough away from it."

The boy pursed his lips, leaned back, and tapped his chin in thought. "I should probably buy a torch before setting off, then."

The innkeeper's stern face melted into one of bafflement. "Do what now, boy?"

"Hmm?" He looked up. "A torch. Most of what you have described are creatures that live in darkened areas. It must mean that the forest is dark enough for them to be there so it would probably be wise for me to take a torch."

The innkeeper wanted to holler in the boy's face that he simply didn't understand, that if he wanted to be 'wise,' he wouldn't go there at all. But his skepticism made him stutter his words before one of his daughters ran to him and tugged his shirt. "Daddy, Mommy says we have more customers and you need to get back to working the bar and main parlor."

"Huh? Uh...sure, darling. Tell her I'll get right on it." He stood, slid his chair in, and turned to point at his young patron. "Stay right there. I need to tend to something before I come back and smack some sense into you, boy."

Devol cocked an eyebrow. "Why would I wait for that?"

The innkeeper shook his head as he went to tend to his new customers. The youngster pushed to his feet and waved goodbye. "Thank you for the hospitality, Mr. Bernard!" He smiled with his silver eyes wide, sat again, and adjusted his blue-and-white jacket and black slacks. After a moment, he decided to close the coat over a white shirt.

Bernard sighed. He should probably have smacked the auburn-haired boy to put an end to his craziness before he left him. A little anxious, he hurried to finish his tasks as quickly as he could lest the hospitality go to waste when the boy got himself killed.

Bernard took the last orders hastily and passed them to his wife. That done, he told his kids to clean the tables of the guests who had finished eating while he took a map off a shelf near the bar, found a pen, and marked it to show a clear path around the woods. Maybe this would help to persuade the boy to not venture through that accursed place. If he needed more convincing...well, he had said he would smack some sense into him and only slightly in jest.

When he came out from behind the bar and entered the side room where the youngster had been seated, however, his place was empty. On the table lay a note and the cobalt splinter. The man looked at the hastily written letter with a scowl.

Mr. Bernard,

Thank you again for the room and food. Sorry I could not say goodbye to you and your wife and children, but if this forest is as bad as you say, I probably want to make the journey through it with as much sunlight as possible. Please keep the splinter for being so nice to me. Hope to see you again if I come through.

Devol Alouest

The innkeeper ran a hand down his face and released a deep sigh. He wondered if he should go and look for the boy before he got too far. If something befell him, even if it were as a result of his stupidity, he would feel terrible. But a part of him was sure that he would hightail it back to town once he saw the woods. No sane person would see even the forest line and think it safe in any way.

He collected a few coins from nearby tables and decided he would give them to the kids. They had earned a little extra and he would tell them it was from Devol. It would at least help them to remember him fondly when the boy returned that night—and he was sure he would have a much more exciting story to tell about the woods when he did.

"A torch was the right call," Devol mused and snapped his fingers to light it as he began his journey through the Wailing Woods. He had to admit that they certainly looked the part of a creepy forest. It was rather dark, even with the sun now properly out. Shadows lingered along the closest thing to a path that he could find, which mostly meant those sections of the woodland floor with the least shrubbery and potential hiding places for snakes, of which he had seen a few. He'd encountered no flesh-eating insects or likan yet, but he had found the signs of the rodents—pawprints and droppings along the way. The trees were odd as well, with dark-gray bark and some with unusual white stains akin to chalk or ash. He did not have a clue where that could come from.

He did keep the warning of flayers in mind. Those were particularly nasty. He had only read about them and seen the bones of one at a museum, but even most assuredly dead, they were unnerving. They had long, angular heads with a lean physique and curved arms and legs with giant crescent-shaped claws that they used to strip the skin of their prey. From what he understood, that meant anything with blood and meat, so he would certainly qualify as prey if he encountered one.

His senses alert, he strode along his rough path until he heard a noise. Well, several noises, but the breathing in particular caught his attention. He huddled behind one of the trees, extinguished the torch quickly, and slid it into his pack as he scanned the forest in front of him. The sound was garbled, harsh, and almost wheezing, which suggested that whatever made it was struggling although he couldn't be sure of that.

He caught sight of a round, dark object—a hairy blob with a pink-white tail—and noticed two more behind it. The first reared its head to reveal a large, puffy, furry face with pale, fleshy lips. Two pointed front teeth protruded and round gray eyes darted keen gazes in all directions. They were, quite unmistakably, the giant rats.

Were they hunting or scavenging? Despite their size, they were not the most ferocious of hunters, often prey for bigger beasts than them or packs of smaller ones. They traveled in small groups whenever they ventured out of their domain, and Devol doubted this was a morning stroll for them.

Then he noticed something else far ahead of the creatures but in their path. It appeared to be a man, although he was too far away to see details, and he wore what he thought might be a dark-gray or black hooded cloak. He was crouched in front of some shrubbery and seemingly studied it or looked at something within. The boy looked from him to the rats.

This would not end well if the stranger were caught off-guard. Giant rats were not terribly agile, but they made up for it with quick, vicious strikes on unlucky prey, and their girth was not merely fat but well-muscled as well. He realized that the heavy breaths were the last lungful of air the beasts would take before they began to creep up on their potential meal.

His first instinct was to shout a warning to the man, but that would draw their attention and he was a closer target. He had no problem facing them if he had to, but it wasn't his best option and it would be better to do so while he had the advantage.

With that in mind, he reached back for his sword. After the first day he had wielded it, he had not fought anything or anyone with it, only used it for practice before his parents sent him hurriedly to find those who could help him—the Templars. Well, it seemed like now was a good time to break the blade in properly.

CHAPTER TWO

Devol drew the sword and couldn't help but look at it for a moment. The blade was broad and the tip was pointed and angular and sloped forward. What made it unique in his eyes, however, was what it was made of. It did not appear to be metal and had looked like glass the first time he saw it.

Even now, it was almost translucent. In the light, he could barely discern a shimmer of some kind of light within of a pale gold or white color, at least when it was in his hands. When he wasn't holding it, the blade almost looked like nothing more than a showpiece. It was dangerous, though, as the dire wolf that had attacked him and his mother could have attested to if it was still alive and could speak.

He crept quickly but quietly toward his quarry. Now only a few yards behind the rats, he was careful to not step on any twigs or scuff against any of the trees and reveal his presence. If he could strike without them noticing, he could potentially kill one of them immediately and leave him with only two to deal with. He inhaled quietly, closed his eyes, and let his Mana flow. It surged through his body and connected to his muscle and his skeleton. He instantly grew more energetic and felt lighter.

When he held his weapon up, he barely registered the weight. The light inside seemed to glimmer and he lowered it hastily, hoping he hadn't given his position away. The rats continued their advance toward the stranger, unaware of him for now. He stepped behind a tree for cover, knelt, and noticed a small rock on the ground. Cautiously, he picked it up, located another trunk beside the rats, and lobbed the stone at it.

It struck its target with a sharp clunk and left a noticeable crack. The rats responded with confused growls and their heads looked around as one. Devol leapt as high as he could. His jump took him up more than ten yards. Still, he could not have been more than a third of the height of the trees when he turned his blade to point it down as he began to drop back to earth. The creatures looked around and tried to find the source of the noise as he landed and drove his weapon into the center rat's head.

The animal uttered a pained shriek and he yanked his sword from its head as the two others bounded to the side. Startled, they watched their mischief mate convulse and fall still and silent. The boy turned his attention to the one on the right and lunged toward it with his blade aimed at its chest. It jumped back as he tried to strike, then responded with an angry hiss as it retaliated with a vicious pounced attack. The one behind him pounded its feet on the forest floor before it jumped into the fray and the two tried to pin him between them.

He flung himself aside and they both missed him and narrowly avoided colliding with each other. Devol darted away and glanced over his shoulder to see if the racket had alerted the man. He could no longer see him, assumed he must have run off in fright, and sighed with relief. At least he only had one person to worry about now—himself.

His furred adversaries crept cautiously toward him and he held his blade up. He inched back slowly, looked over his shoulder again, and noticed a small clearing in the woods a short distance behind him. Instinct told him he should get to it in case other giant creatures nearby were summoned by the pained cries of their brethren.

One of the rats launched into an attack, its claws and teeth ready to sink into his flesh. Devol flipped his blade on its side, pushed forward to catch the rat's claws, and parried to the right of the oversized vermin. As it landed, he flipped his blade and stabbed it down and behind him, deep into his adversary's back and through its stomach.

It responded with a pained hiss and its tail waved wildly and almost tripped him. Thankfully, the young swordsman managed to sidestep the erratic appendage and ran toward the clearing with the other creature in pursuit.

The glade was almost circular with an odd extended area at the north end. Dead branches and pieces of bone lined the edges of it. The boy bounded over what appeared to be a large broken femur and slid on the wet, brown, and sickly-green grass. He spun as his would-be attacker hurdled its large body over the bone. Once it landed, its head jerked from side to side and it made a nervous clicking sound with its teeth.

He didn't know what caused the sudden change in behavior but decided not to waste the opportunity. His Mana flowed to soothe his legs and seep into the muscles, and when he felt he was ready, he bent at the knees and launched himself at the rat. It snapped its head toward him and opened its maw as it stood on its hind legs, surprising him. As it began to fall forward, he wondered if it had anticipated the charge and been ready for it. He stopped a few feet in front of the rodent and thrust his blade forward as its claws lashed at his face. This was a moment when the winner would be decided by who made the killing blow first.

The light in the blade flared and the sword enlarged and lengthened. Devol was shocked and told himself it was merely a trick of the light. Or perhaps the shadows in the woods? It sank into his adversary's head and stopped it in its tracks. The large claws dangled mere inches from his throat, lifeless and pointing uselessly at the ground.

The rat made no sound as it fell heavily on his sword. He had to wedge his boot against its stomach and push hard to free his weapon. Once he'd shaken his weapon to get some of the viscera off, he took a handkerchief out and ran it along the blade to clean it more thoroughly. He checked the sword while he did this. It seemed to be the same measurements it had always been—the blade about thirty-two inches in length and slightly longer than a standard sword.

Nothing seemed out of the ordinary except for the shining blade itself, but he was already aware of that. He grimaced at the handkerchief, a little queasy at the thought of keeping it in his jacket pocket, and wondered if it was even salvageable. The sound of someone clapping behind him distracted him from his debate.

He spun with his sword raised and frowned at the man in the dark cloak who applauded him, as far as he could tell. Devol was somewhat surprised to see him as he'd thought he had run off. This close, he was able to see more detail. The stranger was dressed all in black—a long-sleeved black shirt and trousers with black boots and gloves to match his cloak and cowl. On his back was a large pack, and around his waist, a leather belt held a white gourd filled with liquid that sloshed when he moved and something else wrapped in a black cloth attached to either side. The boy couldn't get a good look at his face as it was obscured by his hood and the shadows from the forest.

"Well done," the man said and lowered his hands. He had an incredibly deep voice and it rattled as he spoke like his throat was producing its own echo. "That only took you a couple of minutes. For a boy your age to not only wander into this nasty place but to fell three giant rats with little difficulty means you are very gifted." He folded his arms and inclined his head as he stared at him. "Not to mention that you have something special with you as well."

"Who...are you?" Devol asked hesitantly, not sure if he should lower his blade in a show of peace or hold it ready.

"Me?" the man asked and took a few steps forward—not toward him but to the center of the clearing. "I suppose today, I am something of a groundskeeper."

Before the boy could ask him what he meant by that, he heard more breathing, this time sharper than the rats and very agitated. He spun and held his sword with both hands as he and the stranger looked toward the odd narrow extension of the clearing directly ahead of them

He saw eyes before anything else—broad, somewhat bulbous, and white. The next thing he noticed was a glint from long talons caught in one of the few beams of pure sunlight streaming into the woods. A beast stalked into the clearing. It walked hunched on all fours and stepped over the branches and bones.

When it stopped several feet away from them, it leaned upon two angled legs and stood easily at over seven feet tall. A long, curved maw held thin, spike-like teeth and pale, ashen colored scales covered its flesh. It extended its sinewy arms and its long claws moved closer to them.

"A flayer?" Devol asked quietly and steadied his hands after a moment of surprise at the sight of it. This one was much larger than the bones at the museum had led him to believe them to be.

"Indeed, and an alpha at that," the stranger stated. He removed the gourd from his belt and took a quick sip before he replaced it. "Although that may be by default. It seems only a few flayers take refuge in these woods at a time and quickly eliminate the others who are weaker. They aren't particularly good neighbors, even with their kin."

As if in response to the comments, the beast's head twitched from side to side and it clicked its teeth together a couple of times before it uttered a loud, shrill shriek. The boy gritted his teeth rather than trying to cover his ears. He would prefer to not let his guard down at this moment.

A NEW LIGHT

"Think you can take it?" his odd companion asked and fixed him with what might have been a challenging look.

He broke his determined gaze briefly to glance at him with an exasperated expression. "I'd rather not," he admitted and braced his legs in preparation for either fight or flight. "But even with my Mana, I don't think I can outrun it. So if it comes to it, I will fight." He focused on the spindly creature again and his sword began to glow as if to corroborate his words.

The stranger chuckled, unfolded his arms, and motioned for him to lower his blade. "I admire your resilience and your courage, but you can try your hand at it some other time." He proceeded to walk forward toward the creature with what seemed like suicidal calm.

Devol almost dropped his blade in his panic. "Wait, don't!"

The flayer shrieked again as it lunged at the man, its front limbs stretched to either side. The arms moved together toward his head so fast that Devol could barely comprehend its speed. Unperturbed by the fact that he was about to be beheaded in moments, the stranger ducked quickly, and the massive curved talons missed his neck and each other. The trace of wind created by their passing dislodged the man's hood as he placed one finger under the flayer's chin at the point where the creature's head and neck met. "Bolt."

In a moment, a red arrow made of Mana pierced its head and protruded at a point where it looked like it came out of the man's fingertip. The beast seized instantly and gurgled for a moment as its attacker stepped to the side and let it fall to the earth with a loud thud.

The boy was speechless, not only at the sight of the terrifying creature felled so quickly and casually but at finally seeing the man, if that was what he was. His skin was as dark as ink but with white markings around his eyes, the curves of his ears, and the bridge of his nose. Devol couldn't tell if it was some kind of paint or natural. He had narrow eyes—silver like his but with no irises—and his long, thin alabaster hair was tied into a bun. Something was different about it, though, and it looked more like twine than healthy hair strands. He looked at his young companion, amusement on his face when he saw his bewildered expression.

"Their scales offer them some defense against blades and the like, but the flesh on the underside of their head is surprisingly thin." The stranger held his gaze and grinned. "Why so surprised, my friend?" he asked and slid his index finger and thumb under his chin as he observed him. His slightly pointed teeth were more noticeable when his grin turned to a smile. "Have you never seen a mori before?"

"A mori?" the boy asked, his blade in his hand but pointed toward the earth. "You're a realmer?"

"Indeed, and from the sounds of it, you haven't seen one before, have you?" the man asked and took another sip from his gourd.

Devol shook his head. "Not a realmer, no. I've met wildkin and even seen a fleuri—well, I think it was but I don't remember if they are purple."

"If they sprout in the winter, it is a possibility," his companion told him, placed a hand on his chest, and extended the other arm as he bowed. "But I suppose I should introduce myself properly. My name is Vaust

Lebatt, formerly an Archon of House…well, I suppose it doesn't matter with it being formerly." He stood and folded his arms. "I am more of a drifter now. Care to share something of yourself with me? What brings you here?"

Despite a little inward hesitation, the boy sheathed his blade. "My name is Devol Alouest, son of Victor and Lilli Alouest. I'm here because I'm on a journey to the Templar Order and this forest is on the path I was told to take."

"The Templars?" Vaust questioned and stroked his chin thoughtfully. "Not many look for them these days. Usually, it is the other way around. What reason could you have to look for such people?"

He scratched his head and sifted through his memories. "Well, a couple of weeks ago, I was with my mother in the Emerald Forest outside Monleans, and a large dire wolf attacked us—the biggest I've seen in person." He drew the sword again and held it up, and his reflection caught in the blade. "It immediately attacked us. I wanted to protect her but I had no weapon. I…well, something happened only moments before it struck. A flash of light almost blinded me, and I felt something or someone take my hand. When the light disappeared, the wolf was dead and I was holding this sword."

Vaust studied the blade curiously and didn't initially see anything of note. After a few moments, however, he saw it gleam— perhaps it had caught a beam of sunlight? He shook his head when he realized it was still in the shadow of the forest. The shimmer flared to a bright achromatic light, and it encompassed the blade before it grew to an uncomfortable glare and glowed around the edges of the blade.

It was magical, without a doubt, and it was not only for illumination. He could tell right away that the sword was far more than the standard exotic. When the boy looked at him, the sword still bright in his hand, Vaust nodded. "I see you have something special indeed," he said, his voice almost a purr. "That, my young friend, is a majestic."

CHAPTER THREE

"It's what?" Devol asked as the light faded from the sword.

"You've never heard of a majestic?" Vaust asked as he approached him. "Given your talent with Mana, I assumed you'd had some training... Well, that and the blade itself."

"Oh yes, I have." He lowered his sword and focused on the mori. "My mom taught me the basics of Mana, but this isn't anything like what I've seen someone use before—at least outside some of my father's comrades, and even they don't talk to me much." He looked at the weapon again and slid his hand over the flat surface of the blade. "And as I said, I've never seen this before it appeared a few weeks ago."

The man considered this as he stared absently into the trees. "I suppose there is still something of a stigma attached to them in this realm." He focused on his young companion again. "So you discovered this blade—which appeared magically out of nowhere in a time of need—and your first instinct was to go on an adventure to the Templar Order?"

Devol slipped his pack off. "It wasn't my idea, to be honest," he said as he rummaged through his belongings. "My parents suggested I go to the Templars and said it was important." He took the folded map out and handed it to the mori. "They said a friend of my father's gave this to him around the time I was born and after they had done a mission together or something like that. He said that if anything odd happens or they need a favor, to search them out."

"Well, this certainly qualifies." Vaust took the paper, opened it, and glanced casually at the map until something caught his eye. He frowned slightly as he registered a symbol on the bottom of the page that depicted a nine-pointed star. "This is…" he said, his voice almost a whisper. "Indeed, I most certainly see…" He folded the map again and handed it to him. "Tell me, Templar-hopeful. What do you hope to achieve once you reach the order?"

"Achieve?" the boy asked as he slid the map into his pack, flipped the top over, and tied it down. His face contorted in thought while his fingers were busy. "I…uh, I guess to learn more about this sword—or majestic, right?" He slung his backpack on. "Maybe get some more training in arms and things like that."

"You have no desire to join the order?" the mori asked.

"I don't know much about it," Devol admitted and shrugged as if joining the order was a decision he could make later when he did know. "My father told me what he could. He said that at one point when he was young, he wanted to join the Templars. But even with that, he did not know much. He seems to trust his old friend, though, and said that this would be for the best and that I should trust their instruction."

"It depends on the instructor," his companion muttered. Although he'd spoken to himself, the boy's sharp ears caught it.

"What do you mean?" he asked.

The man gestured vaguely. "It's merely my personal biases. Tell me, young man, would you like some company to their keep?"

He raised an eyebrow quizzically. "With who?"

Vaust rolled his eyes. "With me, obviously."

"Really?" He gasped. "I thought you said you were this forest's groundskeeper?"

Vaust was sorely tempted to slap either himself or the boy. "That was something of a metaphor. I was here on a mission to keep the forest relatively clear. There isn't much a single man can do about that, in all honesty, but I was entrusted to eliminate anything too dangerous." He approached the dead flayer and retrieved a large sack and a dagger. "With that done, I have to return to Fairwind, where I was given the task."

"Oh, so you're heading that way?" he asked with a smile. "That would be very helpful. I've made the trek alone, for the most part, but it would be nice to have company for the rest of the journey."

"Agreed." The mori severed the head of the flayer and shoved it into the sack, which he tied to his belt. "We can probably be there by tomorrow if we hurry."

"Do you know a quick way out of this forest?" Devol inquired and looked around dubiously. "To be honest, I don't think we're even that far in and I feel a little disoriented."

"A skill to work on, then," the man reasoned and drew his hood over his head. "Later, though. I do know the way out of the forest, but we still have much ground to cover today." He hopped a few times and the boy noted that he had kept his Mana flowing the whole time. "I wonder if you can keep up."

Devol smiled and let his Mana flow a little. "Back in Monleans, I was the best user of Vis amongst all the kids, even the older ones." He hopped a few times as well to loosen his limbs and muscles. "Show me what you can do."

"All right." Vaust spoke from behind him and he spun in alarm. The mori had seemingly teleported and now laughed at his reaction. "Sorry. I was merely having a little fun." He walked a few paces ahead toward the edge of the clearing. "It shouldn't take us very long to get out and from there, I'll let you set the pace. I'll do so until then." He looked over his shoulder, his face shadowed by the hood. "Let us see how much you can push yourself."

He composed himself and responded with a challenging grin. "Let's go!"

The mori made good on his promise and they were out of the forest in no more than ten minutes. Devol kept pace but it had been a long time since he had been pushed this hard and he almost lost sight of his guide a couple of times before they stepped beyond the tree line. Not since his races with his father—the serious ones, at least—had he felt so winded. Once they were a few miles out, Vaust stopped to let him catch his breath. They then plotted a course that would be almost a straight line to Fairwind and set off with the boy leading the way.

After several hours of travel, his companion noticed a cave and they decided to make camp. After a good rest, they could start early and possibly reach the town before noon the next day.

They split up to prepare their camp. Devol cleaned the area, made a fire, and fetched water from a nearby spring while his companion went to hunt their dinner. They both finished their respective tasks in under an hour and soon feasted on a young boar the mori had killed, along with some berries and nuts. He chose the ribs and flanks of the beast while Vaust seemed to prefer other parts of the animal such as the eyes, cheeks, and even a few pieces that made him somewhat skeptical as to whether an average person should eat them.

Either out of curiosity or the desire for conversation, the mori decided to question him. "So, Devol, tell me," he began and leaned back while he held a piece of boar cheek between his fingers. "How much do you know about Mana?"

He finished chewing a large mouthful of boar flank and considered the question thoughtfully. "I think...a fair amount. My mom has a degree in the arts of Mana, and she has taught me ever since I was a toddler."

Vaust nodded slowly, picked up the gourd next to him, and removed the stopper. "So how would you define it?"

Devol took another bite of his food and tapped his chin as he thought. "My mother usually said that it is the 'second blood' of the Magi. It flows like a river through you, one that you control. It is crucial to think of it as an essential part of you, not as something to perform silly party tricks with."

His companion chuckled, finished the meat hanging between his fingers, and swallowed some of the liquid from the gourd before he straightened. "Believe it or not, Devol, if you have taken your mother's words to heart, you are already far more prepared for the life of a Magi than most."

"So you think the same way, Mr. Lebatt?" he asked.

The mori shrugged and sipped his water. "It is not how I would put it, but your mother's advice is similar."

The boy finished the flank and placed the bone beside him. "Then how do you think of Mana?"

Vaust shrugged. "I could speak for quite some time on that subject, but we need to rest soon and I don't wish to bore you. I would put it simply like this…" He held a hand out and formed a ball that hovered slightly above his palm. It was a white core of light surrounded by a red shell. Devol had never seen Mana like that and was enchanted.

"In the realms," the mori continued, "Mana is the birthright of all who live in them, but that does not mean all truly understand the gift we possess." The orb grew in size and changed from the shape of a single grape to that of a cantaloupe. "To most, it is simply power—energy, or as your mother put it, something to perform silly tricks with. But a true Magi knows better." The orb changed shape and took on a humanoid form before details etched themselves in quickly and it looked like a miniature rendering of Vaust himself. "A true Magi knows that Mana is the essence of their spirit."

"Oh…" was the only response the boy could make, still focused on the image in his companion's hand, before the man snapped his hand shut and the vision disappeared. "Wha— Hey, can you teach me how to do that?"

The mori clasped his hands together and hung them over his knees. "Do you want to learn a silly trick or something more?"

He felt a little sheepish and he scratched his cheek and looked away in embarrassment. "Let's go with something more. Although it would still be nice to have a few tricks in case I ever need one."

Vaust laughed. "I'll admit, I don't disagree." He studied him again. "To continue, are you familiar with the trinity of Mana disciplines?"

Devol nodded vigorously. "Oh yes." He leaned back on one hand and held the other out to count by raising his fingers in turn. "There's Vis, Vita, and Vello."

"Indeed. And what are the meanings behind them?"

The boy held his first finger up. "Vis is using Mana to enhance your body, which will enable you to be stronger and faster and able to endure more, things like that."

"Increasing your natural stamina," Vaust summarized and pointed at him. "Don't forget that if you focus only on adding power to your strength, you won't be able to strengthen your power."

"Right!" He nodded and now held two fingers up. "Vita is the ability to control the flow of your Mana so you don't expend more than is necessary."

"Correct," the mori agreed and held two of his fingers

up. "It's not the most dramatic discipline but an important one, nonetheless." He held a third up. "And the last?"

Devol mirrored him with three fingers. "The last is Vello, the ability to transfer Mana, which enables you to cast cantrips and even strengthen or control simple objects."

"They don't necessarily have to be simple." Vaust clarified and lowered his hand. "But it's a good way to learn it. And a quick check—are you familiar with cantrips?"

He raised a hand and tilted it from side to side. "I know of them, obviously—like the bolt cantrip you did in the forest to create an arrow from Mana and solidify it. They are simple spells that many Magi learn over their years of training and include the basics that almost anyone can use and those that fall into different classes. But for me…well, they aren't one of my stronger abilities. My mother is very skilled, though."

"There is no shame in that. It comes easier to some rather than others," his companion said to reassure him and placed a hand on his chest. "The mori are taught cantrips from a very young age and have much more time than humans to learn them."

"I've heard that the mori are some of the most gifted Magi among all the realmers," Devol stated.

Vaust smiled. "That is true, something many hold in high regard, although the angeli would argue that point."

The boy looked at him, his curiosity piqued. "I'm sorry, who?"

The man waved a hand. "Nothing to be concerned about now." He rested his arm on his leg while his other hand stroked his chin. "I have to say, you are very well taught for your age."

Devol nodded and smiled. "See, I told you I know a lot."

"You certainly have the basics," his companion replied and raised an eyebrow. "Now, what about Anima?"

"Hmm?" He hesitated and his face fell. "Anima? I don't think I've heard about that. Is it a mori specialty?"

"Not quite. It's more of an advanced discipline," Vaust clarified, pushed to his feet, and stretched. "Since we're now well-fed, come with me for a moment, would you?"

"Um…sure, okay." He stood and followed him out of the cave. They walked in silence onto the wide plain under the night sky.

"Would you like to see that something more I told you about?" the mori asked and turned to him after they had wandered a few yards away from the cave. He pointed past him. "Move a few feet away."

The boy complied and turned toward him as his companion held his arms apart. "You may wish to brace yourself," he warned and drew a sharp breath before Devol noticed a red shimmer around his body, one that promptly exploded outward. It raced through the young Magi and made him feel like he would be thrown back dozens of yards or lifted off his feet.

In an instant, it was gone, but he could still feel a heaviness in the air that was almost tangible. It seemed like he could barely move his arms or legs. He looked at Vaust and frowned at the faint red shimmer that faded quickly—or, rather, it looked like it was absorbed inside him.

"What is…going on?" he asked and struggled to remain standing.

"This is my Anima, Devol," his companion explained as he continued to stare at him.

"Anima?" the boy asked and panted from the pressure. "It feels so heavy. What are you doing?"

The mori straightened. "You use your Mana to surround yourself like you would with armor. It creates a field that makes it more tangible and easier to use for protection and to access its power. That heaviness you feel is my Anima suppressing your Mana."

"Is that so?" he responded irritably as his breathing became weaker. "Do you mind toning it down a little, please?"

"I could but I think it would be more useful if you did it yourself," Vaust countered.

Devol tried instinctively to adopt a questioning look, but he did not have the best control over his muscles at the moment. "What do you mean?"

"I think you can manifest your Anima, my friend," the man declared. "From what I've seen so far, you're almost there."

The more tenacious part of him agreed that this was probably a good time to try, but the more reasonable side asked, "Can I have a hint?"

"Certainly. In fact, I'm giving you a big one at this moment." Vaust pointed to him. "There are several ways for young Magi to first manifest their Anima." The boy wasn't sure if it was a tease or purely happenstance, but he held three fingers up as he had before. "Through specific training, breathing exercises, working on your Vita discipline, and things like that, although that takes a long while and we don't have time for that." He lowered one finger.

"Another is to force it, which isn't recommended. Even in the best circumstances, it usually causes great pain and stress to the Magi."

"This doesn't count?" Devol asked.

Vaust shook his head and an amused grin spread across his face as he lowered his second-to-last finger. "The last one is to coax it out. It's somewhat tricky compared to the other two, but this is one of the more standard ways," he explained. "Even in the few hours I've spent with you, Devol, I can see you are gifted. Either that or you're the product of good training, but there is a limit to how far that will take you."

"I assume there is a flight or fight factor here?" he asked and used his Mana to access the strength to stand taller.

"Of course." The mori chuckled and stared a challenge at him. "But what you are doing—able to use Vis even under these circumstances—tells me you are at the door, Devol. Just open it!"

"And how do I do that?" he demanded.

"Like we've discussed, Mana is your 'second blood'—your 'spirit,'" Vaust reminded him. "It is the manifestation of your life and will and you have to draw it out." He clapped sharply. "Focus and bring it all together within you, then let it pour out—but don't let it consume you. Your mother compared Mana to a river, correct?" Devol nodded. "Then expand it into an ocean and form a tidal wave."

The boy balled his fists and lowered his arms to his sides. He focused on his heart, a trick his mother had taught him—to think of his heart as the center point of his Mana and its home. Even in dire times, being able to remember that would keep him calm. He could feel it pooling and let it coalesce into one point as he battled against his companion's Anima. It was something he had never tried before. He'd spent all his time focusing on manipulating and making the Mana flow that he never understood what it felt like to bring it all together. The comparison to an ocean was apt.

Now, he would release it.

With a determined cry, Devol let his Mana explode outward. It instantly filled his entire body before it pushed through to include the outside of his skin and the air around him. He suddenly felt light. His sight also seemed to improve and the night was no longer so dark. The pressure of Vaust's Anima was pushed back and a white glow surrounded him with the edges tinted silver.

"There you go," the mori said too quietly for him to hear as he was too preoccupied with the new experience to pay attention to anything else. The man noticed the silver glimmer around the edges of the boy's Anima. All Mana was white with a color strain that was unique to the user. Scholars and philosophers alike had debated the significance of these colors. Were they an indication of the person's personality? Or were they developed over time and based on experiences? Mana was a gift from the Astrals, so was it connected to them somehow?

Vaust had never paid too much mind to that. He preferred results and absolutes and wading into a debate that had lasted for centuries seemed a waste of time, even for a long-lived mori. But he did note the silver color of Devol's Mana. That was unique. In fact, he had only seen it in one other person. His thoughts returned to the symbol he had seen on the map, the insignia of the only man with silver Mana.

He observed the boy, whose face lit up as he began to move freely again and stared at the Anima he had produced. The mori saw wonder in him that he had not seen in a long time. It was a shame. A boy like this did not deserve to live a life believing a lie.

CHAPTER FOUR

"Mr. Lebatt, I did it!" Devol shouted and raised his arms ecstatically.

"Indeed you did," Vaust agreed. "But you shouldn't get comfortable. You'll pass out if you keep going like that."

The boy's face fell into a small frown. "Huh?" Now that he thought about it, despite his newfound lightness and jubilation, he felt a tad off.

"You've brought your Anima out, but it's now pouring out of you," his companion explained and approached him. "You need to rein it in. Otherwise, you'll pass out from Mana depletion and perhaps even die if you pour too much out."

"Well, that would certainly bring the mood down." He sighed in exasperation, stood tall, and exhaled a long breath before he focused on himself again. Vaust stopped in his tracks. He had intended to explain to him what he needed to do but was now curious as to whether the boy could correct it himself.

Devol closed his eyes and began to pull his Mana in a

little. It felt different than usual and Anima made it seem more tangible. He inhaled slowly, focused on his heart again, and reeled the Mana in. When he opened one eye slightly, the colorful light around him faded and shrank slowly. It looked like his attempt was working. He noticed Vaust observing him—surely he would say something if he was doing something wrong? Then again, he seemed to be a very trial-by-fire type of teacher, so maybe he should not depend on that possibility.

The Anima continued to shrink but it did not weaken. It continued to surround him and more importantly, he could again feel his companion's being held at bay. But when he recognized this, he thought of something else. If pushing his Anima out like this was a risk to him and Vaust's felt so much more powerful, he did not seem concerned at all. The thought was intriguing but it was probably best to not dwell on that.

After he decreased the expanse of his Anima to the point where it felt like it only surrounded his immediate area, he opened his eyes fully and shook his joints to test them. He still felt good and remained strong. The last time he had experienced something this exciting was the first time he had properly accomplished Vis. He looked at Vaust, who nodded in approval.

"Congratulations. You successfully used Vita in combination with Anima."

"Is that tricky or something?" Devol asked, his gaze focused on the taller Magi.

His companion nodded. "Certainly more so than simply using it with Mana. It is a useful skill, as when your Anima is out you are protected and stronger. But, as you felt for yourself, it tends to draw attention. Being able to use Vita to control your Anima so that you don't overuse it and even to hide it in certain situations is quite useful."

"Oh, okay." He nodded and held his fists up. "So I can use Vis and Vello in combination with Anima as well?"

"Indeed you can, although it will take a while to get used to it." The mori folded his arms. "We have a little more time. I can show you something a little more practical if you like."

"Sure," Devol agreed and placed his fists together. "I'm ready."

Vaust grinned and extended an arm toward the cave. "I hope so." An object hurtled toward him from within their shelter and he caught it in his open hand.

The boy watched as he unwrapped a black cloth from around the item and stared when he held something up in the moonlight. It appeared to be a weapon of some kind with a curved blade of darkened metal and a zig-zag pattern embossed on either side of the blade. It was attached to a black rod a little longer than Devol's arm, and golden rings jingled at the bottom where white leather binding acted as a handle.

"What is that?" he asked as he admired it. The metal glittered both hauntingly and beautifully under the moonlight.

The mori slipped his fingers into the rings at the bottom of the weapon and spun it a few times. "This is a kama," he stated, flipped it, and snatched it by the handle. "Or, rather, that is what the weapon is called. This is my majestic."

"You have one too?" he asked.

His companion nodded "This one was passed down to me when I earned the rank of archon in my realm. I kept it after I departed as a…keepsake."

"They are special, right? It doesn't seem like the kind of thing one simply gives away."

"I didn't mention it when I left." Vaust chuckled and rested the kama on his shoulder. "So, what do you know about exotics?"

"Oh, that's an easy one," Devol said. "Exotics are weapons that are made with special materials and magical enhancements like runes and incantations. There are different types and varieties and each has a unique property that can be accessed by trained Magi. My father has a very special one, and all the guardsman get an exotic gladius as recruits—or one of three or four other weapons."

"Correct again," the elder Magi affirmed. "But even the rarest and most powerful of exotics can pale in comparison to majestics. With exotics, almost anyone can use one and the user will imbue it with Mana as an energy source. The majestic is connected to the user themselves and not everyone is capable of wielding one. In fact, it can be rather dangerous for someone who cannot resonate with a majestic to use it."

"So my sword is connected to me?" he asked. "What does that mean, exactly?"

"It means you need to be careful," Vaust warned and his tone grew more serious. "Majestics are more than the weapons or objects they appear to be. They are powerful and very few weapons can survive even a clash with one. But should they become damaged, they will injure their users as well."

"What?" He gasped and wished he had known that before setting off. Without a doubt, he would have brought an extra sword to use instead.

The Magi began to twirl his kama. "It's something to keep in mind. But each majestic also has a unique power—one that even the greatest Magi cannot learn or bring forth themselves, although many have tried."

"Can you tell what mine does?" the curious boy asked.

Vaust shook his head. "Not without a demonstration. Although I'm sure someone at the order can answer those questions." He rested the kama against his shoulder. "We could keep talking but I assume you prefer a demonstration?"

Devol's eyes lit up. "You're right!" He extended his arm toward the cave and within seconds, the sword that seemed to have chosen him so mysteriously streaked into his hand.

"Impressive Vello control," the Mori said and tapped the base of his kama. "But I didn't intend for us to spar."

"You didn't?" he asked, having already partially unsheathed the blade.

His companion chuckled. "If you wish to, we can." He pointed his weapon toward the boy. "But understand that there is a limit to how much I can hold back. Myazma is only so tame."

"Myazma?" He looked at the kama. "You named your weapon?"

"Technically, I renamed it. The original name was from an old mori tongue and translating it was more along the lines of a poem than a real name. I searched through the common tongue and this seemed more fitting." He turned the weapon to the side as he and his young opponent locked gazes. "Are you ready?"

Devol held the sword in both hands and drew a deep breath as he assumed a battle stance. Even with Vaust's warning, the thrill of combat was overtaking him. "When you are."

The mori nodded, unmoving. "Very well. Come at me."

His Mana flared and when his Anima enhanced it, he felt stronger and faster than he could have imagined. Common sense reminded him that he should probably steady himself. If he tried to attack without understanding his new power, he could launch himself into one of the rocks in the distance. He lowered slightly and moved his blade to the side before he surged forward and launched himself at his opponent with a challenging shout.

Vaust did not move, but as the boy's blade swung, he retaliated with his kama. Their blades clashed and Devol stopped several yards behind the mori. He spun, as did his companion, who twirled his weapon casually at his side. With a bewildered frown, he caught a glimmer from his blade. It had seemed like his adversary had merely parried the blow, but when he turned and looked down, his vision blurred slightly. Confused, he shook his head and stared at what looked like a long black mark sliced into his blade.

He paused to examine it. What had happened and how was it possible? It must have come from the mori's weapon. He held his sword a little higher but his head began to swirl. Was he getting sick? He had been fine a moment before. Then, he began to cough and fell to one knee as he sputtered.

"So, point proven, then?" Vaust called as he examined the boy's reaction.

Devol grunted and his Mana flared as he pushed to his feet, once again prepared to strike, even with a broken blade. "Neat trick," he responded. "I don't suppose you will tell me how you did it?"

"You've proven you can be smart," his adversary pointed out, flipped his kama, and caught it by the handle. "Where would the fun be if I simply spelled it out for you?"

"Then I won't stop until I work it out," he declared and surged toward the older Magi.

"Doing the wrong thing repeatedly…" Vaust sighed and readied himself to counter. But before the attack completed, the boy suddenly stopped his charge, slid along the grass, and kicked dirt into his eyes to obscure his vision. Momentarily surprised, he almost missed a bright flash from above as the young swordsman vaulted upward, ready to strike. He leaned back as the weapon arced and the blade narrowly missed his chest.

Startled, he jumped back and scowled at a small cut on the lapel of his jacket. If he had not cut through the other blade, that could have been a clean strike.

"Well done, Devol," the mori complimented and his eyes widened when the boy barreled toward him.

"I'm not done!" he shouted and prepared to thrust with the blade before another coughing fit slowed his approach.

Vaust almost laughed. He had to concede that the youngster had tenacity, but it was getting late and the point of setting up camp was to rest. "Yes, you are," he responded, flipped his kama again, and took one step back. The attack slashed at nothing but air and he brought his weapon down on the back of the young swordmaster's head to knock him into unconsciousness. "For the night at least."

Devol awoke to birds chirping and the smell of the meadow. He rubbed the back of his head where a dull pain nagged at him as he glanced to where Vaust strode in through the cave entrance. The Magi offered him honeycombs and more berries.

"Good morning." The older Magi greeted him cheerfully and pointed behind him to where his sword was sheathed not far away. "Don't forget that."

The previous night's events rushed back to him and he sighed and continued to rub his head. "I guess I didn't win, huh?"

"You did well, especially since it was your first time using Anima and your weapon was slightly damaged." The man showed him the nick on his jacket as he popped a few red berries into his mouth. "It's not like you have been trained in how to correctly use a majestic. It is a sword and swordsmanship is important, but it is more than merely a pointy stick."

"So you won't tell me what happened?" he asked around some of the honeycomb. "I don't know what your majestic is able to do but I don't fall ill like that. I haven't had to see a doctor in two years."

"A robust constitution." His companion selected a few berries and popped them into his mouth. "If you had used a regular weapon or even a lower quality exotic, it would have been rendered useless. Your majestic endured but that doesn't mean there wouldn't be ill effects."

"So that's a no," Devol mumbled and retrieved his blade. He unsheathed it halfway and looked for the black mark, but it was no longer there. "So it must have been the power of your majestic, then?"

Vaust poured a little water into his tin cup and sipped it. "An accurate guess," he remarked. "And no, I won't explain it yet."

"Why not?" he asked with an edge of impatience in his tone.

"It's simple." He looked the boy dead in the eye. "As I said, all majestics are unique. I'm not saying you will run into another who has one, but should you ever run into an enemy or hostile Magi and are forced to deal with them, do you think they will simply explain the fine points of their abilities?"

A little angry at that response, he ate a few berries and looked away from the mori's gaze. "I suppose they wouldn't," he admitted finally as he chewed.

"Smart boy." Vaust chuckled. "Neither you nor I know what the future holds. I don't know if you'll stay with the Templars or lead a life that brings you into confrontation with other Magi. But if there is even a tiny part in you that is considering it…well, it's best to be prepared, is it not?"

Devol swallowed his food, sighed, and nodded. "You're right. I'll work on it."

"You should do that for you, not me," his companion stated, finished his meal, and began to pack. "Come on, we're a little behind because I let you sleep, but we can still get to Fairwind shortly before noon if we hurry."

At this announcement, the boy all but inhaled the remainder of the fruits Vaust had brought and packed his belongings. He slid the other end of his blade into the side pocket of his satchel. The mori glanced at him and considered the advice he'd given him. He hoped he'd choose a life where he could use his abilities for good. The life of a Magi was dangerous, but it was better to pursue it and be prepared for it than have it come for you.

And if he was right, the boy would not have much of a choice.

CHAPTER FIVE

Devol smiled as the cool breeze blew in from the sea. They were close to their destination and Fairwind already lived up to its name. He and Vaust had covered dozens of yards in seconds and sprinted to the village. He grew ever more excited and briefly surpassed the mori's speed as they crested a hill.

He paused on top of the hill and looked out with the sun shining on him. The settlement might not have been one of the major cities of the kingdom, but it was one of the most prosperous fishing and shipping ports in the world. Looking at it, even from afar, was enough to confirm that.

It was a village not of tall buildings but vast ones. Large storehouses for fish, tools, ship parts, and more to maintain the workflow and valuables of the village stood alongside equally large dock houses for the numerous ships being built, repaired, or coming in with goods for the market. Most of these clustered around the docks, a vast network of buildings where he could see at least a few hundred men and women going about their busy workday.

Behind the docks, a grid-based collection of streets were paved in rough blue, white, and gray cobblestones. Each thoroughfare was lined with tailors, restaurants, blacksmiths, and other shops ready to serve the populace and visitors passing through.

Devol clasped his hands behind his head and continued to admire the view as Vaust walked up beside him. "We made it." He beamed and looked at his traveling companion. "Do you think we can find something to eat before we go to the order?"

"That would not be a bad idea," the mori agreed and studied the scene below as he removed the stopper from his gourd. "The seafood is fresh here, and I know of a few restaurants of great repute you would probably enjoy."

"Sounds good!" the boy exclaimed and scanned the village again in search of buildings that stood out. "So which one of those buildings houses the order?"

"None of them," his companion stated and drank thirstily. Devol lowered his arms in confusion as he looked at him. The Magi glanced casually at him as he put the gourd away. "Why so surprised?"

"But the map said…and you said…" He fumbled for words and tried to decide if this was a trick or not.

"Ah, yes, the map." Vaust smiled and placed a finger on his chin. "You might want to have another look at that."

Devol whipped his satchel off, opened it, and dug the map out. He unfolded it and examined it quickly. "Look at the line—it leads right to Fairwind!" he said, almost shoved the parchment in his companion's face, and pointed to the emblem marked *Fairwind*.

The mori took it and turned so they could both study it. "Right up to it," he corrected and pointed to the line that stopped at the edge of the town. The boy leaned closer to study the mark. Although it seemed to lead to Fairwind, a small divot off to the side of it seemingly pointed to the east of the village. "I considered simply making you search for it to see how long it would take you to realize your mistake." He folded the map and returned it. "But we'll already have to waste time as it is."

"Then…if it's supposed to be that way…" He turned his head to look at the other side of the hill but saw only a large formation of stones down the slope and much farther in the distance, a large group of trees before the plains stretched on for miles again. "There's nothing there!"

"At first glance, no," Vaust agreed and set off down the hill toward the town. "Are you coming?"

"Where are you going?" Devol demanded.

His companion pointed toward the settlement. "Fairwind. I thought you were hungry."

"I want to find the order first," the boy stated and turned to walk toward the stones on the other side of the hill.

The older Magi chuckled. "Rather capricious, aren't you?" He turned to follow the boy, who leapt on top of one of the stones.

A large patch of dirt in the center of the ring of rocks made him even more confused. "Maybe…" he mumbled, slid off the rock and onto the dirt, and dropped to his hands and knees to search.

Vaust walked around the side of the rocks and leaned against one as he watched him scratch around. "What are you doing?"

"There has to be a secret hatch or something, surely?" Devol responded, continuing to test the soil. "I'll try the forest next, but if it was somewhere in there, the line would have been more obvious."

"A decent deduction," the mori admitted and tapped the side of the rock. "And while watching you scrabble in the dirt for an opening that isn't there might be amusing for a time, it would only be for a very short time. I will tell you that you are in the right place but looking in the wrong area."

He grunted in annoyance and settled on his knees to glare at his companion before his eyes widened and he peered at the face of the rock Vaust leaned against. The markings were faint, but he could see what appeared to be etchings in the stone. He scrambled to his feet and moved closer to examine them.

They seemed relatively simple—a large circle with three triangles, the heads pointing in different directions, one up, one left, and one right, along with large dots in the spaces between each triangle, and one under it. If there were other markings, he could not see them due to how faded the etchings were.

"It seems you've found something most interesting now, Devol," the older Magi said quietly and startled him when he stepped close beside him.

"Uh, yeah, I assume so." He traced his fingers along the grooves. "They look like some kind of symbol but I can barely make them out."

"You wouldn't be able to see them at all if it weren't for the fact that you've kept your Anima up the whole day," Vaust told him.

Devol looked incredulously at the mori, then at his hands. Sure enough, his Anima was still present, albeit at a much smaller scale. He had not meant to maintain it but he felt almost no drain on his Mana. It lingered on him almost like a subconscious thought.

His companion folded his arms and looked at him, his expression somber. "I'll keep this brief as we have another challenge awaiting us. As I explained, the trinity has to do with the control and use of Anima and Mana. Anima naturally enhances one's abilities, including those that cannot be normally targeted using Vis." He pointed at his nose. "You seem like a curious boy, Devol. Have you ever tried to increase your senses? Smell, taste, touch, anything like that?"

He nodded. "A few times, I used Vis on my tongue to increase the taste of a roast my mother made but all I accomplished was to bend the fork." He frowned at the slightly embarrassing story. "I tried other things like increasing my hearing or smell to help at hide and seek but it never worked."

Vaust nodded. "Using Mana to try to target such pinpoint areas isn't an easy task, even for experienced Magi, but Anima surrounds the body, internally and externally, and makes this process easier." He pointed toward the etching. "Focus on those marks. You can barely make them out due to the residual increase in abilities your Anima grants you. Now, increase your Anima and focus on your sight."

Devol drew a breath, straightened, and looked directly at the symbols as he let his Mana pool in his eyes. In moments, the symbols became clearer like the ages of dust that had made the markings fade began to blow away. As they became more prominent, he could even see faint shimmers surrounding them. "There's Mana on the symbols!" he cried in surprise.

"Indeed," the mori confirmed, his arms folded over his chest as he watched him. "This is what is known as an anchor point."

The boy remained focused on the sigils and the Mana that continued to flow through them. "What are they?"

"It is in the name," his companion told him, stood in front of the rock, and held a hand out. "Since you told me as much, your familiarity with the other realms is rather limited. But I'm sure you've wondered at least once how one travels from one realm to another." He balled his hand into a fist and placed it at the center of the point, and the symbols began to glow red. "There are a few ways to do it, but anchor points are the most prominent, at least in your realm."

Devol watched in fascination as the triangle pointing upwards glowed brighter than the others. A faint image appeared above the mori and displayed what appeared to be a city floating above orange clouds. The man began to rotate his fist to the right and the bright glow moved to the right dot between the triangles. The image changed to an ornate-looking house that stood on a hill of purple grass. "They can also be used to travel to individual dimensions—rifts as some call them—that are created by Magi for their personal use, although most are protected by wards that can only be accessed by them or with their permission."

Vaust continued to turn his fist and the glow moved to the right triangle. This time, a lone tower appeared, backdropped by a sky of black and dark purple and surrounded by what appeared to be a forest of blackened trees with white lights or leaves covering them. "This leads to my home realm, Avadon." The mori chuckled and continued to move his fist until it pointed to the single large dot at the bottom.

An image of a large castle appeared, seemingly on top of a mountain or other rocky area. It gleamed white with a large drawbridge drawn up, and fires burned on the tops of two large spires on either side. "And this is the domain of the Templars."

"This is their hall?" Devol asked with a grin. He had made it. Thoughts raced through his mind. What he would say when he finally met one of the Templars and from there, what would he do? He had come to get help and training, but after that, could there be more?

"It is," the older Magi stated and moved his fist away from the rock. The picture vanished as the symbols lost their red glow. "I hope you get to see it soon."

"Wait. What?" the boy shouted and leaned closer to the symbols. "What happened?"

"I closed the gate. It should have been obvious," Vaust said flatly and strode out of the rock formation.

"But why?" he asked as he followed. "I came here for the order."

"I'm quite aware," the mori acknowledged and registered the impatience in the boy, which reminded him how young he was. "Think about it like this. If you and I had not met, how long would it have taken until you noticed your error with the map?" He spun and stared at him. "Would you have been able to decipher the instructions on the side of the map that explained the anchors?"

Devol stopped in his tracks. Instructions? He swung his satchel in front of him, fished the map out again, and studied it. After a moment, he noticed a small diagram on the left edge which included the symbols he had seen on the rock with the bottom dot circled. "Oh, how did I miss that?"

"You are determined but somewhat narrow-minded. That would be my guess," Vaust responded calmly and began to roll his right sleeve up. "I can appreciate your willingness to seek the Templars out and learn things for yourself. But you are young, and if this is what you want to do, you need to mature, Devol."

The young Magi wanted to retaliate against the veiled insult, but he had to admit that he was right. He simply nodded and awaited the mori's next words.

When his companion had finished rolling his sleeve, he glanced at the rock with the anchor. "As it stands, this is your first challenge to becoming a Templar—setting foot in their realm."

"So you want me to open the anchor myself?" Devol asked, folded his arms, and sighed. "Well…fair enough. You are right. I would probably have spent days discovering this on my own even when I got here. But I have to ask why you would try to test me at this point?"

"That's simple. I care about the reputation of the order,"

Vaust explained and showed him the underside of his arm. A golden tattoo of a circular shield inlaid with a triangle set with an inverted eye met his curious gaze. "After all, those who join the ranks would be my brothers-in-arms as well."

CHAPTER SIX

"Uh, sir. We have another customer," the hostess of the famous Fairwind seafood restaurant, Azure Oasis, notified her superior.

The head Manager frowned. "Then why are you talking to me, Melony? You are the hostess for the day. Go and host."

"Well, the gentleman isn't exactly dressed to our standards," she said smartly, pulled back the curtain that blocked the entrance of the room, and peeked outside again. "And to be frank, sir, something seems a little off about him."

"Is he causing a ruckus?" he asked, stood from his desk, and strode to his office exit.

"Not exactly, sir," she admitted. "But if you could deal with him, I would be most grateful."

He sighed. "Fine. Everyone deserves a favor now and then." He pushed the curtain aside and stepped through to the main dining area, walking carefully on the dark-blue carpet to the white marbled floors that lead to the entrance. The hostess followed. When he reached the front, he looked around. "Now, where is this...oh."

It was very easy to see which of the few waiting diners the hostess was concerned about. The man was dressed in dark garb—not entirely unusual as gentleman usually preferred darker colors for their formal dress—but his clothes were far from formal, especially the cloak and hood.

He took a few steps closer to the dark figure. "Can I help you, sir?" he asked, his arms folded and chest out—not exactly a posture that suggested a willingness to be of service.

"I should hope so," the man replied. When the manager noticed that under his hood, a cloth hid the patron's mouth and dark glasses obscured his eyes, he began to feel a little on edge. "I was looking to acquire some food. I've heard your restaurant has some of the best fish in Fairwind—particularly high praise in a fishing village."

"Well, you've heard right," he stated and relaxed somewhat. The man didn't seem to be there to cause problems. "But this is a fine dining establishment, and with that comes a few rules—"

"Oh, no need to worry. I'm not hoping to dine in," the man explained and slid his hand under his cloak. At that, both the manager and hostess tensed cautiously but the concern eased again when he withdrew a piece of paper and a small red pouch. "If you could prepare these items for me, I'll be on my way."

He took the paper and bag and heard a jingle. The hostess stepped alongside him. "We don't allow food to be taken away. You have to have—"

"Hush, Melony!" her superior ordered and she looked at him in confusion before she realized that he had opened the pouch to reveal a rather sizeable, glittering cobalt. He looked at the would-be patron with a large smile. "Of course, sir. We shall do our best to have it ready as quickly as possible. Would you like coffee or a glass of wine while you wait?"

"A glass of wine would be lovely." Vaust nodded and sat on one of the benches near the front door. "Take all the time you need. I have some time to kill."

The mori carried his order on his back in a rather large bag generously provided by the Azure Oasis staff. He left Fairwind and strode up the hill to the field beside the stone formation. When he drew close, he sensed a flare of Mana behind the rocks. A loud shout followed before a crack preceded a body being flung back and skidding on the dirt. He sighed, placed the bag down, and retrieved one of the containers of water before he advanced.

His young companion sprawled ignominiously in the dirt and groaned in pain as he rolled from side to side. Vaust opened the top of the pitcher, splashed a little onto him, and frowned when a slice of cucumber plopped onto his cheek. Devol coughed and shook his head. The older Magi looked inside the container. "Oh, cucumber water," he commented and took a sip. "Quite refreshing."

With a grimace, the boy shifted so he could lean back against the rock behind him. Water dripped off his hair. "You got the food already?"

"You've been at this for a few hours now," he pointed out and set the pitcher down. "A couple of questions. First, how does it feel that I can order several courses worth of meals and bring it here before you were able to discover how to activate an anchor when I did it right in front of you?"

Devol pursed his lips, looked away, and made no attempt to answer. "Well then, second question. It's more personal curiosity, to be honest." He looked at the anchor point and noticed another small pattern above the top arrow in the shape of a rectangle with several smaller ones inside and stitched together with lines. "Why did you think punching the anchor would get it to work for you?"

The youngster rolled his head to look at him with weary eyes. "I was merely eliminating all my options."

"As you might have noticed, all you managed to do was trigger the protective ward," he retorted and indicated the rectangle that faded slowly. "And you are lucky it is there. If you had managed to damage the anchor, be it the symbols or rock, it would have simply made it deactivate."

"The symbols or the rock? I thought the symbols were the anchor," Devol muttered and narrowed his eyes at the large stone. "That's not simply a rock, then?"

Vaust shook his head slowly. "No, that is not 'simply a rock.' If it were that easy to make anchor points, they wouldn't be so valuable."

"A fair point." Devol sighed, straightened a little, and rested his hands on his knees as he stared at the symbols. "I wasn't eliminating options. The truth is that I got angry."

The mori chuckled and offered him the pitcher. "It took a while but you are honest, at least."

With a self-deprecating grimace, the boy took it and drank some of the water. "I tried doing the...oh, that is refreshing." He took another gulp and wiped his lips with his jacket sleeve. "I did exactly as you did, but the symbols didn't light up for me. Then I tried letting my Mana trickle in. That got them to light up a little, but when I poured more in, nothing happened—they didn't even get brighter."

He is close—or at least on the right track. This was not a test for him to get into the Templars' keep. He had said that purely as motivation. What he was trying to do was get him to understand how much Anima enhanced the trinity. He had hoped that he would catch on given that he had already seen what Vis and Vita could do. It wasn't unreasonable to expect that he would come to the final conclusion on his own—what were the possibilities of Vello?

But he imagined the boy was getting hungry and there was no use to continue the training if he would pass out from hunger and exhaustion. He stood, took a swig from his gourd, and went to retrieve the large bag of food. In silence, he returned with it and placed it on the ground. He was about to address his companion when he saw he had drawn his sword and now stared at it. "What's on your mind?"

"I'm gonna try something," Devol said, pushed to his feet, and approached the symbol.

"You can have more time once you've eaten," he told him and sat with his legs crossed. While he was not exactly sure what the young Magi was contemplating, he was fairly certain it would not work.

"What's one of the differences between you and me?" the boy asked and held his blade up.

"Well, there are so many," Vaust responded as he undid the knot on the bag. "Most aren't kind—at least to you. I don't think you need to bruise your ego any further."

Devol looked at him with an exaggerated frown. "Thanks for that," he muttered and turned toward the anchor. "But in this case, I thought the one thing you have that I don't is that you are used to your majestic."

"That is one thing, certainly," he agreed and selected a tin which he opened to reveal herb-buttered salmon. "Are you sure you wouldn't care for a bite? One of the things your realm does better than mine is food, although that may be due to the big difference in diet."

The boy's blade began to glow with the same white light as before and Vaust was grateful that he still wore his shades in this enclosed area. It seemed brighter than he remembered. "What are you doing?"

His companion did not answer and instead, placed the blade against the rock. With that, his purpose suddenly became clear. He thought the majestic acted something like a key and that one needed to have it on them or active to open the anchor before they could control it. It wasn't a bad train of thought, but it was a futile one. After all, not every member of the order had a majestic.

He lifted a piece of fish to his lips to take a bite but a loud roar was immediately followed by another burst of bright light. Vaust dropped the tin and almost drew his kama as his eyes widened.

Devol now stood in front of an open gate. The image of the Templar castle was visible on the other side of the large portal. He could feel the wind from the mountains and the distant heat of the flames that adorned the hall but did not understand how the boy had accomplished it. There was only one way to control an anchor point.

The young Magi looked at him and beamed as he held his sword aloft. "It looks like I passed the first test, eh, Mr. Lebatt?" he shouted victoriously.

The mori relaxed, moved his hand away from his weapon, and simply gave the boy a nod. He had indeed passed his made-up test, although he wanted to accuse him of cheating. Unfortunately, he was unsure of how he did it.

Still smiling, his young companion ran toward him, placed the tin Vaust had taken out into the bag, and tied it again. "We'll bring this with us," he said happily as he shouldered it. "Maybe we have enough to share with your Templar friends." Oh, there would be, the mori realized caustically. He'd bought enough to last three days for the two of them, convinced that this would take at least that long.

He shrugged as the boy ran merrily through and chuckled at his enthusiasm. Most first-time portal-users were incredibly hesitant to walk through and he had no experience with them to his knowledge, yet he hurried through with excitement rather than fear.

The older mage followed, stepped into the gateway, and made a note to examine it when he returned. He had to know what Devol had done.

Although perhaps it would be better to simply watch the boy.

CHAPTER SEVEN

Devol took several cautious steps toward the Templar guildhall and studied it curiously as the howling winds of the mountain pushed against him, although it did little to slow his march to the gates. Vaust stopped in front of the portal and watched him move closer to his destination.

As the gate closed behind him, the mori noted a small change in the boy. He was still determined but he saw an apprehension in the young Magi, whom he had only seen cycle through feelings of excitement, belligerence, and curiosity. He seemed almost humbled at this moment as he approached the gates but he did not falter.

His demeanor was reassuring. He had wondered if he would race merrily toward the hall once he had arrived but this display, no matter how brief, did show that a part of him understood the gravity of the situation ahead of him.

The young Magi reached the edge of the moat that surrounded the castle. He stared down what was at least a fifty-yard drop into the chasm, and the water looked deep. After a moment, he focused on the castle and studied it more thoroughly. Even with the picture the portal had provided, he could not have imagined its scale at the time. It was massive—well beyond any of the halls he had known even in Monleans, where it was said that the hunter and knight halls were the largest in the world. This eclipsed even them.

He counted seven spires in all, four at each corner of the castle and three that were stationed in a triangular pattern and built into the center of the façade. Numerous pennants fluttered over the front entrance, and he recognized the green, white, and golden ones with the large tree and sun emblem—those of Arkadia, the realm of humans, wildkin, and fleuri.

At the bottom of the banner were seven other insignias and one was a sword pointing to the same sun emblem that adorned the insignia of his realm. It was that of Renaissance, his kingdom. He was more than familiar with it, given that he had seen his father in armor almost every day of his life, where the emblem shone proudly on his chest plate.

The other icons were probably from the other kingdoms and meant to show that this was a realm of seven kingdoms united together—although with what he knew of history, that seemed to be a more noble goal than actual reality. He turned his attention to the spires and noted the large bowls that sat on top, each with a large fire that the wind from the mountain did nothing to extinguish. In fact, it might have helped to keep them ablaze.

Slowly, he shifted his gaze to the gate in front of him. The large drawbridge was raised, waiting to be lowered to invite visitors inside. In the small space above the entrance and the bridge, large spikes provided hints of a gate that could be used if the castle was ever attacked.

Devol released a long breath, placed the bag of food at his feet, and rested his hands on his waist as he watched his companion approach. "Hey, Mr. Lebatt?

"Yes, Devol?" the mori asked, stepped beside him, and let his gaze trace the familiar structure. "It's quite a sight, is it not?"

"Oh yeah, it's amazing," he replied but a questioning tone still lingered in the compliment. "But I…"

Vaust looked at him in surprise. "Yes?"

He scratched his head a little sheepishly. "Is this another test?"

"Not one I've devised, why?"

The boy frowned and gestured at the castle. "Then shouldn't the bridge come down?" he asked and pointed at it. "You said you were a Templar too, didn't you?"

His companion frowned. "Yes, and I have to say you've taken that information with rather less enthusiasm than I expected."

"Yeah, sorry about that." He smiled a little awkwardly like the thought had only now occurred to him. "I thought it was a joke at first, and I was in a foul mood at the time." He looked at the bridge again. "But in that case, why haven't they lowered it? I know they don't know who I am, but they should lower it for you, right? Is there a password or call sign or something?"

Vaust chuckled. It was amusing to see him in the moments where his knowledge and understanding gave way to childish myths and games. But he did have a point. "Why yes, there is a password." He opened one of the pouches on his belt and retrieved a small purple crystal with a silver band around it. "Give me a moment and you'll hear it."

Devol gaped as the crystal began to glow as Vaust raised it to his head. A voice resonated in his mind. "Eh, who is it?" the speaker demanded and the boy looked around to see where it was coming from.

"It's me, you dullard," his companion replied with mirth in his voice, although his lips did not move. "Lower the bridge. Isn't that your responsibility? Am I interrupting a nap?"

"Vaust? Well now, you're alive!" The man dissolved into laughter and the boy now realized it was being emitted by the crystal. "It looks like I owe Zier a splint now. But why are you all bothered? You were supposed to be here yesterday."

"I had an interesting meeting," the mori explained with a smile at Devon. "I've brought a visitor with me—a young Magi looking to meet the Templars."

"Is that so?" The man evidenced genuine curiosity in his tone. "We don't have many of those these days. Let me meet the little scamp."

"Certainly. Let us in and you can do exactly that," Vaust stated crisply.

"Aye, aye, I'm on it. Hold on a wee moment—been helping with the smithy," the man replied. "I'll be there in a minute."

The mori nodded and lowered the crystal from its position close to his lips.

"Who was that?" Devol asked as the glow in the gem

faded before Vaust stowed it in the pouch. "And what is that?"

"The crystal? You've never used an apperception stone?"

"Apperception?" He shook his head in confusion before his thoughts came together and he realized what the crystal was and pointed at the satchel. "Oh, an A-stone!" he shouted, shaking his head. "No, we mostly use voxboxes to communicate. A-stones are expensive. My father has one but he won't even let me touch it, much less try to use it."

"Oh, that's right," the mori conceded. "They are rather pricey in some realms. As they were originally created in Avadon and the stones are rather plentiful there as well, they are considerably cheaper. They work better for our line of work than your voxboxes, so we each have one. They are one of the few materials that can hold Mana."

"Like cobalt?" he asked.

Vaust nodded. "Yes, although they are not nearly as valuable as they only store rather small amounts, but they can hold dozens of different types of Mana at the same time. So you merely need to connect your Mana with one stored inside and you can communicate with that user."

"Amazing." Devol gasped, impressed and a little envious.

His companion nodded. "Should you decide to join us, I'll make sure you get one."

"Truly?" The boy grinned. "That would be wonderful."

"It's something to consider. And as for who that was…" A loud clang issued from the castle, and both looked up as the drawbridge began to lower. "Well, it appears you are about to meet him."

When it settled, a man appeared and the boy's eyes widened. He was certainly larger than any man he had ever encountered, easily over seven feet with large shoulders with a span that was easily as wide as Devol's body was tall. A large blond beard was perfectly matched with long, unruly hair with several braids woven into it.

He wore an eyepatch that did not quite cover a noticeable scar on his right eye. The other showed a deep-set eye of a dark color and its gaze drifted from Vaust to the visitor. His large arms folded, he strode across the bridge. He wore a long brown jacket that reached his ankles, below which black boots with metal tips were visible. Beneath the jacket, some kind of gray or dirty silver armor could be seen when he moved but was mostly obscured by the garment.

The wind whipped at the giant of a man and his jacket was tossed and tugged at relentlessly, but his approach seemed unstoppable. The young Magi stood a little straighter with his arms at his side.

"You don't need to be so formal," the mori told him and folded his arms to mirror the man, who was now only a few yards away. "Despite appearances, he is quite a gentle giant. Well, make sure you do not do anything to make him your enemy. Start on the right foot."

Right foot? What would that be? Devol had been very casual with Vaust. Was that the right approach? Should he offer a handshake or a bow? He had grown up around the royal guard thanks to his father and his mother had instilled proper manners. Although he admittedly might not have used them to the best of his ability, now would be a good time to recall those lessons.

The man stopped a few feet from the arrivals. The boy lowered his head—less of a bow and more of a polite nod that lasted far too long—and awaited the response.

"Damn, does it always have to be so bloody cold out here?" the giant protested. Devol pursed his lips, confused by this. It was a little chill with the wind but it didn't seem that bad. He raised his head cautiously. The large Templar tightened his jacket before he slapped his comrade on the back. The mori seemed unmoved. "How have you been, Vaust? Took you longer to finish those gigs than I thought!"

Gigs? He was only aware of the one the older Magi had in the woods. Were they all like that? Vaust nodded and smiled at his friend. "It was mostly the travel. I don't get to enjoy the realm that much when I'm here, so I took a slower pace. Also..." He moved his arm and gestured with his hand toward Devol as if presenting him. "This is Devol Alouest, the young Magi here to train with the Templars."

The man looked at the youngster and noted his stiff demeanor. "You all right, kid? Nervous about being in the presence of the Templars, are ya?"

That might have been a factor but it was mostly this so-called gentle giant he was worried about. "It's an honor to meet you, sir," he blurted, straightened, and thrust a hand toward him.

"He wasn't so nervous around me." Vaust chuckled and glanced at his friend. "And he had never seen a mori before. Perhaps you should think about your appearance, my friend. You could be scaring potential recruits away."

The man returned his gaze with a crooked smile, and

Devol noted sharp canines amongst his teeth. "I should look into finding a jacket with some bunnies in it, then?"

"Designs or hides?" Vaust asked.

The man frowned and scratched his beard. "Does it matter?"

The mori sighed. "Yes, but let us not dwell on that or we will be out here for quite a while." He placed a hand on the boy's shoulder. "Devol, I would like you to meet Captain Baioh Wulfsun, my friend and one of the commanders of the Templar Order."

Wulfsun waved a large hand dismissively before he immediately brought it back to hold his jacket tightly against him. "I don't need that title crap. Not much use for it nowadays. You can call me Wulfsun, lad."

Devol nodded. "A pleasure to meet you, Mr. Wulfsun!"

"Just Wulfsun. Come on now." A sheepish grin appeared on his face. "All Templars are brothers and sisters here, and we will be soon enough if you've come to join us."

"He's merely here to train," Vaust interjected. "He hasn't made his mind up about whether he will join us or not."

The giant frowned and stroked his beard as he studied the young Magi. "Is that so? Only to train? There are many academies and guilds to look into for that. What made you seek us out, then, boyo, if you don't mind me asking?"

Devol took his pack off. "No, it's all right." He retrieved the map and handed it to Wulfsun. "I was told to come here by my father and Mr. Lebatt helped me on the way."

"Is that so?" The man's smile widened and he darted a glance at the mori as he took the map and unfolded it. "It's not like you to take strays in, Vaust."

"I saw him in action and he's hardly incompetent if

that's what you are implying," the other man countered. "In fact, he was able to draw his Anima out in one night."

Wulfsun whistled, clearly impressed. "That's quite a feat!" He scrutinized the map. "And I wasn't saying nothing bad, only that—" His eye widened and he stopped in mid-sentence and darted a glance at Vaust, who responded with a nod. "Huh, ain't that like him," the giant muttered, folded the map, and handed it to Devol. "Tell me, lad…that blade on your back wouldn't happen to be a majestic, would it?"

He nodded and drew his shining blade "I'm not sure what it does, but it's a big reason why I'm here." He held it aloft and let his Mana flow through it and in moments, it shone with the ethereal light.

The Templar commander observed it with astonishment, his mouth agape. "That looks exactly like—"

"Something you've seen before?" Vaust asked and cut him off. His comrade looked at him in bewilderment, but when he caught his gaze, he merely nodded slightly.

"Aye, something like it." He gestured to Devol. "You can put that away now, brother," he stated as he turned. "Let me welcome you to the Templar Order hall. I can tell things are about to get quite interesting today."

CHAPTER EIGHT

The entrance hall of the main building was adorned with several paintings, large and small. They all seemed to capture vital moments—battles, victories, armies standing ready, or a lone warrior preparing to fight a monster. Devol guessed that they were historical pictures and noted that many of them also bore the circular Templar insignia that he had seen on the castle entrance and Vaust's arm.

Wulfsun pushed a pair of large doors open. The room within was large and two curved staircases at the end led to two separate floors. A large desk stood near the stairs. No one was seated there, but he was surprised at how ornate it was. In fact, much of what he had seen of the castle had a sense of splendor to it.

He saw a few more large canvas paintings, and when he looked at the ceiling, a large version of the insignia was inscribed there in gold. He was not too familiar with architecture or any type of building design, but he could tell this structure was quite old yet remarkably well-maintained.

"So then, where should we head to first?" the captain

asked and placed his fists on his waist as he looked at Vaust.

"I'll leave that to you," the mori replied as he gestured to one of the staircases and walked toward it. "It would appear that the madame isn't here, so I'll have to search for her."

Wulfsun snorted. "You simply gonna head off, then?"

His comrade waved dismissively. "You are in charge of the new trainees, aren't you? And you are capable." He stopped at the foot of the stairs and looked over his shoulder. "I'll catch up. I need to drop my bounties off and report. For now, get to know the boy. I think you two will get along famously." With that, he began to ascend the stairs and left the two of them alone.

"Always shifty, that one," the giant muttered with a scowl. "It took quite a while for the two of us to see eye-to-eye, even when I had both of them." He turned and looked at Devol. "He didn't give ya too much grief on the way here, did he?"

The boy shook his head. "Mr. Lebatt was quite helpful. He traveled with me, showed me Anima, and even helped me with the first test."

"First test? What test?"

"The one to open the anchor," he said cheerfully. "You know, to get in?"

Wulfson folded his arms and uttered a surprisingly soft chuckle for a man of his stature. "Heh, that was no test, boy. At least not one for the order."

"Huh?" Devol shook his head in confusion. "But there were instructions and everything on the map. How was I supposed to get in without using the anchor?"

His protest met with another chuckle. "I saw the instructions and I assume you didn't read them through properly." He held his hand out and spread his fingers. "You were supposed to place your hand on the anchor and let your Mana flow into it. Someone would have come through eventually."

"But I did that when I was trying to open it," he stated.

"For how long?" Wulfsun asked.

"I tried it multiple times and I poured a lot in!" he confessed.

The man shook his head again. "Ah, I can't tell if he was honestly trying to test you or merely having a laugh. You simply had to position your hand and let your Mana flow for about one full minute. It is a signal that someone is looking for us—like ringing a bell. Most guilds that use rifts do something like this. Otherwise, how would potential clients and recruits make contact? It's not an easy feat to open an anchor." He clicked his tongue in thought. "So how did you get here, then? Did he eventually take pity on ya?"

Devol shook his head and pointed at his blade. "No, I eventually worked it out. I had to use my sword."

"Your majestic?" Wulfsun asked and raised an eyebrow. "You used your majestic to open the portal?"

"That's right." He smiled. "I feel a little embarrassed that it took me so long to discover it. Mr. Lebatt even demonstrated how to do it."

The commander was intrigued. Opening an anchor had nothing to do with a majestic. While some had abilities that affected portals, that wasn't the norm. Was this boy's power something like that? That would be a hell of a find. He was quite thankful that Vaust saw fit to bring him there. It could be a dangerous thing for others to find out.

"I see. It's something to think about," Wulfsun mused.

"What's that?" he asked.

After a moment, the man turned and approached another pair of doors in the lobby that led to the west wing of the castle. "Nothing for now. Come along."

"Where to?" He ran behind the Templar, who held them open. The two slipped inside and the doors shut with a loud clang behind them. Now that he thought of it, almost all of them made the same sound when they shut.

"I'm gonna show you the training hall," Wulfsun stated. "It's the closest thing we got to an academy here."

"There is a Templar academy?" he asked. He had never heard of such a thing and might have gone there first if he had known.

"Not an official one," his guide admitted as they walked down a narrow hall with many doors on either side. "We haven't had one of those in more than a couple of centuries."

Devol nodded and glanced at the man. "Oh yeah, I wanted to ask—what does a Templar do, exactly?"

The giant stopped in his tracks. He was a few steps ahead of the man before he did as well and looked over his shoulder. Wulfsun caught him by the back of his coat and lifted him so they were eye to eye. "You came here knowing nothing about the Templars?"

"Um…not really," he admitted. "I know my father respects you and that Templars are skilled Magi warriors. But compared to other Magi guilds like hunters, knights, and sorcerers, I can't say I know much. I don't think I ever met a Templar before you and Mr. Lebatt."

Silence followed for a short moment while the man considered that. Finally, he nodded, put him down, and patted his shoulder. "You're a trusting lad, I'll give you that. I'm not sure I would ever go to a place I didn't know anything about, much less search it out."

"As I said, my father respects you," the boy repeated. "And both my parents said this would be the best place to learn about my new weapon. That's all I need."

"Is that right?" Wulfsun's frown turned to a smile as he continued to walk. "Best not let your pappy and mummy down then. In here." They reached another set of doors, these etched with a sword on one and a fist on the other. "Most of those other rooms are for individual training and meditation, but this is where many of us get real work done." He pushed them open.

Inside was a massive open domed area that contained about a dozen round arenas, each themed differently. Some contained large trees and shrubbery akin to a forest. Another had rockier terrain with cliffsides and spikes on the ground. One was filled with water and a platform in the middle was only a few inches above the surface. The water flowed around it like it was an ocean tide and splashed onto it periodically.

"This is incredible," Devol said as he studied the area in awe. Long walkways led to each arena and bronzed archways above them were roofed to block the sunlight. About thirty men and women either walked around or sparred with one another. Both human and wildkin were present, along with another mori like Vaust, although he was black with red eyes and a few white marks. He chatted to another realmer with pale golden eyes and smoother features who looked less haunting and more gentle than his companion did. Was he a mori too?

Another humanoid appeared to be female and stood almost as tall as Wulfsun with deep-red skin. Coarse gray hair almost like straw flowed down her back. She had large glowing red eyes and curved horns and was dressed in dark armor with the Templar crest in the center of the chest plate. She was in conversation with another humanoid with sleek light-purple skin and large, round black eyes, fish-like in appearance. Devol could see webbed hands and some kind of device around its neck that flowed with water. He was dressed in blue robes with the Templar insignia on the left of his chest.

"More realmers," he whispered, enchanted. "That's a daemoni and tsuna, right?"

"Indeed." Wulfsun nodded. "Our order welcomes people from all realms and ways of life as long as they hold to our values." He pointed to an arena in the distance. "There are a few more."

The boy narrowed his eyes and studied a slim figure dressed in leather with scaly green skin and large round eyes that could move in every direction and a large fin on its head. He was in a battle with two others, a shorter, stocky figure that looked a little like Wulfsun but with fiery, short, and well-kept red hair instead of blond and a braided beard.

When the man smiled, he revealed stone-like teeth and he held two large axes aloft, one in each hand. The third figure—who observed the other two—had bronze-colored flesh, a slanted face with pretty green almond-shaped eyes, flowing green locks, and a single horn on her head. She was dressed in pale-green robes with browns and blues woven in.

"Those are…a squama, dwarf, and dryad?" Devol asked.

"Aye. They are more impressive in person than as pictures, eh?" the captain commented. "We've got realmers from all nine of the known realms, although not all are here today."

"I wanted to ask…" the boy began but trailed off for a moment as he considered his question.

"What is it?" Wulfson responded encouragingly.

"This castle is huge and there are so many people here." He turned to look at the Templar. "But given the size, it feels like there should be more."

The giant nodded and gestured for him to follow him to a stone bench near the forest arena. "Aye, and there are, but not all are here in the arena. I'd bet you a splint most are in the tavern right now, while others are off on missions." He sat and folded his arms as the boy put the bag of food down and sat next to him. "But even if we had every Templar here, you would still be right. The order is somewhat light on bodies. It has been for a while."

"But why?" Devol asked. "My father spoke so highly of you and from what I saw of Mr. Lebatt, you are amazing."

"We certainly can be," Wulfsun said with a smile. "But that doesn't mean that many are flocking to our gates. I won't bore you with all the details given that you don't know what you want to do yet. But I'll say that our order is ancient—hells, all other guildhalls were based on our example. But with that long history comes some dark times, and those can overshadow all the good you do, unfortunately."

"What happened?" He felt sorrowful as he sensed the commander's forlorn demeanor.

The Templar forced a grin, straightened, and clapped him on the back. The friendly blow almost knocked him off the bench. "Ah, don't worry about it for now. The thing is, that incident is old news but it caused some shake-ups in the order. That and the establishment of the guilds meant we lost esteem, but we still remain. We have a duty to."

"Establishment of the guilds?" the boy repeated. "So does that mean the Templars aren't a guild?"

"We aren't but most people call us that since those are the norm nowadays," Wulfsun replied. "The Templars are an order. It might be a minor difference to most but it's a statement to us. We are an order connecting to all realms. There is no other Templar order but ours, and although some tried previously, they didn't last." He leaned forward and peered skyward. "We have a duty to defend the realms from evil, and it isn't a matter of philosophy. Anything that seeks to destroy or corrupt is our foe."

"The knights and chevalier guilds work similarly, don't they?" Devol pointed out.

The commander shrugged. "As I said, all guilds foundations are based on ours, but there are important differences." He glanced at him. "Including a mission we have been in charge of for centuries."

"And what is that?" The boy leaned closer, wanting to hear more of this.

Wulfsun straightened and folded his large arms behind

his head. "It's something the Templars have to deal with for now. You needn't worry about it."

Devol frowned. It seemed both he and Vaust shared the habit of withholding information they didn't think he should know.

"Now tell me something, boy," the captain began, "what kind of training are you looking to get here?"

He leaned back as he considered it carefully. "I'm not entirely sure. Um…I guess focusing on my majestic would be the most important."

"That would be wise but beyond that, I mean we can teach you weapon combat, Mana arts, all the usual things. But unless you have a goal, I don't see why you would need to stay here to learn all that specifically," the Templar replied.

"A goal?" He placed his hand on his side and touched the hilt of his blade. "I do know that I want to be a warrior like my father. I feel that if I do have something special about me, I should use it to help others, right?"

Wulfsun uttered a loud laugh but in merriment, not mockery. "That is the best way to use it, I think. Yours is better than some of the responses I've heard over the years."

"I'm glad you think so." His gaze drifted to the different Templars and absorbed a few more details. "This is beyond what I even imagined it would be. I…I think…" The words trailed off and he paused and wondered if he was merely caught up in the moment. He didn't want to make a promise he couldn't live up to or would regret.

The Templar sensed something weighing on the boy and assumed that Vaust had dropped hints to him that he should join them. He was somewhat guilty of it himself and he had only known him for about fifteen minutes. With a reassuring smile, he patted him gently on the shoulder. "Don't worry about too much right now. You can get some rest and think about it. Feel free to stay with us and train, then see what you think."

Devol nodded, closed his eyes, and drew a sharp breath. "Thank you, but I'm fine. I came here to train and if you'll take me, I'm ready to start right now." His speech was punctuated by a noticeable growl from his stomach and his eyes widened as he shook his head. "Well, maybe some food first." He lifted the bag and began to undo the knot. "Do you want some? Mr. Lebatt bought so much."

Wulfsun chuckled and nodded as he helped the boy open the large bag. He had spirit, without a doubt. That was something many lacked, so he already had a significant advantage.

CHAPTER NINE

Once he had shared much of the food bought by Vaust with Wulfson, Devol still had leftovers, which he gave to the other Templars in the battlegrounds nearby. The commander guided the determined boy deeper into the training grounds for him to begin his "tests."

As they walked, he asked questions about the test and the man simply responded with some variation of, "Wait and see." A little frustrated after each gentle rebuff, he turned his attention instead to the arenas and other Templars nearby to keep himself occupied. When they seemed to draw closer to the end of the path, he saw a rather simple arena, at least when compared to the others —a smaller square platform made of white marble.

Three figures occupied the combat ground. Two were older Templars from what he could see and he studied them with interest.

The man had wolf-like features—long, pointed ears, a pronounced nose, clawed hands, and tanned skin, with a long shaggy mane of curled brown hair. The other was a woman—or at least had the figure of a human woman—but had long blue arms with rows of feathers, a black pointed beak, and deep-set black eyes and a crown of blue and green feathers for hair.

They were both wildkin but two different varieties, the man belonging to the more human-appearing homina species and the woman of the verte species. Both had the more pronounced features of their animal counterparts.

The third figure—which the two older Templars were observing—was a young girl about his age from what he could see and was also a wildkin. She was a little shorter than him with long black-and-orange hair with white spots and similar sharp, pointed ears to the man. Her ears, however, were on the top of her head and almost blended in with her hair. She had fair skin and one eye was green while the other was blue.

Dressed in a simple baggy white shirt and pants, she practiced punches and sweeping strikes with her claws. He stopped and watched her draw back and noticed a pair of bracers or gauntlets on her arm, although he couldn't make the details out. A yellow light flashed briefly before she leapt forward and slashed the air. Devol's eyes widened as three large claw marks gouged the ground of the arena despite the fact that he could not see her touch it. She wouldn't have that kind of reach anyway, which left him confused.

When he looked at her, she had focused her gaze on him and he nodded sheepishly as he jogged to the commander's side. "Hey, Mr. Wulfsun."

"I told ya, boy, just Wulfsun," the Templar stated in a

pointed tone, but the boy was reassured by the easy smile still on his face. "What do ya need?"

"I wanted to ask…are you a wildkin too?" the boy questioned, he didn't have the more noticeable traits of either species, but the sharpened teeth, great height, and well, he might be a little presumptuous, but the name could have pointed to that.

His large companion laughed and shook his head. "Ah nah, boyo. I'm as human as you. I was raised and trained by one, though," he revealed. "I was left on the Templar Order doorstep as a lad and my master was a wolf wildkin similar to Freki there." He nodded at the man Devol had observed. "Baioh was the name I was left with in the letter—no family name obviously. I decided to exercise a little humor and named myself in tribute to my master, although he didn't find it as amusing as I did. Still, I think he appreciated it."

"Is he here?" the boy asked. He wanted to meet the man who had trained such a confident warrior.

Wulfsun shook his head again. "Nah, he left on a mission over a year ago and won't be back for quite some time."

"You didn't want to go with him?" he asked as the two passed under a large open gate into another room with dark-brown walls. Orange orbs hung from the walls to illuminate the area and Devol noted several weapons and pieces of armor beside them.

"Of course I did!" the captain admitted and frowned at the thought. "But that's how I came to have this command. He said someone needed to watch over the training since he would be gone for so long. I didn't like to think about it at the time, but he was right. There were others who could have taken the mantle, but if I wanted to consider myself his kin, I should also be prepared for the responsibility."

The young Magi nodded. "That's very admirable."

The two stopped at a pair of metal doors and Wulfsun folded his arms and released a bellowed laugh. "I thought so too. I mostly got called sentimental and such at the time, but I eventually got the hang of it. I'm starting to see why he did this for so long—you get attached to the young buggers when you watch them grow and go after their ambitions, although we don't have many youngsters to speak of right now. It's heartwarming. I guess I am a little sentimental." He scratched his beard, briefly lost in thought or memories before he nodded to his companion and flicked his thumb toward the doors. "Well then, if you are ready, we are here."

Devol turned to examine the doors. They looked heavy—dark metal with a bronze Templar insignia spread across them both. "The test takes place in there?"

"This is the first test!" the commander corrected and smacked one with a large hand. It clanged noisily and the boy resisted the temptation to cover his ears. "This is a test of mettle. I'm not sure how much attention you've paid, but I should tell you right now that Templars are in a constant state of training, even during off-hours. Every door in this castle weighs anywhere between a couple of hundred pounds to seven hundred, although one or two are a little heavier."

"All of them?" He gasped and recalled the loud thuds along the way every time the man had opened one.

"Aye. It helps with potential thievery as well." Wulfsun

chuckled. "It's hard to be sneaky when every door slams with the subtlety of a dragon's fat ass pounding into a town broadside, although Vaust and a few others have found a way." He frowned slightly but gestured with his hand. "Anyway, this door is one of the heaviest in the castle. Each side is one thousand, seven hundred and fifty pounds, totaling three thousand five hundred pounds."

"By the Astrals, what?" Devol gawked and studied them more closely. "So my test is…"

"To make it through," the Templar declared and held three fingers up. "You seem hesitant so I'll give you a hint. Only a handful of the strongest men in the world such as yours truly can open these doors naturally, so don't think about it like that. There are three ways you can accomplish your task. The test is to get through, and I'll leave the rest to you." He folded his arms again. "Still wanna start right now? As I said, you can have a few days to think it over."

Devol responded by removing his pack. He stared at the man for a moment with determination in his eyes before he stepped closer to the doors and studied them. He had options, he thought cautiously and assumed that pushing them was the simplest, which meant using Vis. That triggered an idea and he paused to consider it.

There were three ways to open them and three uses of Mana in the trinity. If he was right, there was not only a way to accomplish it Vis but with Vita and Vello as well. He examined the metal more closely. How was that possible? His gaze settled on a large keyhole between each door just before the Templar insignia. He traced it with his fingers and discerned the faint presence of Mana.

Wulfsun had not said anything about a key so maybe he

could open it with his Mana? That would be using Vello so it was an option, but Vita? He stepped back again, took a deep breath, and summoned his Anima around him before he focused on his eyes.

The Templar noticed this with great interest. Vaust had mentioned that the boy had only learned Anima the night before. It seemed the young Magi had a knack for it as he barely felt it flare. He almost chuckled at the irony. The boy approached this cautiously, but if he was already familiar with Anima, he was making this harder than it needed to be.

Devol stared at the door and studied the inverted eye of the Templar insignia, which seemed to look directly at him. Some type of rune or ward was traced in Mana above the eye and it latched onto him somehow, but he felt no malicious intent.

If he had to guess, it was a tracking rune of some kind and perhaps measured his Mana. That would be a measure of Vita if he was right. So to even start the tests properly, he concluded, he had to show that he had learned the basics. He began to realize that Vaust's prodding and coaching might have been to determine if he could get past this point. A little ruefully, he acknowledged that he should have been more thankful when he had the time with him.

He let his Anima subside and exhaled slowly as the silver-and-white light faded around him. How should he approach this? Should he perhaps simply use Vis and test his theory? He was not sure he could open it with Vis alone, however. Maybe part of the way, but he had yet to see how strong he was with the aid of Anima, so it was potentially possible.

A NEW LIGHT

The boy straightened with his arms at his sides and let his Mana flow through him. As it built, he closed his eyes to focus better. If he intended to try Vis, he needed to harness as much Mana as he had available.

His concentration was broken, however, when he heard the shriek of metal. He opened his eyes and narrowed them on the eye of the Templar insignia. It glowed and the doors began to move apart.

Wulfsun clapped loudly behind him. "There you go, boy! You found the solution in no time at all."

"Wait. I had only begun to build my Mana up—" Devol protested but stopped himself. He had used Vita to do it and had somehow summoned enough Mana to empower the door to open. It had been successful, even if not as planned.

"Ready for the next part, then?" the commander asked and waited for him to step through, but he caught the man's arm to hold him back. The Templar looked curiously at him.

"If you don't mind," he said with a glance at the doors, "I want to see if I can open them the other two ways."

Surprised, the giant raised an eyebrow. He had not heard the request before and most were satisfied to have simply opened the doors. But if the boy wanted to make the attempt, why stop him? He grasped the handles of the large doors and closed them easily. He ran a hand over the eye to deactivate the ward and stepped back. "I like to see spirit like that. Try to your heart's content."

Devol nodded and approached the keyhole. If he had enough Mana to get through with Vita, then Vis would probably work with no issues. Vello was his weakest discipline in the trinity, so that would be the next one he would try. He peered inside the keyhole and noticed small, glowing blue spikes in the darkness—cobalt? So was he supposed to use his Mana to activate those?

It seemed like a more complicated way to display his flow of Mana, and he had already done that. He straightened with a frown. There must be something more, but he couldn't even begin to guess and would simply have to try and see if it worked. He extended his hand with his fingers spread apart and let small trails of Mana flow out and into the keyhole to attach to the cobalt spikes within. He allowed more to trickle in and when he neither saw nor heard any change, he decided that flooding the spikes with Mana wouldn't achieve the desired result.

It was a keyhole, so perhaps he should treat his Mana as if it were the key. That made sense when he thought about it and he held his open hand with the other, closed his eyes to focus, and used the Mana attached to the spikes to try to turn the lock. He regretted it almost immediately as he could feel his fingers bending with it.

The Mana strands were too thin. He probably had the right idea but needed to strengthen the bond. Pushing his impatience aside, he focused on building the Mana trails to strengthen the connection between him and the lock. The process relieved his fingers somewhat when he tried to manipulate the lock again, but when he had turned it almost a quarter of the way, the resistance returned. He frowned and tried using his other hand to create a second set of Mana strands to help relieve the stress of the bond and unlatch the door.

Wulfsun observed the boy's struggle, a little surprised

that he still had to use Vello in that manner. In the same way he knew from watching him use Anima that he could open the doors, he knew from this display that it wouldn't work. Most Magi who were advanced in Vello did not use it as an extended limb or digit. This type of action was accomplished purely through mind and spirit. It was not necessarily bad that he used Vello in this manner for simple things like moving objects and the like, but he would not get through the lock like that.

Eventually, Devol released his hold, backed away from the door, and shook his fingers. He stopped after only a few steps and sighed in frustration before he shook his head, returned to the door, and placed his palms on it. His face a picture of concentration, he let both his Mana and Anima flare and stared at the Templar eye as he gritted his teeth and pushed. With an angry yell, he took a step forward and thrust the doors apart.

This earned an approving whistle from Wulfsun, who placed a hand on his shoulder. "Two out of three. Well done, lad," he complimented him. "Most are happy to get through the first time. You have certainly shown some fire."

The boy nodded and checked his fingers. "I guess I still have more to work on," he admitted, picked his pack up, and slid it over his shoulders. "What's next, Mist —Wulfsun?"

The Templar let that slide and pointed into the dark hall behind the doors. "Now we get to the part that makes things fun," he stated with a toothy grin. "We'll learn about that pretty sword of yours, brother."

CHAPTER TEN

They proceeded deeper into the darkened space and moved toward a light that indicated a second chamber.

"This is one of the spires in the center of the castle," Wulfsun explained and pointed to the opening ahead. "We refer to it as the treasury and it's where we keep most of the valuables we've procured through missions, negotiations, that kind of thing."

"And it's where you keep the majestics?" Devol asked.

"Not all, boyo," the Templar corrected. "We have some in there but majestics are unique and we can't simply pass them around like we would a work mule. This is where we keep artifacts, exotics, trinkets, curios, those types of things. Rivets as well."

"Rivets?" He frowned as he searched his memories. "I don't think I've ever heard of those."

The commander chuckled. "It's something of a local term around here. But more importantly than those, this is where a friend of mine is usually hiding. He'll help you get everything in order for the next part of the test."

So he would meet another Templar. He wondered if he was a commander too and where he hailed from. Was he another human or perhaps a realmer he had yet to see? He'd had so many new experiences today and yet he was thrilled about another. It was probably a habit he should work on before he went into another haunted forest in the future.

When they walked into the chamber, Devol paused to study the high white-and-silver walls contrasted by dark marbled floors. Several large bookcases were filled with tomes and a few banners displayed the familiar Templar insignia. A massive fireplace provided a calm, flickering fire and in one of the corners of the chamber, the foot of a spiraling staircase leading farther up the tower was visible.

"It's probably the fanciest looking room in this castle," Wulfsun told him. "My friend managed the decorations and renovations over the years, something of a pet project."

"Given that it might as well be my abode…" a steady, studious voice began and the boy turned. The speaker was a dryad, a male this time and taller than the female he had seen earlier. His pale red skin highlighted his bright yellow eyes. Flowing blue robes covered his form with white wrappings around his hands and what appeared to be wooden rings on two fingers of his left hand, but they were immaculately crafted. His hair was long and hung to the middle of his back. It was a snowy white but more vibrant than Vaust's, and his white horn protruded from the top of his forehead with another wooden ring adorning the base.

He folded his arms behind his back as he approached the two visitors to his domain and his gaze lingered on Devol for a moment before he turned his attention to

Wulfsun. "I would argue that making it more homey helps with my work."

"And hello to you too, Zier!" The captain greeted him with a large grin and turned to his young companion. "This is Zier Nightbloom, head of scholars in the order." He turned to the dryad and gestured toward the boy with his head. "This young Magi is Devol. He came looking for us."

"I see." Zier looked at Devol, who saw a faint glimmer of white and green in his eyes. "Hmm...impressive for your age. You are here to train?"

He nodded and drew his blade. "Yes, sir. I recently acquired this majestic and need help to determine its origin and abilities."

"A majestic? Are you certain?" the scholar asked.

He shook his head but immediately nodded, a little confused by the question. "I've shown it to others like Wulfsun. They agree that is what it is."

Zier closed one eye and peered at the sheathed sword. He removed a hand from behind his back to stroke his chin. "To come here for that? It's rather unorthodox."

"He's here on good authority," the commander explained and stared into his comrade's opened eye. "Trust me. Vaust brought him in himself."

"Ah, so he has returned then," the dryad commented. "Good, I need to speak to him. But before that—"

At a loud clatter in a room behind him, the scholar sighed and looked over his shoulder. "Is something amiss in there?"

"Everything is just fine!" a young male voice called in response. The speaker had an accent and stretched the j's and i's, but Devol could not place it. "I'll be there in a second." A moment later, a boy emerged through the doorway, dressed in blue and white robes. He had dark skin, sharp green eyes, and hair twisted together in long braids.

The large tome under his arm looked almost flesh-colored from age and wear, and a newer book with a dark leather binding and a golden eye embossed on the cover was clasped shut and bound to his belt. "Is this what you were looking for?"

Zier took the tome and examined it. "Indeed it is. Well done," he said with a nod and opened it. "How you manage to find these long-lost treasures is astounding."

"You were reading that a month ago, Zier," the youngster replied and shrugged with a small smile on his face. "Not long-lost so much as misplaced, although why you left it in the map area is a mystery to me."

"Humph." The scholar sniffed and flipped through the pages. His assistant finally noticed the visitors.

He nodded at the giant Templar. "Hello, Commander." His gaze shifted to Devol. "Oh, someone my age." He approached him and proffered his hand. "Nice to see another boy here."

"Nice to meet you," he replied and took his hand. "I'm Devol Alouest."

"I'm Jazaiah Filsaime, but you can call me Jazai." They shook hands and studied one another curiously. "So what brings you to the order?"

"He's here to train," Zier answered before the others could. "He's showing some initiative, unlike a certain someone."

Jazai frowned and rolled his eyes. "You know, Zier, when you're that obvious, you can merely say 'you.'"

"I'm trying to leave you some dignity," the dryad retorted and continued to flip through the pages in the book.

His assistant sighed and focused on the newcomer. "My father and he were buddies in the academy or something. He brought me here to keep up with my studies when he had to go abroad."

"And have you done your part?" Zier asked. "Do remember I'll be writing to him soon."

"You don't write," the boy replied. "You send him messages with an A-stone."

"We're both busy men," the scholar countered and peered at him for a moment. "And the question still holds weight. I'll be testing you by the end of the month."

"You still need to teach me more about rune placement and functions," Jazai retorted and smiled wryly.

"Indeed so." The dryad nodded and returned to his book. "I'll make sure you can call yourself an expert by the test, so it will be no blame on my part if you fail."

"That hasn't been a problem so far." The boy chuckled, stepped beside Devol, and leaned closer. "I think he was hoping I was a wide-eyed know-nothing he could simply lecture all day. He's become somewhat irritated about the fact that I've excelled in every trick and test he's thrown at me."

"Certainly not, young Jazaiah," Zier responded. "Your intellect is a sign of your talent and your father's teaching. It's merely the ego and personality around it that irks me."

The boy chuckled again. "He's basically saying I'm a

jerk but a smart one, at least." He looked at Wulfsun. "So is he your new apprentice or something, Commander?"

The giant shrugged. "We haven't gotten that far. We came here to start the next part of the tests."

"Really?" Jazai's attention turned to Devol. "So you just did the doors?"

He nodded. "Yes. Did you take the tests too?"

The boy nodded with a broad grin. "Yeah, little over a year ago. I got through using Vello on the keyhole and it took me less than ten minutes."

"Vello?" he asked and frowned when he recalled his attempt. "That was the one I couldn't do."

Jazai nodded a little smugly. "It's probably the hardest one, but I thought— Wait, the one you couldn't do?" His smile faltered and he gave the newcomer a bewildered look. "So you got through with both Vita and Vis?"

Devol nodded. "Yeah. I think Vis was the easier of the two." He screwed his face up in thought. "Although I didn't mean to open it with Vita. It simply happened."

The other boy's expression was incredulous, and he looked at Wulfsun for confirmation. The Templar now wore a sly smirk as he nodded.

"That's…uh…well, it's damn good," Jazai acknowledged. "It looks like I might have some competition around here."

"Oh yeah. But you did say it was nice to have someone your age," Devol recalled and gestured over his shoulder. "And I saw a girl—a wildkin—who looked about my age."

"Asla?" the young assistant frowned and peered in the general direction of the arenas as if he could see her through the walls "Well…she certainly counts, but she's not exactly a very extroverted person.

"She's been staying in the order for a few years now, being looked after by her guardian, Freki. She's begun training hard over the last year or so. Can't say too much, partially because it's not my place and partially because our conversations are usually pretty brief."

"Give her time," Wulfsun stated with a small frown. "The reason she's here isn't as simple and comfortable as yours."

Jazai nodded. "I know. I've not pushed her." He looked at Devol. "How old are you exactly, though?"

He pointed to himself. "Me? I'm fourteen, turning fifteen in a couple of moons."

"Oh, then you are closer to her age than mine," the boy responded, lowered his arms, and gestured at himself with a thumb. "I'm fifteen, turning sixteen during the awakening moon."

"Let us hope that is the start of you earning some wisdom," Zier remarked, shut the book, and focused his full attention on Wulfsun. "So I assume the reason you are here is that the boy is trying to learn about his majestic's abilities, then?"

The commander nodded. "Aye. The lad doesn't know a damn thing about it."

Jazai raised an eyebrow. "Can I see it?" he asked and held his hand out. Devol nodded and handed it to him. The apprentice drew it and Zier studied it for a moment before his eyes widened. "Oh, that's a majestic indeed," the other boy muttered as he examined the blade's surface and the light under it. "Have you seen something like this before, Zier?"

"I believe I have." The dryad glanced at Wulfsun, who

nodded curtly. He thumped the book onto a nearby table. "Come with me."

Jazai seemed surprised by his mentor's reaction. He turned to Devol and shrugged, slid the blade into the scabbard, and handed it to him. Zier took the group to the other side of the room and into a larger chamber, this one with a stone floor and a large table in the center. "This is where we will hold your kinship trial," he stated.

"Kinship trial?" the new young Magi inquired as he looked a little warily at the large cupboards, racks filled with various tools and scrolls, and a massive chandelier above.

"It's another test, basically," Jazai explained. "This one will help you to discover its origin and ability."

"Oh, that would be useful," he said, a little distracted by the numerous and very different objects on the table. "So will we have to look through books or something?"

"Nothing that mundane," Zier said and approached him. "You will speak to your majestic."

CHAPTER ELEVEN

"The majestic will speak?" Devol frowned at his sword. "Are they...alive?"

Zier's eyes closed for a moment before he turned his head slowly to look at Wulfsun, who shrugged with indifference. Jazai chuckled and slid an arm around the young Magi. "Nothing like that. He means resonation."

"Resonation?" That meant little and he felt more confused than ever. "Vaust said something about the fact that not everyone can use a majestic so I assume it has to do with that?"

The scholar nodded. "Indeed, although in this case, we can see that you are already forming a connection to yours. What we will attempt to find out is what power it has." He gestured to the table.

Devol examined the items again and noticed over a dozen weapons and instruments, although none looked particularly ready for battle. "Are those training weapons?"

Wulfsun shook his head. "Nah, boyo, those are the rivets I told you about." He walked closer and selected one that resembled a mace but was almost all black and made of a rough-looking material. "I guess you can think of them as practice exotics. They use enough special material to contain the magical enhancements but aren't practical for battle unless you are trying to show off."

"On occasion, we find someone who is worthy of a majestic," Zier continued and stepped beside the commander. "We have several stored awaiting a master, but even in our current condition, we are not in a position to merely hand them to someone who shows promise. Majestics are powerful, and while they may not be sentient as you suggested, young one, they can connect themselves to another."

"Mr. Lebatt said something about that too," Devol recalled. "He said that if it bonds itself to you and it gets damaged, that could affect you as well."

"Aye." Wulfsun nodded. "And worse, if you try to force a bond with a majestic when you aren't compatible or ready to wield one yet…well, people have lost things to the process."

"Lost 'things?'" he asked a tad nervously, although he tried to not let it show.

Jazai leaned closer. "Mana, limbs, lives, things like that."

His eyes widened in surprise. "Oh, that's unfortunate."

"Indeed," Zier agreed and examined the other objects on the table. "This is a simple study. You are to try each weapon in turn and see which one resonates with you the best. In normal circumstances, this would tell us what kind of power the user will best work with. You see, while majestics and exotics are different, there are some similarities. The abilities of exotics and the Mana that fuels them are similar, almost like a person's biological—"

"I think you're wasting your breath, Zier. Not the time for a lecture." Jazai interjected with a glance at the other boy. "Basically, discovering which power works best with you might be a clue as to what your majestic does. It isn't always right but as he said, it is a simple study."

"I see." Devol sheathed his sword on his back as Wulfsun tossed him the mace he held. He caught it, surprised by how light it was. "Are all rivets this light?"

"Many are." The commander folded his arms. "Although they are made with the cheapest special materials, as much as that sounds like a contradiction. But that mace's power is to increase and decrease its weight depending on the wielder's control. Try it and see what happens."

Without hesitation, he let a trickle of Mana flow into the mace. He had some experience using exotics as his father had given him some lessons, although he never let him keep one until the sword appeared. He saw a small silver glimmer in the head of the mace and it became weightier in his hand as he connected to it.

"You see the color of his Mana?" Wulfsun whispered to Zier.

"I did." The scholar nodded. "Another sign, it seems."

Devol swung the mace to adjust to the change in weight, then raised it and increased the weight as he repeated the arc. This time, it almost made impact with the floor and he grimaced. He did not doubt that he would have cracked the stone with the rivet if it had done so. He used both hands to lift it and noted how heavy it was now. As he struggled with it, he wished he hadn't made it so heavy and it lost weight drastically so he was able to raise it easily over his head.

"Well, that seems to work as expected." The commander tapped the table. "Put it down and try another."

Devol nodded and complied. "I'm curious," he stated and looked at the two Templars. "Do either of you have a majestic?"

Wulfsun grinned. "Aye, both of us do."

Zier glared at him for a moment before he sighed. "Indeed, we are among a handful of Templars who have a majestic. Most here make do with exotics."

"Can I see them?" he asked excitedly. "I saw Mr. Lebatt's. While I'm not sure what it does yet, it looked impressive. I want to see some others if I can."

"Don't bother." Jazai snorted and glanced at the scholar with an aggravated tone to his voice. "He's never shown me, no matter how much I pester him about it."

"Mine is an orb," the dryad responded and his apprentice's jaw clenched. "My realm of Daosith holds majestics in high regard, as many do. We have about forty known majestics, and each noble family is blessed with one or more. In my family, I was chosen to take care of one of ours."

Jazai folded his arms as he stared at his tutor in exasperation. "Why do I have the feeling you did that to spite me?"

"There is no need to be so vague, Jazai," Zier responded cheerfully. "I did do it to spite you. Now go and fetch a kinship scroll, if you would."

The boy rolled his eyes and exited the room. "Perhaps I should write to my father about you."

"I'm sure he could use the laugh," the scholar retorted before he returned his attention to Devol. "Now then, continue with the others. Once you have tried them all, we shall work on the next part of the trial."

He nodded and examined the different objects available —a shield, a pair of glasses, rocks in several different colors, a rifle, scissors, a doll made of cloth and one of plastic, a deck of cards, a long wooden staff, and a number of other odd objects as well. "Some of these would make poor weapons."

"Truly a warrior, aren't you?" Zier sighed and received a questioning look from the boy and an irate one from Wulfsun. "This is a world of Magic. Just because something may not appear to be practical…well, that falls into the hands of the user rather than the object itself."

The commander looked around the table and he frowned at the dolls. "Even I have to admit, some of these are weird choices. I did tell them to make the rivets simple, I suppose."

"Keep going until you try each one, young Magi," Zier instructed. "And let us know if one appears easier to use than the others. Remember, we're looking at the abilities and connection, not the items themselves."

He looked at the long table with a frown. This would probably take a while.

Jazai returned to the chamber and watched in silence as Devol tried to resonate with what appeared to be a camera. He stopped beside Wulfsun with his arms folded and a scroll in one hand as he observed the attempt with a mixture of amusement and sympathy. "He's still at it?"

"Aye." The giant Templar nodded. "Zier is making him try every last one of them."

The assistant shook his head. "He made me do the same thing, although I found mine after only a few different items." He patted the book attached to his waist. "Kind of convenient that it turned out to be the same type of majestic."

Wulfsun nodded again. "We had that in the vault for a long while. I'm glad it finally found a user."

He smirked. "Glad to take it off your hands. However, Zier keeps making me use it for menial tasks."

The commander gave him a knowing glance. "It's probably his way of training, yes? Besides, it's not like you can keep it if you merely have it for appearances. Gotta get practical use out of it eventually."

Jazai sighed. "I know, I know."

"There are only a couple left," the Dryad stated. "Finish this and we can continue."

"Hey, Zier!" his assistant called and held the scroll up. "I'm back."

His tutor looked at him over his shoulder. "Just now? Where have you been?"

"Looking for one of these damn things," Jazai retorted and waved the scroll in the air. "We have very few left. I had to get this from the supply you keep in your quarters."

Zier nodded and returned his focus to the young Magi undergoing the trial. "I'll make a note to order more."

Jazai lowered his arm and looked at the scroll. "When was the last time we had a kinship trial? Asla, wasn't it?"

"And you before that," Wulfsun told him. "But before you…probably two or three years before you arrived."

"We aren't exactly using them at a frenetic pace," the boy muttered. "I didn't see Asla's trial, so this will be my first time to see someone else go through theirs."

"I'm interested to see which one comes up," the commander mused and stroked his beard. "I got a splinter on some kind of transmutation ability."

"You also have a gambling problem," Jazai retorted and ignored the Templar's somewhat offended scowl by looking away to gesture at the other young man. "If I had to take a guess…I would go with evocation."

"Is that so?" Wulfsun asked as Devol picked up the last object. "Many majestics are that so it's a safe bet, but not everyone falls into a class so easily."

"Agreed, but did you look closely at that blade?" the young apprentice inquired. "That light inside… I might not be a smithy or majestic researcher yet, but that looks like it channels a power source of its own. Many evocation-type majestic have something similar to that."

"Similar yes," the giant agreed. "But not quite like it either."

"So, am I finished?" Devol asked as he put the mace down. "They were all different but none felt quite right."

Zier nodded. "It would appear so. Did any of them feel unique?"

The boy shrugged. "They all felt about the same, to be honest. I don't think I had any problems controlling any of them, but I don't think I was exactly great with any either."

"Not that I noticed." The dryad frowned. It would appear that they would find no hints there and he felt a small surge of excitement. This had rapidly become something of a mystery, one he was eager to solve. He beckoned to Jazai, took the scroll from him, and unrolled it. For a long moment, he studied it in silence before he nodded at Devol, who stepped forward hastily.

"So what's next?" he asked eagerly.

Zier turned, stretched the parchment, and knelt to place it on the ground. "We try to discover the class of your majestic."

"Class? Like its type or attribute?" the boy asked, his gaze fixed on the scroll as the scholar stood.

"Nice deduction," Jazai commented. "Think of it as what category the power of your majestic falls under—like cantrips. Usually, this is for the user to see what magic class they are most in tune with to help to choose a majestic or exotic for them. But in this case—"

"We would normally do something like this over a period of time," Zier interrupted and earned his apprentice's ire. "You would use these scrolls several times over months or potentially years if you were a novice. Gradually, a symbol would develop on the scroll that indicates your class."

"Oh, I see." Devol nodded and regarded the blank page with both excitement and nervousness. "But it won't take that long for me, will it?"

The dryad shook his head. "You already have a majestic. We are merely trying to find out what it does." He gestured to the scroll, which was entirely blank, and then at the boy. "Funnel your Mana into it through the blade and it should produce the symbol immediately."

Without hesitation, he unsheathed his blade and looked

from it to the parchment. He would finally have an answer to what the light could do. A part of him felt eager while another part felt a little uneasy, and he did not know how to describe the odd contradictory sensations. So much had been thrown at him so quickly, but he reminded himself that this was the main reason why he'd come. He needed to find the answer as soon as possible so he could look to his future without doubts to hold him back.

"Place your majestic on the page," Zier instructed.

"Make sure to not stab through it," Jazai warned.

The scholar shook his head and sighed. "I truly hoped that was self-explanatory."

The boy nodded and placed the tip of the sword gently onto the scroll, letting his Anima gradually gain power as he transferred his Mana into the blade and through it onto the page. The others gathered closely and awaited the results to see what future this young Magi had in store.

CHAPTER TWELVE

Devol removed the sword from the scroll and bent to pick the parchment up as the others took a step back. He could see nothing other than a faint shimmer of silver from his Mana. Disappointingly, no words or symbols had appeared.

Wulfsun scratched his head, his expression confused. "Did we get a bad one?"

Zier shook his head firmly. "No, even if Jazaiah had chosen a defective scroll, I examined it myself before we started."

The other boy glared at his mentor. "I think I hear a faint tone of sadness that you can't blame this on me."

The scholar brushed his protest aside and extended a hand toward Devol, asking for the majestic. He handed the weapon to him and looked on with concern as the dryad ran his hand over the sword and checked the tip of the blade thoroughly. "Odd. It seems fine and the boy was obviously able to use it." He frowned and returned it. "Well then, it is not impossible for the scroll to not work, merely quite rare."

"Want me to get another?" Jazai asked, his arms folded. "Do remember I'm getting them from your personal supply."

Zier pointed to the scroll in Devol's hand and the boy handed it to him. He examined it carefully to be thorough before he shrugged and rolled it. "Nothing seems the matter with this one. It looks like we'll need to try other methods."

"What other methods?" the boy asked and rested the blade on his shoulder.

"You'll see in a moment," he promised, pointed to the other boy, then indicated one of the cabinets in the far corner. "Jazaiah, I'll fetch a crystal. Get the pedestal ready, would you?"

His apprentice whistled in surprise. "You gonna use the crystal now? I don't think I've seen one of those used yet." He continued to mumble as he and his mentor went in separate directions. Devol followed the younger scholar.

"What's this about a crystal?" he asked and peered over his shoulder to where Zier and Wulfsun looked in different cupboards on the opposite wall.

"Don't worry about it too much," Jazai said reassuringly. "It's another way to potentially discern the class of magic your majestic fits into. Although I should mention that this one is trickier."

"Oh, got any pointers?" he asked, a little worried about what made this one different than the scroll. If he failed the easy trial, would this go any better?

"It'll require Vello," the other boy explained, opened the

large doors of a cabinet, and searched through the contents. "You will pour some Mana into a crystal, which will charge the Mana with its essence and react to it in a unique way, depending upon what class it falls under. It's basically a curio."

"A curio?" Devol remarked but the answer did little to resolve his confusion. "I've had curios before but they are simply magical knick-knacks—toys. I don't think something like that can be of much help."

"That is more common nowadays, I guess." Jazai chuckled as he continued to search through the cabinet. "But curio is a very generic name. It is better to think of them as exotics that are not meant to be used as weapons. They aren't always souvenirs for people passing through the big city."

He regarded his companion with a raised brow. "That sounds like a judgment."

The boy chuckled again and shrugged. "More an observation. I guess I'm a city boy, technically." He finally retrieved out a bronzed, three-legged pedestal from the depths of the cabinet. "Here it is. I doubt we'll have any problems with it being defective. This used to be the only way to discover a Magi's talent a couple of centuries ago."

The two rejoined their elders. Zier now held a fist-sized clear crystal and once Jazai positioned the pedestal securely, he placed it on top and motioned for Devol to sit on the floor. The boy did so and, his nervousness seemingly forgotten, studied the crystal. On closer inspection, it had what could be a glow in the center that he had not noticed before, or maybe it hadn't been there until this moment.

"Place your hands on either side of the gem," the scholar instructed. He nodded compliance and moved his hands slowly to the sides of it. Immediately, the light inside began to shimmer faintly. "Now, this should not be difficult, but it will require concentration and might be taxing on your Mana supply," the dryad continued as he sat opposite him. "You need to send your Mana through the outer shell of the crystal so it connects to the light inside. That light is what we refer to as a Mana cell, something that can absorb Mana."

"Like what is inside cobalt, not so?" Devol asked.

"Not exactly." The Templar seemed to prepare himself to begin a lecture until a slight tap of Wulfsun's boot on his back stopped him. "Humph. Well. For now, it is close enough. But this has been modified to take Mana in and search it. As a result, it will have a different reaction depending on the type of power your majestic has."

The boy nodded and noticed his hands shaking a little. "Wait—shouldn't I hold my majestic or something?"

Zier shook his head. "This is for people who are still discovering what type of majestic they could wield so holding your weapon serves no purpose. But in your case, you already have a majestic that has connected to you, albeit lightly from what I can tell but enough to leave a type of imprint on you. This crystal will be able to detect that imprint and react accordingly."

"Oh. That makes sense." The boy frowned in concentration. "So what kinds of reactions are we looking for?"

"Well, if it is in the constitution class, it will form a tight ball of light. If it is the conjuration class, it will form into a kind of mist and swirl around the inside of the crystal," the

Templar explained. "Things like that, but since we haven't gone through what each class represents, we'll hold off on that for now and attempt to discover what your class is first."

Devol drew a breath and moved his hands slightly closer. "I'm ready."

"Good, now take a deep breath and concentrate," Zier ordered and watched closely. The boy obeyed, his eyes closed, and thin trails of Mana flowed from his fingers onto the side of the crystal. "Send a little more now and remember that the Mana cell is your target, not the crystal itself."

With a small nod, he scrunched his face and focused more intently. The thin strands of Mana grew thicker and finally pushed through the crystal and seeped into the light. He continued to push more into the crystal, where it was drawn in by the light. Zier, Wulfsun, and Jazai all looked on eagerly, waiting to see the reaction from the cell.

"You doing fine," Jazai murmured. "It might take a couple of minutes but keep going."

Devol responded with the slightest nod, now almost fully focused on keeping his Mana in check. He didn't want it to grow weak or even to potentially overload it, although he was unsure if that would create a problem. Maybe a large amount was needed to cause a reaction.

A sense of tension settled over the group. Zier noted small changes and studied each one carefully. The light began to glow brighter and shifted its form, but nothing conclusive resulted. He should have had more patience, but his patience had begun to wear thin. He was oddly invested in the revelation of the boy's majestic's power and now decided he would step in and help him.

"Go ahead and increase the flow of your Mana," he instructed. "Don't overdo it but send a surge in and let us see if that yields something."

The young Magi immediately released a pulse of Mana that traveled into the cell, and it flared brighter than it had previously.

"Looks like we're finally getting somewhere." Wulfsun smiled and leaned closer. "Now let's see what it looks like —huh?"

The trio gaped as the light formed into a ball that suggested it might be constitution until it did something rather unexpected. It began to enlarge and a torch-like fire enveloped it as it stretched before it bounced around the inside of the crystal and began to divide itself into small copies.

"By the hells, what is all this?" the commander demanded.

Zier shook his head as he clasped the boy's hands. "I honestly have no idea. Devol! That's enough. You need to stop."

Devol opened his eyes and his eyes narrowed on the crystal as the light began to swirl rapidly inside. The flames formed a halo that began to rotate. He backed away hastily, along with the rest of the group. Even though he had cut the flow of Mana off, the Mana cell did not stop.

"Uh...are we in danger?" Jazai asked.

"Shield!" Zier called and an illuminated shield of green Mana formed in front of him.

Jazai frowned and reached a hand out to drag the other

boy closer. "An unusual way to provide a hint, friend. Shield!" he snapped to create a barrier, this one of blue Mana.

Wulfsun remained in place with his arms folded as they continued to stare at the crystal. It began to glow even brighter and everyone wondered if it would erupt or collapse but awaited whatever would happen with bated breath.

It turned out they had been too anxious. After one final burst of light, the Mana cell inverted itself quickly and faded, surprising all of them. Jazai and Zier took a moment to observe it and make sure it would not have one last surprise in store before they dropped their barriers. The scholar stood, walked cautiously to the crystal, and prodded it a couple of times before he picked it up and examined it.

"So, does that tell ya anything there, head scholar?" the commander asked and looked from the dryad to Devol.

His fellow Templar nodded, silent for a moment before an amused laugh caught Wulfsun and Jazai off guard.

"What is it Zier?" the apprentice asked.

He gestured dismissively. "My apologies, but it's been so long..." he muttered and turned to address the others with a smile. "I do indeed know what class he is now," he revealed and smiled broadly as his gaze settled on the young Magi. "It has been quite a while since we've had a perplexion amongst us."

CHAPTER THIRTEEN

Though Zier stated his words with the air of someone who expected a rather shocked reaction from those present, he instead drew an amused look from Wulfsun and Jazai and a bewildered one from Devol.

"A perplexion?" the boy asked, drew his sword, and rested the blade on his shoulder. For some reason, having it there brought him confidence. "What is that? Are you saying I'm weird?"

"No, no, not weird. Special would be more appropriate," the dryad responded with a smile the young Magi assumed was supposed to be calming. Given his rather terse personality until now, however, it seemed more creepy than comforting.

"Well, if that's all done and settled," the commander began, stepped closer, and clapped the boy on the shoulder. "We can continue with the test—"

"Now, now, Wulfsun. No need for that, is there?" the scholar interjected. "There is so much more the boy needs to learn, and he came here for training if you recall."

The giant regarded his comrade warily. "Aye, but the whole point of learning his class was to determine where we should start his training."

"True, but that's precious time we are burning," Zier pointed out and placed a hand on his chest. "I propose that we begin his training immediately and I will, of course, lend a hand to—"

"Oh no, you don't," the commander snapped, stepped away from Devol, and jabbed a massive finger into the dryad's chest. "I see your plan now. You found something new to play with, and you want to hurry this along for your sake."

The other Templar frowned, grasped the finger, and jerked it aside. "This is far from 'play,' Wulfsun, and I don't see how this is not beneficial to the boy. I might have my own interests, true, but that does not mean—"

"The boy is here for training, not to be your study specimen!" the giant countered and folded his arms obdurately. "He's only learnin' this stuff, and if he's going to train, he needs to do it right."

Zier's scowl deepened and matched the furrowed, angry expression of the Templar commander. "Honestly, how often do we have a majestic in the perplexion class? We are not even quite sure what it does, so what use is there in conventional training right now?"

The two continued to argue and Jazai stood beside the bemused young Magi. Both boys watched the argument escalate. "So…uh, what's happening, exactly?" Devol asked in a low tone that their superiors were unlikely to hear.

"Something you will probably get used to around here," his companion admitted and gestured with his head at the bickering Templars. "I'm not saying Zier and Wulfsun hate each other or anything, but they are different enough that if they spend too much time around one another, they eventually butt heads over something."

"I see..." he replied although it wasn't entirely true. The opponents wagged fingers at each other and Wulfsun now looked a tad red in the face. "So can you tell me what a perplexion is?"

Jazai nodded. "It means you are special, but not in a condescending way. Although when Zier says it like that, I understand how one might be confused." He chuckled and unlatched the book from his belt. "We were trying to discover your majestic's power and perplexion is a rare class of Magic. The fact that the test reacted in such an odd way means you don't fit into any of the normal classes, which makes it unique."

"Oh, that seems logical." Devol nodded and held his sword up for a moment to look at it. He released a trickle of Mana and the light began to float around it. "Is that a good thing?"

"Usually, but I could not tell you outright," the other boy admitted. "You see, there are six classes as we know them—conjuration, evocation, transmutation, divination, manipulation, and constitution." The apprentice opened his book and pursed his lips as he glanced at it. "I can give you a more thorough explanation of each later, but they are an easy way to find out how your majestic relates to your Mana. For example, a spell or power of the conjuration class can make something—an item, element, or things like that—from Mana."

"I know that one fairly well," Devol said. "My mother is

adept at conjuration cantrips. But there are only certain things you can make, aren't there?"

Jazai nodded. "There are rules and you can't make something like an invincible shield or a bow that never runs out of arrows. But since that isn't your class, you can learn more about it later."

"That is true. So what does perplexion mean mine can do?" he asked and rested the blade tip on the ground.

His companion shrugged. "Well, that's the tricky thing, isn't it? Also, it's the reason why my typically composed mentor is so excited."

The two young Magi looked at the arguing Templars again. Zier had stepped so close that he almost touched Wulfsun's chest and continued to argue his position while he tried to slip sly insults past the giant. By the way the commander narrowed his eyes, however, he noticed each one.

"That's how he acts when he's excited?" Devol asked and gestured at the dryad. "I'd hate to see him angry."

"Different circumstances." Jazai sighed and shook his head before he returned to his book. "Because you're in the perplexion class, you don't fit neatly into any of the other classes. It means your power is probably rather interesting but more difficult to pinpoint and train for."

"Oh. Well, that is a problem," he muttered and glanced at his weapon before he focused on his companion. "So… do you have one?"

"One what?" the apprentice asked and looked up from his book.

"You know," he responded and shook his sword. "I overheard you talking about the time you did the test. So does that mean you were trying to see what majestic you could wield? Or was that only advanced Magi training?"

Jazai smiled and nodded. "Mine is divination," he revealed, held the open book tied to his waist, and tilted it toward him. Devol assumed that the magic within it made it light enough to carry this way when it should have been far too heavy. "My majestic was one my father found before I was born. It sat in the vaults here in the order until I arrived. He sent me a letter to personally congratulate me on being the one to claim it. Divination is the magic class that affects the mind or astral plane." He showed him several lines written in the pages that he didn't look at very closely at first.

"Astral plane?" Devol asked and squinted as he focused on the words. "What is an... Wait, this is about me!" He gasped. Within the tome, he could see words being written in front of his eyes. The pages showed his full name, date of birth, and paragraphs mentioned details of his life, his practice in swordsmanship, his wins in foot races with other children, his favorite meals, and even his best stories.

"It's impressive, isn't it?" the apprentice asked with a smile. "The more I get to know someone, the more I am able to tap into their memories and my majestic can probe more deeply into their minds. Usually, I can only learn things they are thinking about in the moment or pieces of information that are ingrained in them—like their name, personality type, things like that. The more I am around them and the more they let their guard down, the more my book can discover."

"My guard down?" He considered that for a moment and decided to try something. Without saying anything, he drew out his Anima again as he followed the words being written. They began to slow. The record of the memory of going into the Emerald Forest outside Monleans with his mother changed to a description of the room and the events that had just taken place.

"A good guess," Jazai said with a nod. "If your Anima is up, that reduces my majestic's ability to 'discover' more about you, at least your past. But if you want to get around it, you have to be thoughtlessly aware."

"Thoughtlessly aware?" He didn't quite grasp what the boy meant with that. "You mean empty my mind?"

"You have the right idea," his companion agreed. "For example, if you only focus on what you are doing right now, all I can retrieve is your basic information and whatever you are doing at this moment. Although it only works if you aren't far away." He turned the page to reveal that it was now blank before he flipped it back. Some of the words had disappeared, but his details and some of the memories it had already written down remained. "It stays unless I erase it or the person or thing dies."

Devol nodded and felt very uneasy. "That's honestly terrifying. You could learn anything you wanted about a person without talking to them."

Jazai shrugged. "Again, there are rules. It only worked well because you didn't have your guard up and I had time to get to know you a little already. By the way, I only explained this because I feel like we'll get along if you stay," he told him. "Whenever we decide about what your majestic can do, you'll want to keep that between you and your allies. In battle, an opponent knowing your tricks is a huge disadvantage, although I'm sure you can see that for yourself."

"You're right." He nodded and smiled at the apprentice. "Thank you."

"For telling you?" the boy asked.

"For saying you think we'll get along," he stated, flipped his sword, and rested it on his other shoulder. "I think we could be good friends too."

The apprentice's eyes widened before he smiled and nodded. "It would be nice to have someone who is close to my age," he admitted. "But that all depends on how long you are gonna be here. Still, those are questions for later." He gestured to his book. "I was trying to see if I could learn anything about your majestic's ability."

He pointed to the left page that showed an inked picture of Devol with his name and basic information written next to it. "I've worked with my majestic over several months, and I have it set so that if I have the chance to learn about someone, the specifics of their majestic is one of the first things to come up. Of course, not many people have one so I'm somewhat lacking in practical experience." He moved his finger to the section titled *Majestic* that read *emits a bright, unnatural light*. "As you can see, I unfortunately had no success. If my tome can't deduce it, my observations are stored so it can build on them later."

"Is it because I don't know much about it?" Devol asked.

"Probably. There have been a couple of times where I've discovered something my target forgot or didn't know about before. I hoped it would work like that here, but no such luck."

The young Magi sighed and his frown returned as he looked at the Templars, who seemed to have resolved none of their disagreements. "Then it looks like we'll all have to find out together," he stated before he strode toward the two opponents.

Jazai reached a hand out in an attempt to stop him. "I wouldn't interrupt them when they are like—"

"Hey!" he shouted and immediately drew their attention. With his free hand on his hip, he stared at them and let his exasperation show. "Thank you for helping me thus far, but I want to know more about this sword and we won't find the answers any sooner if you stand here and shout at each other. So please, can we get back to the tests?"

The apprentice lowered his hands and managed to control a laughing fit when he saw the perplexed expressions on the two elders' faces. Zier coughed into his hand and backed away from Wulfsun, who rubbed the back of his head sheepishly. "Eh, sorry about that, lad—a civil disagreement between a couple of old comrades," the commander muttered in a subdued tone.

"Quite," the dryad agreed. "I suppose I was caught up in the excitement. Majestics are quite rare, and anything in the perplexion class is extremely rare and I wanted to—Oh, it does not matter at the moment." He turned to Devol and nodded. "You are right. We need to learn more about your ability before we can get any real work done. And the next part of the test should at least provide us with a starting point."

"Which was exactly my point," the giant Templar muttered. His comrade darted him an irritated look.

"Wonderful, then let's get to it!" the boy exclaimed and thumped his fist against his chest. "So what's the next part?"

Wulfsun placed his hands on his waist. "We'll head into the arena so you can show us your skill, and you'll get to try your majestic in a more...hmm...visceral setting."

"I'd like that," he said with an eager nod. "So will I spar with a beast or something?"

"He has been called that before." Zier snickered and the commander cast him an angry look.

"Context is important there, scholar," the giant retorted and turned to the boy. "But I'll give you better than some beastie. boyo. Your opponent"—he placed a thumb against his chest plate and gave him a broad, toothy grin—"will be yours truly!"

CHAPTER FOURTEEN

"I have to slay you?" Devol asked and stared at the Templar, his eyes wide. "That seems like it could be…awkward."

"You don't have to slay me, boy." Wulfsun sighed and shook his head.

"I would not mind it," Zier mumbled loudly enough for the Templar commander to hear.

"Shut yer trap," he retorted and looked at the boy again. "It's only a sparring match. We'll try to see if using your majestic will provide more information in battle."

"It's a chance to see what your power might be," the dryad added as he bound the hefty tome Jazai had retrieved for him previously with a length of leather around the waist of his robes.

"Aye, that too." The giant thumped his chest with one of his hands. "Take this match as an opportunity to go all out. We're here to see how far you've come until now."

Jazai lowered his head down and whispered to Devol. "Gonna spoil the big secret here. The test isn't to determine whether you're worthy to join the Templars or not."

"It's to see how strong I am, right?" he responded. "Where I need to focus my training?"

The apprentice nodded and straightened. "So you caught on?"

"Yeah. I've heard them saying things like that for the last little while," he replied. "It's been so much process, but my ears are sharp."

Wulfsun clapped sharply. "All right, are you ready, boyo?" he asked eagerly.

Devol nodded and pointed to him. "Will you use your majestic as well, Wulfsun?"

The Templar smirked. "Of course. I can't make this too easy. There would be no point to it if I did."

"So do you need to go and get it first?" he asked.

"No need." The commander shook his head and his smirk became a broad grin. "I've almost always got it on me."

"Oh, can I see it?" he asked and scrutinized him to see where he might have strapped it on his person.

"You'll see it soon enough." The chuckle that followed seemed a little ominous. "Come along now."

Wulfsun marched past the boys and back to the outer room with Zier on his heels. The two young Magi soon caught up and Devol wondered what the man's majestic could be. He'd said he already had it on him and it could be any number of things. Vaust's was a kama and a rather ornate one at that.

He did mention that they typically had an elaborate look about them, and looking at the large man now…well, it certainly wasn't his coat. He noticed his gauntlets—black with an intricate, looped pattern in gold. His thoughts returned to the wildkin girl he had seen earlier. She also used some type of gauntlet or gloves and when she attacked, she seemed to strike with invisible claws of some kind. So the gauntlets were a possibility but unless he knew what they did, he had little opportunity to prepare.

Before he realized it, they had left the spire. Wulfsun pushed a massive pair of doors and they opened into a large dirt arena. A couple of stairways led to a large platform above and Zier and Jazai ascended the right side.

"Good luck, Devol," the apprentice said as he turned and gave him a thumbs-up. "We have good healers, so don't be afraid to go all out."

The boy nodded and returned the gesture. "That's good. I don't have to worry about hurting Wulfsun too badly then."

Zier snickered as the commander smirked. "If the boy didn't sound so earnest, I would say he was mocking me."

The young Magi discarded his pack at the edge of the entrance to the arena and moved to the right side as his opponent went left. His focus settled into calm and he swung the blade a few times to make sure he had acclimated to it. While it still felt entirely natural to wield it, he was again amazed by how weightless it felt to him given that it was much longer than the other weapons he was used to.

Satisfied, he faced Wulfsun, who had undone his jacket and tossed it aside to reveal a large chest plate with a similar pattern to his gauntlets. The giant crouched, clapped sharply, and extended his arms. "All right, boyo.

Whenever you are ready, come at me with everything you've got!"

Devol nodded and held his blade with both hands on the grip. When he looked at the massive Templar now, he felt a little of the intimidation he had experienced earlier when he first saw him stride across the bridge. The man's expression didn't contain even a hint of anger or even seriousness, but rather a confident smirk and even a tinge of eagerness for battle. It made him realize again how gigantic he was, not only in stature but in sheer presence.

Despite this, he straightened, focused on his target, and let his Anima come forth. Wulfsun nodded approvingly and mirrored him. His shimmered a bright yellow-and-white. It was as wide as Vaust's had first felt and not as oppressive but certainly fierce. The young Magi drew his blade to the side. He did not know what to expect from his opponent, but he had to be careful. Even if he was a simple brawler, a man his size combined with a Mana-infused strike would be enough to end this test very quickly.

Devol drew in a long, quiet breath and let his arms lower very briefly before he attacked the Templar. When he was a few yards away, he leapt to the side and struck at Wulfsun's left arm. His adversary reacted with ease and merely raised his hand so his gauntlet blocked the blow, but Devol had feinted and now spun in place and swung so his strike aimed at the giant's chest.

His sharp ears heard a chuckle from the commander when his blade met the armor. He slid back while he checked the chest plate with narrowed eyes. Surprisingly, he couldn't see a single scratch so it must be fairly durable.

But from what he had been told, a majestic could destroy even exotics.

Calmly, he stopped his slide and used the momentum to sprint forward as he drew his arm back to thrust the sword toward the Templar's head. Wulfsun brought his right gauntlet to block but it seemed unlikely that it would be enough—it was not a shield after all. This assumption proved erroneous when the tip of his blade struck the gauntlet and it refused to budge an inch more.

The boy's eyes widened as he landed and glanced at his opponent, who extended his palm and prepared to swipe. He ducked and a meaty hand whistled above his head with a rush of air. Without pause, he stepped back as he took his blade in both hands again and used Vis to summon as much Mana as he could in a short time. His opponent was unknown so he needed to test how much abuse the Templar could take before he showed even a hint that he would give. He brought his blade to the side before he swiped it again. Wulfsun blocked it with both gauntlets and a loud crash sounded through the arena. Zier and Jazai's robes billowed from the wind kicked up by the impact and dust flurried around the two combatants.

When it settled, Devol strained against the commander's defense. He noticed that his blade chafed against the metal of the man's gauntlets, lowered his sword, and took a few steps back as he breathed deeply and narrowed his eyes. "It's the armor itself, right?" he asked and his Mana flowed in his eyes. "That's your majestic, isn't it?"

The man's smirk returned. "Aye, you've got it," he replied and straightened. "But it protects more than only that."

The truth soon became clear. Now that he had collected himself and used Vello to analyze his opponent, he could see that his Mana was centered on the chest plate and gauntlets but flowed out from there to his body as a whole. From the top of his head to his feet, it enveloped him in what appeared to be a full-body suit of armor created from his Mana.

"It looks almost exactly how Anima looked on Mr. Lebatt," he noted and focused on the brighter light from the armor itself. "But it's more solid. I should have noticed even before we started the match."

"You did rush in a little too fast," Wulfsun agreed. "But see here, boyo, this isn't the typical defense Anima provides. It is far stronger than anything you are used to—which I would assume is not very much given that you only discovered it a day ago." He chuckled and regarded him with kindly amusement. "I guess I should be a little sporting since I know your class and all, however much good that does me." He gestured toward himself with his thumb. "My majestic falls into the constitution class—the one the scholar refers to as the 'boring' one."

"I typically say basic to be more polite," Zier interjected and beside him, Jazai sighed.

"Constitution is about pushing your Mana beyond the limits of normal Magic. You don't get many of the special tricks of the other classes but you can use your natural talents in ways they couldn't without decades of training." He flexed his arms and the yellow light condensed even further to coat his entire body in a sheet of Mana. "In my majestic's case, it can create armor tougher than almost any material out there, but don't think it is only a shiny suit of armor." He held one arm up and clenched his fist. Mana began to swirl around it. "With every physical strike you have given me so far, my majestic has absorbed some of that impact."

Devol retreated a few steps and watched in astonishment as the man's already large arms began to expand and grew even more substantial. "And I can take that force and use a little of it myself." He swung his arm back as he took a massive step forward. "I hope you are ready for a demonstration."

The boy raised his sword to guard as the Templar launched his fist forward. Even though he was several feet away, a force pounded into his blade, thumped the flat side into his chest, and hurled him back several feet and almost knocked the wind out of him. When he was able to touch the ground again, he tried to scrape his feet along the dirt to slow himself but was only able to lessen the impact slightly when he inevitably careened into the back wall of the arena.

Wulfsun placed his fists on his hips and laughed loudly. "Ha! You really came at me, boyo! I only added a little of my strength to that punch. Most of that was the energy you gave me. I recommend you try something a little different with your next attack. You're beating yourself up here."

"Would this be considered Wulfsun bullying the new kid?" Jazai asked as he leaned against the railing and frowned.

"He's getting too into it," Zier responded. "It's not very

surprising, of course. The boy has tremendous natural talent and shows advanced skill in swordsmanship for his age, but that won't be enough for him to win against someone like Wulfsun."

"Are you saying he has a chance otherwise?" the apprentice questioned with a furrowed brow.

The dryad shrugged, adjusted the cuffs of his robe, and brushed off some of the dirt that had been kicked up by the giant Templar's assault. "Under normal circumstances, not a chance in the hells. Wulfsun is among the top warriors in the order, which would make him one of the top warriors in this realm and a good many of the others."

"You have to be leading to a 'but' at some point," Jazai remarked.

"However…" Zier began.

His apprentice rolled his eyes. "Cheeky bastard."

"Devol's majestic class is a perplexion, and since we don't know what that exactly entails…well, I cannot say for certain if it is impossible."

"Well, that is neat and all." The boy looked at the young Magi, who had scrambled to his feet and now rubbed his left shoulder. "But he needs to use it for it to make a difference. And since he doesn't know what it does and only learned about all this in general not too long ago, it is still a very tall order."

"So do you think this is a pointless exercise?" the scholar asked and regarded him with interest.

Jazai smiled. "Not at all. I think it is exciting and want to get all the details right. It could make a fun story someday."

"Humph." Zier snorted and returned his focus to the arena. "You sound like you want to make a bet."

The apprentice laughed, then shrugged. "I wouldn't be opposed. What are you in for?"

"I won't do your chores for you," the dryad replied and smoothed the neckline of his robe. "Not again."

"Dammit."

"So, you coming at me again there, boy?" Wulfsun goaded, his fists clenched. "I'll tell you right now, I won't merely defend against your attacks from here on out."

Devol had already assumed that. He shook his head to clear it and hefted his blade again. While he would not be able to match Wulfsun with sheer force, he had been sure of that even before the fight. His real purpose was to test his majestic's power, so maybe he should focus on that rather than on what he knew he couldn't do. He looked at the sword and stilled his mind. It offered no hint of what its ability was—aside from simply looking appealing—but he would never find out if he didn't try.

He held the blade skyward and concentrated. Wulfsun and the others watched as the glowing white light enveloped the sword and it expanded dramatically and became a vast, sky-touching blade of light at least fifteen feet tall. The massive Templar's smirk did not disappear but his armor began to strengthen reflexively in anticipation.

"So you finally brought it out proper, eh?" he remarked, hunkered down again, and spread his arms. "Very well then. I said this at the start, but now maybe you'll understand what I meant. Come at me with everything you've got!"

The boy lowered the blade to chest height and held it in front of him. The dust at his feet began to swirl around him as he took a step forward. It was time to see what his sword could truly do. He walked forward slowly before he uttered a challenging roar and lunged forward to swing the blade of light at the Templar.

CHAPTER FIFTEEN

The light of Devol's blade began to fade and he breathed heavily as he tried to peer through the dust that swirled around the arena. Zier waved his hands and Jazai shielded his eyes, although he tried desperately to find a way to peek through the haze to see what had happened.

The boy brought his sword in front of him defensively and waited for Wulfsun's reaction. He was not sure what had happened to the commander, but he imagined that if the attack was as powerful as it felt and looked, he would be mightily pissed if he was still standing.

A spark of yellow light caught his attention before the dust blew out of the center of the arena, past him or into the air. He raised a hand to stop the dirt from getting into his eyes, but after a few moments, he peered through the cracks between his fingers. The Templar stood strong in the same position where he had been before, utterly unmoved. He cursed under his breath. Had his assault accomplished nothing? Was his majestic nothing more than a sword with a fancy type of light?

Jazai grimaced and leaned against the railing again. "Damn, was that nothing more than sparkles and prayer?" He drew a deep breath. "I know we still aren't sure what it does and Devol isn't properly trained yet, but it looked impressive, at least."

"Just because it did not have the reaction you expected does not mean it did nothing at all," Zier responded, his head inclined slightly as he observed Wulfsun.

"What do you mean?" the apprentice asked and looked from his mentor to Devol. "Did I miss something?"

"It appears the attack did not harm Wulfsun in any physical way," the scholar said, his expression thoughtful as he stroked his chin. "But that look on his face is not one of anger or even disappointment. He looks almost…rattled?"

Jazai stared at the giant Templar, who stood firm with his arms folded again. He took a moment to study his face and scrutinize his features. Zier was right. He did not know him as well as his mentor did, but from what he could see, Wulfsun did have an odd expression. Most wouldn't say rattled perhaps, but he did look a tad confused, even if it seemed he tried to mask it behind a façade of indifference.

Although the man stood motionless, he considered everything that had happened in silence. He felt lighter and heavier at the same time. For a very brief moment, it had felt like his Anima had almost given way. He took stock of his Mana. It had certainly drained although not by much. Perhaps he'd charged his armor a tad too much. No, he would have noticed something as obvious as that. And something else was missing too—the power his armor had siphoned from the boy's strikes. He had used most of it while showing off before, but some had remained and he could no longer feel it.

Devol also thought things over—and most importantly, what he should do next. He had accomplished something with that attack. While he was certainly more fatigued now than a moment before and his Mana was weaker, it appeared that whatever he had done was ineffective.

Should he simply go on the offensive again? Maybe the strike did do something to Wulfsun and it was not obvious. Perhaps he had created an opening he should exploit. But if he was wrong and the Templar kept his word about not holding back, he would find himself most likely pounded into the dirt very shortly. What should he do now?

"Is that it, boyo?" the commander roared and snapped him out of his thoughts. "Unless you got something else to try, I'll be coming for ya soon enough!"

If his strike had done something, it sure as hell was not enough to deter the Templar. Devol glanced at his blade and contemplated setting it down. In sparring matches with his father and friends, it was a sign of respect to know when one had been bested. It meant you had that much more time to train. But seeing the man's bravado, he felt he probably would not take it that way.

"You're taking an awfully long look at that sword there," Wulfsun noted and stroked his beard as he arched an eyebrow. "You do realize what it is, right?"

Devol looked at him. He wanted to say he knew and that was what he had spent all that time learning. But then he realized that more often than not, he referred to it as a blade or sword in his head. It certainly was meant to look and feel like that, but a majestic was far more than that.

Maybe his power didn't work right because he didn't use it correctly.

"Starting to dawn on ya, then?" Wulfsun asked with a snicker. "One of the things we'll need to train you in is to not be read so easily. A majestic is more than whatever item it happens to take the form of. It is the channel of your power to grant abilities far beyond what almost anyone is capable of. It is a majestic!" He pointed a large finger at him. "Take note of the name, boy, and focus."

The boy looked at the weapon in his hands. He could summon the light easily enough, but he could do that even with a regular sword and a cantrip. If he wanted to take advantage of having a majestic, he should use it in a different way. He held it aloft and brought the light forth again.

"He's going to try another big swipe?" Jazai sounded exasperated. "Maybe something clicked?"

"You still need to work on patience," Zier noted and gestured at the young combatant. "Watch closer."

Devol watched the light form around the blade but this time, he did not simply let it spool around the edges. Instead, he did his best to reach out to it and draw it in. The light responded to this desire and began to flow into it to course through it, consume it, and become the blade itself.

His mouth gaped as he stared at the sword now made from the light inside it. He held it out in front of him, examined it, and watched as the light danced through the blade. It shimmered in his hands and while it looked incredibly fragile at a glance, it felt like something so much more—far beyond any cantrip he had seen cast before and even different than Wulfsun's armor. He finally understood why Zier and the others had shown such an interest in it.

"Well, it certainly looks pretty," Wulfsun taunted. "But unless your plan is to distract your opponent with a shiny toy, it won't be much good if you don't put it to use."

Devol moved his gaze from the blade to the Templar and responded with a small nod. "I agree," he answered, took the weapon in both hands, and adjusted his stance to indicate that he was prepared to attack. "Once more, Wulfsun!"

"Aye, there you go!" his opponent bellowed and bent his knees as he clapped once. When he opened his hands, an orb of yellow light appeared that began to grow and surround him. "This defense of mine is absolute," he declared and the barrier around him shimmered. "I can't move while I keep this in place but nothing has ever broken through. Think you can be the first, boyo?"

Devol's response was to swing his sword back as he leaned forward and prepared to charge. He stared at the man, who returned his gaze with his now-familiar smirk. In silence, he inched forward rather than initiate a running attack. His focus remained on keeping the light in place, but now that it filled in the entire blade, it seemed to fit naturally.

It felt right to see what it was capable of. His pace increased and soon, he pushed into a full sprint. He did not yell or utter a challenge but surged toward his adversary's barrier with all the zeal he could muster.

Wulfsun placed his hands against the barrier as the boy approached and drew a deep breath. Now that the light-created weapon bore down on him, he felt more apprehension than he had when the blade was double his size. The boy planted his feet just short of him and drove the blade toward the barrier to strike it dead center. A blast of light flared from the sword and his shield turned a brighter yellow.

"By the Astrals, that is bright!" Zier yelled and Jazai shielded his eyes as he squinted to see who was winning through the flurry of light and Mana around the combatants.

The young Magi's majestic remained thrust firmly against the front of the magical barrier. The shield remained a deep yellow color where the weapon had struck, and the area around it glowed a slightly less bright yellow hue. Devol continued to press the blade forward and took a couple of steps so the weapon was positioned against his ribs, which enabled him to press it harder against his opponent's resistant magic.

The Templar was surprised by the power he faced and even struggled a little. Not only could he feel the blade push slowly into his shield, but the entire front half of his barrier also felt like it was under strain. He had been able to withstand cannons, giant monsters, and all manner of different weapons with this defense and a simple sword thrust shouldn't cause it to buckle like this.

He attempted to use his Mana to strengthen it as much as he could, but using it already took an immense amount of concentration to maintain and stretched his Anima to its limits. There wasn't much Mana to spare for repairs and reinforcing his defense at this point. He looked through the blinding light at the boy, who continued to press his attack.

The young Magi gritted his teeth with more determination than he had seen in an adversary in some time.

If the blade pushed through, he wasn't in any position to avert its strike quickly and it was pointed directly at his chest. It was somewhat disconcerting. If it could wreak havoc on his shield, he did not want to imagine what it would do to his insides.

Devol could feel the weapon digging with relentless slowness into Wulfsun's barrier and was determined to persist with the pressure. Everything he had been taught about majestics rushed through his head. They responded to his desires and were an extension of himself. If that were true, it would not buckle before he did and he would not let that happen until he showed the commander everything he had.

Quickly, he moved his bottom hand over his top, pressed both against the top edge of the handguard, and finally bellowed another resolute challenge and pushed with everything he had left. The blade of the majestic dug in deeper and cracks appeared in the shield. His opponent began to back away a little and Devol took a large step back before he lunged forward and drove the blade through. The resistance shattered and he took another step and maintained his momentum with a forward thrust to pierce his opponent's chest plate.

The giant clasped his meaty hands together and with a roar, pounded his gauntlets into the blade. His attack was powerful enough to force the weapon toward the ground and it dug into the dirt. The boy gasped in shock and stepped back to draw the blade out, but Wulfsun looked at him, his fists still clenched together, and swung them to catch him in the chest. The majestic was yanked out of the dirt and the young Magi was catapulted several feet. He almost flipped entirely before he plummeted to a hard landing. His weapon landed a few feet away from him.

Devol coughed a few times before he grimaced and tried to catch his breath. He wiped the dirt from his face as he retrieved his sword, planted the blade into the dirt, and held it by the grip to use it as a support to help him to clamber to his feet. When he managed to stand, he looked at the Templar, breathing deeply. The man's ragged breaths were as labored as his were, although he stood firm with his arms folded again.

"So…" he began as he removed the blade from the dirt and held the weapon firmly in both hands, "did I pass?"

Wulfsun was silent for a moment before he looked down, his shoulders shaking. Devol could hear him stifle a chuckle before the man dropped the act and released a loud laugh that echoed throughout the arena. "You are certainly something, Devol!" he responded and laughed again. "That wasn't exactly one of my strongest attacks, but it should have been more than enough to leave a kid like you on the ground for longer than that."

The young Magi responded with a faint smile. "I can be stubborn, I guess," he admitted and began to chuckle a little as well.

"Aye, but you are the best kind of stubborn," the giant replied. He nodded and lowered his arms to reveal a large hole in the chest plate of his armor. With a grimace, he slid his hand under the plate and when he removed it, the fingers were stained with blood.

Thankfully, this seemed like a good time to end the

bout. The damage to his majestic had left him drained and a little disoriented, but he'd had years in which to learn how to hide it from his foes and push past it. "I can say this with confidence—had this been a test to join the Templars, you would have a ceremony this very night."

Devol nodded happily. "Thanks, Wulfsun," he said before he stumbled and fell heavily. He dragged in a couple of large gasps of air as he smiled warmly, held his majestic firmly, and hoisted it high. "I'm glad I made it."

CHAPTER SIXTEEN

"Well, that was certainly a grand finale," Jazai said and beamed as he pushed off the railing and folded his arms. "Do you think we should get down there and congratulate him?"

"I would think so," a deep and appealing voice replied. The two spectators turned to where Vaust stood behind them. "Battling Wulfsun and pushing him that far certainly deserves praise."

"So you finally caught up?" the apprentice asked and nodded to the mori Templar. "I would have thought you would have had more interest in how this went, given that you brought him in from what I heard."

"I was optimistic," the new arrival responded, moved past them, and leaned on the railing. "Plus, I already had a taste of what he is capable of, so my opinion wasn't that important."

"You wanted everyone else to have a look?" Zier asked and studied him with interest.

"The boy made an impression on me. I wanted to see if

he could do the same with others," Vaust admitted with a shrug. "I had to make a report anyway."

"So you went to speak to Nauru?" The scholar nodded as he clasped his hands behind his back. "And how is she? It's been a while since she's left her chambers."

The mori gestured to where the combatants were in conversation. "You can ask her when she's done."

"Hmm?" Zier and Jazai returned to the rails and their eyes widened as a figure in flowing blue, white, and silver robes walked into the arena.

"You all right there, Devol?" Wulfsun asked and proffered a hand to help him up.

The boy nodded a little wearily as he accepted the aid, and the Templar hoisted him to his feet. "That was a good match."

"Hopefully, we can have a few more!" he responded and clapped him cheerfully on the back with sufficient force to almost upend him again.

"You should ask him that after he has properly rested, Commander Wulfsun," a soothing, airy voice replied. The giant looked toward its source and his eye widened. Devol glanced at what had surprised him and his gaze settled on a feminine figure dressed in elegant robes, but her features caught his attention more than anything else.

Her skin was like the smooth texture of a leaf, the color a light, gleaming blue with streaks and patches of pink around her neck and arms. When she looked from the Templar to the new Magi, her eyes danced with teal-colored embers. She did not seem to have normal lips. Instead, the area around her mouth slanted and protruded from the rest of her face when she spoke, but when she was silent, they flattened to give her face an almost mask-like appearance. Her hair—a dark-blue that changed to a brighter pink at the tips—was like vines twisted together into a large bundle that reached her lower back.

"Grand Mistress Nauru!" Wulfsun stated and bowed his head slightly. "It's good to see ya after so long."

Nauru chuckled and her eyes glowed brighter with real mirth. "I need to make rounds more regularly. You act as if I've been away on a mission." She glanced at Devol for a moment before she returned her focus to the giant. "I've told you to not be so formal, Commander. I think you're worrying our new guest."

He raised his head to fix her with a small frown. "You're gonna call me by my title, but it's unnecessary to call you by yours?" he grumbled and shook his head "Right, well, I should at least be civil, I suppose, as befits the Templars."

"Oh, certainly." She nodded, focused on the boy, and smiled. "You should have begun by introducing this young Magi."

"Of course." He placed his hand on the youngster's shoulder. "This is Devol…uh…" He darted a glance at the newcomer, who mouthed his last name. "Alouest, right! Devol Alouest. Devol, this is Nauru, the thirty-second leader of the Templars." He spoke heartily before he patted him on the shoulder, shook him a little, and moved his hand away. "He seeks training with our order."

"Devol?" Nauru asked and extended a hand. "A pleasure to meet you, young Magi."

The boy looked into the warm glow of her eyes and took her hand. "It's an honor, Grand Mistress," he replied.

She chuckled again. "No need for that as I just reminded the captain." She squeezed his hand for a moment before she released it and her hands vanished into the folds of her long robes. "Devol—that sounds like 'devil,'" she stated and her gaze darted to the side as she considered the idea. "I thought humans considered devils to be dark creatures or of ill omen."

"Uh, that's normally right," Wulfsun agreed and ran a hand through his shaggy mane. "I didn't question it much. He's from Monleans and they have different interpretations of—"

"It's 'loved' backward," Devol interjected. "My father said before I was born that any child of his would probably be a little devil—like, rambunctious and all. My mother said she did not think it was funny but when she made the connection, she liked the name and it stuck. I haven't had too many problems with it."

"I see." Nauru's eyes flickered briefly. "That is an adorable story."

"Madame Nauru, may I ask a question?" he ventured.

"What is it?" she responded,

He pointed to her. "Are you a fleuri?"

She smiled sweetly again. "That I am indeed. Is this your first time seeing one?"

"Kind of—certainly my first time meeting one," he admitted. "I thought I saw one a few years ago in the Emerald Forest outside Monleans during the fall. He was purple—that means he was born in the wintertime, right?"

"Indeed, although we use the term 'bloomed' instead of

born," Nauru explained and shifted her gaze to the sky as she continued. "The colors of green, white, and pink are for spring, the summer shades are red, tan, and gold, autumn's are orange, yellow, and brown and, of course, winter is blues, silver, and purple. I bloomed on the cusp of winter and spring and so inherited the colors of both about one-hundred and forty-one years ago."

"Wow, you're so pretty," he marveled before he caught himself and slapped his cheeks in irritation. "Sorry, I didn't mean to—"

"It's all right, child," she said with a giggle. "I'm glad you think so. I am also glad that we can learn a little about each other so soon."

Devol grinned, relieved that she hadn't been offended. "Me too. Feel free to ask me anything you like. I did come to your order, after all."

"Very kind of you," Nauru responded. "I do have a question if you have the time."

"Certainly. We've finished the tests—right, Wulfsun?" he asked the Templar captain, who nodded.

"I caught the end of the sparring match, and you certainly gave it your all," she remarked with amusement. "You seem gifted, Devol, but tell me, what caused you to search us out?"

"Let me show you." He stretched toward his backpack where it had been dropped at the entrance of the arena. It elevated and he pulled it toward him. However, it appeared that his fight with the giant had drained him of much of his Mana so the bag floated only a few feet before it stopped. When he overcompensated with a heave of his Mana, it streaked into his chest and knocked him off his feet and away from the two Templars.

"Ow." He coughed as he sat and patted the dust out of his hair before he retrieved the map.

"It's all right, boy. I'll fill her in," Wulfsun stated with a thumbs-up. "Leave the map and go catch up with the others. I'm sure they want to congratulate you."

Devol nodded and managed to muster sufficient strength to scramble to his feet and approach Nauru. He bowed to her, gave the man the map, and retrieved his majestic before he hurried to the stairs.

Jazai was the first to greet him and held his hand up for him to slap. "Nice work out there!" he congratulated him as they slapped each other's palm. "You got your majestic working for you now, huh?"

"I guess so," he said, although his tone was hesitant. "I'm still not entirely sure what it does but it helped me to get through Wulfsun's shield, at least."

"Certainly more than merely a flashlight, isn't it?" Vaust asked.

"Mr. Lebatt!" He recognized the mori and approached him quickly. "Did you see the match too?"

"I came in with the grand mistress," he stated. "I did see you push through Wulfsun's barrier. I'm sure he gave you the spiel about it being impenetrable and all that?"

"Yeah, he said no one ever made it through before," Devol recalled.

Vaust chuckled and leaned back, his expression amused. "He likes to do a little grandstanding but he is not wrong. The few times I have been with him when he has used it in combat, nothing ever made it through. Assaults certainly knocked him around somewhat and cracked it, but nothing ever broke it. You've accomplished a first and been here for only one day."

"It is a fascinating development," Zier said, his curious gaze on the majestic. "And that was on its own. We should probably see if Macha can hammer something together for him quickly."

"It is a tad early to be thinking of modifications. Besides, Wulfsun will probably need to see her first," the mori reminded him. "But we are getting ahead of ourselves, Zier. That is something for those who are in the order and Devol has not made his mind up on that so we shouldn't rush it." He turned to the boy and raised an eyebrow. "Unless something has changed since I last saw you?"

The young Magi considered the question. Everything that had happened had been very different than he had expected. He had seen the recruits train with the guardsman. In fact, they did not even start sparring until after a few weeks of basic swordsmanship training, and that was usually still instruction.

Here, everyone seemed so nice and they treated him as a comrade. Of course, Wulfsun and the other elders referred to him as "boy" or something akin to that, but it seemed friendly rather than demeaning. He looked at the majestic in his hand. While he did plan to have a life of adventure and protecting people, this seemed like a huge step to take on a whim, even a positive one.

He looked into the arena, where Wulfsun and Nauru were deep in conversation as they studied the map. "Can I ask the grand mistress something first?" he inquired.

Vaust looked at Zier and both shrugged. "I'm sure she would have no objection to that. Go ahead," the mori replied.

The boy hurried down the stairs with Jazai on his heels. The two Templars watched them, their expressions thoughtful. "If he stays, that will make three young recruits," the scholar noted. "The most we've had for quite some time."

"That's certainly true. It is usually older Magi following tales of better times, seeking redemption, or merely trying to find a new home," his comrade replied and smiled as the boys approached Nauru without hesitation. "Like you were at one point."

The dryad turned away. "As I recall, so were you."

"Also true," Vaust said without rancor, "but I've been here for quite a while now." He chuckled as he lost himself briefly in memories. "This is my only home, truly."

"Hey, Miss Nauru," Devol called. The grand mistress and Wulfsun turned to look at him. "Sorry to interrupt, but I have another question if you don't mind."

"And what is that, young Magi?" she asked.

He took a moment to put the words together. "I originally wanted to come here only for training, but I like everyone I've met so far and I think I can gain more than originally thought by studying with you."

"I believe the same," she agreed and glanced at the templar beside her. "And from what the commander has said, he believes so as well."

The giant placed a fist against his chest. "Aye, and we have to have another match after that last one!"

"Right, so I thought…" He paused to take a breath. "I…

may want to join the order someday. But I can't say right now."

Nauru nodded reassuringly. "That is perfectly all right. It is a difficult decision for one so young."

"But I want to help," the boy declared. "I met Mr. Lebatt on a mission he was finishing. If there is anything like that I can do, let me know. I want to be able to help while I stay here and train. Maybe that way, I'll gain understanding of what the Templars do and it will make the decision easier."

Both Nauru and Wulfsun seemed slightly taken aback by this, but they were certainly more interested than perplexed. She pressed her fingers together, closed her eyes, and lowered her head in thought. "It is very gracious of you, Devol. I see how that could benefit both of us." She opened her eyes and looked at both boys. "As it happens, I think there could be a little errand you two could run together."

"Both of us?" Jazai asked and his head jerked to look at his companion before he returned his gaze to meet hers. "Me too?"

"Yes. I think you have something to gain from this as well, Jazai," she stated with a grin.

The apprentice tilted his head to the side before he shrugged. "It has been a while since I've been out of the castle. But if Zier throws a fit, I'll send him to you, madame."

"Noted." She chuckled and looked toward the arena's entrance. "Perhaps...I think it would be best if the three of you went."

The boys looked at one another in confusion and in unison asked, "Three of us?"

CHAPTER SEVENTEEN

Devol and Jazai sat in the middle of the forest arena in the larger training area, brought here by Nauru before she stepped away to talk to some of the other Templars. She did not leave them unattended, however. They were joined by a third member, the wildkin girl Devol had noticed earlier and who had previously been identified to him as Asla. She stared intently at them despite sitting a good few yards away.

"She seems…" Devol began and peeked quickly at her. She narrowed her eyes when she saw his glance. "Studious."

"It's a polite way to put that, yeah." The apprentice leaned back on his hands as he fixed her with an unconcerned look. "Asla, you wanna introduce yourself or should I have the pleasure?"

Her eyes widened before she shifted her focus from him to the newcomer, then away. In silence, she stared into the trees.

"I guess that answers that." Jazai sighed. "Her name is

Asla Baghira. She is a cat wildkin who came to the order more than a year ago, although she has only recently started training with us. I was here with my pops when she first arrived," he explained while she continued to avert her gaze from them. "It isn't my place to go into too much detail about her arrival, although I must confess—even if I am a jerk—that I don't know much. But I can say she is another promising student in the order and she's a few moons younger than you are."

"I see." Devol nodded, stood, and approached her slowly before he stopped a few feet away and extended a hand. "Hi, Asla, my name is Devol and—"

"You smell like fish," she told him, her head still turned away although she cast him a sideways glance.

"Huh?" He pulled his shirt to his nose to smell it. While most of the fishy odor seemed to have been filtered by the smoke from the den and sweat from his fight, very faint traces lingered from the fish they had eaten previously. "Oh, I guess so. Sorry about that."

"It's all right." She shrugged and looked away again. "I like fish."

"Oh, that's good," he said with a smile as he placed his hands casually behind his back. "When we go out on the mission, maybe I can catch you some."

"So we are going on a mission then?" Asla asked and now turned her full attention to them.

"It seems that way," Jazai responded where he still leaned back casually. "I'm not sure what it is yet, but the grand mistress took Devol up on his offer to help and somehow, we were roped into it."

"So who will watch over us?" she questioned and studied the newcomer again.

Devol shrugged. "I don't know anything about the mission yet. But you think we'll go with someone?"

"That's how it is usually done," the apprentice explained. "I have been on a couple of missions, as has she, but we mostly shadow a real Templar or deal with the smaller objectives. For us, it's another way to train."

"Really?" The young Magi sounded dejected. "I hoped they would let us take care of it ourselves."

"Even if they did," Asla began, brought her knees up to her chest, and looked at the grass, "it would mean the mission isn't all that important."

"But it's a mission for the Templars," Devol pointed out. "Doesn't that make it important by default?"

Jazai snickered and shrugged in an offhand way. "Technically, I guess so, but she did call it an 'errand' so it shouldn't be all that big a deal."

"You should take after your friend more, Jazai," Nauru said from behind them as she, Wulfsun, Zier, Vaust, and the wolf wildkin man who had been training Asla before walked closer. "If you do not wish to participate in the mission, I'm sure your instructor would be more than happy to find chores for you to do to pass the time until they return."

The apprentice pushed hastily to his feet and waved his hands frantically. "No, no! Nothing like that, madame! I'm merely saying that I don't think this will be anything like a hunting mission or something that would require supervision."

She nodded. "I see. You are right in a way. This is a

retrieval mission, but that does not make it something to take lightly." She looked at Devol as she ushered the wolf wildkin forward. "First, a quick introduction. Devol, this is Freki Remus, Asla's mentor in the order."

The boy hurried closer and extended his hand. "Nice to meet you, Mr. Remus!" he said enthusiastically.

Freki nodded with a small smile. "Pleasure, little pup. It is good to see another young Magi interested in the order."

"It has been fun so far," he replied and looked at Jazai and Asla, then at Zier and Freki. "So you both have mentors, huh?"

"Most recruits have high-ranking Templars to show them the ropes for a while," Wulfsun explained. "Not for too long as most come to us with at least decent experience. But Asla's and Jazai's circumstances are unique."

"I'm sure we can find you one, should you request it," Nauru offered. "But for now, I would like the three of you to take a few days to get well-acquainted. The others and I will go over the specifics of the mission, and we will fill you in soon. But it is important to begin building a rapport with one another as you will rely on each other's skills and mutual trust for success."

"So we will be going alone?" Asla asked and almost spooked Devol when she stepped beside him, having reached his side without a sound.

The grand mistress glanced at Vaust and Wulfsun before she turned to the youngsters and nodded. "Yes, we believe it will benefit the mission and allow you to have your first taste of responsibility within the order."

"I guess you got thrown into the deep end early, Devol," Jazai remarked as he elbowed him in the shoulder.

"It's all right. I'm ready," he assured him and gave him a thumbs-up. "I only hope it isn't too easy."

"I suppose that all depends on you," Nauru responded cryptically and turned away. "For now, use the time to train together. I'll send Wulfsun this evening to show you to your quarters, Devol."

"Right. Thanks, Miss Nauru!" he called as she and the other Templars began to disappear into the woodland beyond the edges of the arena.

The three watched them for a moment. Asla stretched her arms before she spun and stepped a few paces away from them. "All right. Should we begin?"

"Going directly into a sparring match?" Jazai asked and rolled his eyes. "Devol just finished a bout against Wulfsun. I don't think he can show you what he's got right now."

"Then you and I will train," she replied, held her hands up, and revealed sharp nails. "That is what the grand mistress desires, correct?"

"She wanted us to get to know each other," the apprentice retorted and folded his arms. "There are other ways to do that besides fighting."

"It is the most direct method," Asla replied, although Devol suspected from her tone that she said this out of defensiveness rather than philosophy.

"Are you bitter that I won our last fight?" Jazai asked with a smirk.

The wildkin bristled at the comment and her eyes narrowed. "And I won the four before that," she countered, her gaze challenging. "Besides, that was only due to your use of tricks."

The apprentice threw his hands dismissively. "Yeah, I'm

a Magi as technically, we all are. My skills are better suited to cantrips and information gathering. Not brawn."

"Are you good with cantrips, Jazai?" Devol asked and pointed his thumb at himself. "I can only do a couple. I trained mostly in swordplay and Vis."

"I gathered that much." The other boy nodded. "Yeah, I never got into a martial art of any kind. I focused on increasing my Mana control and learning cantrips. I can perform about fifty of them."

"Fifty?" He yelped in astonishment. "My mom can do about that many and she has studied almost all of her life."

"Well, that's still impressive if she isn't an adventurer of any kind," Jazai responded as he held a hand out and extended his fingers. "My old man travels often, and he works in the services of not only the order but also the academy at home. His majestic isn't great for direct confrontation, so he either had to learn a Mana or martial art. He learned all the basic cantrips and concentrated on the conjuration class cantrips as well."

"So is his majestic in the conjuration class?" Devol asked

The apprentice shook his head. "Nah, he is a diviner like me. But cantrips can be learned by anyone, no matter what their natural talent falls into. It is merely harder outside your class." He smiled as he extended his other hand. "If you think me being able to use fifty spells is impressive, he can do about two hundred—all the conjuration cantrips and some transmutations, and he has all the upgraded basic ones in the constitution class as well."

The young swordsman was taken aback. "Man, that is… huh," he muttered. It seemed logical that scholars who worked primarily on Mana arts would know far more than the average person, but that was still amazing, especially for someone who probably didn't focus on it for their profession, merely as a secondary hobby. He looked at Asla, who had lowered her hands and now stared at them as her tail waved slowly from side to side. "What about you, Asla?"

The wildkin raised an eyebrow. "Cantrips aren't my specialty."

"No, I mean your majestic," Devol replied and gestured vaguely with his hand. "Jazai mentioned you had one earlier on the way here."

"Did he now?" She focused on the young scholar with annoyance and narrowed her eyes.

"I also saw you training earlier," he added quickly in an effort to take the heat off his new friend. "You made a large scratch on the floor like you attacked it with metal claws or something."

Asla pursed her lips. "We aren't supposed to reveal the secrets of our majestic."

Jazai sighed and scratched his head. "Yeah, to nobodies and enemies. But we will be working together soon so he's an ally." The girl refused to meet his gaze and her tail drooped to brush the ground. He grinned a little as he reached for his book. "I can always simply show him, you know."

"Don't you dare!" she snapped and her tail raised almost vertically as she extended a claw. She composed herself quickly, shook her head, and sighed. "Fine. Take a look." She unlatched a pair of dark leather gloves from her belt and placed them on her hand. Devol noted a set of three claw-shaped stones on the knuckles of each glove, pure white with small, edged patterns etched within. "I'm in the constitution class."

"Like Wulfsun?" he asked. She glared at him and he backed away.

She made a visible effort to relax. "Yes, like the captain. However, my majestic is not primarily defensive. It helps me tap into my more…animalistic abilities."

"Most wildkin majestics are like that," Jazai explained. "No one seems to know why, but those that can be traced to the wildkin lands or particular tribes seem to focus primarily on bringing out the more animal traits of the wielder. They are probably the only majestic that can be considered a type or class of their own."

"Pay attention," Asla called. Devol startled when she dropped to all fours. Her irises assumed a sharper and narrower shape and a faint glimmer of orange Mana similar to the color of her hair flickered around her. Curious, he used Vis to enhance his sight and observe her and was shocked when an orange outline formed and took the shape of a large cat.

Before he could ask what it could do, she leapt at him with surprising speed. He drew his majestic instinctively. The claws on her gloves clashed with the edge of his blade and the bright light flared instantly. Her eyes widened as she landed and retreated hastily. "What was that?" she demanded.

"My majestic," he stated as the light faded and he lowered his sword.

"I felt that…I needed to get away," she muttered, pushed to her feet, and shut her majestic down. "What does it do?"

"We don't exactly know yet," he replied somewhat sheepishly.

"Don't know?" She looked at Jazai for an explanation, but he merely shrugged in response.

"It certainly does something," the apprentice stated. "He was able to get through Wulfsun's big shield with it."

"Really?" Asla asked, clearly surprised. "Interesting, but if you don't know what it does, you are handicapping yourself."

"I know," Devol conceded. "That's why I came here to train and learn more about it." He smiled and lifted it again. "Maybe we can find out more together?"

"Are you sure?" Jazai asked. "Are you still in good enough shape to do that?"

"I'm not one hundred percent but I still have some energy and Mana to spare for now. I'm sure Wulfsun will be back soon, so we might as well make use of the time."

The other boy shrugged, approached one of the trees, and sat beneath it. "All right. I'll watch and make sure neither of you hurt the other too badly."

"You'll have to participate eventually," Asla insisted as she focused on Devol and brandished her claws.

"No doubt, but I'll let you two have fun for now." The apprentice raised a hand and lowered it quickly. "And go!"

The three youngsters sparred and trained together for a few hours and the earlier awkwardness between them began to fade as they learned more about one another. Wulfsun, unbeknownst to them, hadn't left. He and Freki were able to conceal themselves in the brush and observe them through the evening, both happy to see the early signs of a team bond forming between them.

CHAPTER EIGHTEEN

Several days passed and Devol and his new teammates continued to train together. This was quite different than the normal sword practice and Mana study he had done at home. Battling a skilled and speedy wildkin and a talented Magi—who could read his thoughts if he was not careful—had proven to be a rather interesting and intense experience. In that time, they awaited word from Nauru on when they were to depart but they had not seen the grand mistress since the day she put them together.

On the evening of his eighth day at the Templar Order, he followed Wulfsun, who had asked him to join him after training while Jazai and Asla went to the dining hall. He complied willingly and asked where they were going, but the giant said he wanted to keep it a surprise for now but that he should bring his majestic with him.

They headed to the eastern wing of the castle and passed many rooms and halls he had yet to see as he'd had no reason to be there until now. In fact, besides the areas he had seen on his first day there, he had yet to fully explore the castle. Training filled most of his time and he was given a temporary room in the scholar's tower across from Jazai. Although the apprentice somewhat disdainfully declared that it was less a room and more a refitted supply closet, it suited Devol for now.

Wulfsun opened a large metal door and motioned for him to enter. As soon as it swung inward, an immense heat issued from within. The boy walked through and paused, a little surprised by several forges and dozens of benches and cooling pools positioned in the large space. Numerous pieces of metal and colored stones in boxes were scattered on the floor or hung on the walls beside weapons and armor.

Three dwarves stood in conversation, while a squama moved a box of supplies quickly across the room. A female daemoni worked at the largest forge, one equipped with two large rocks of cobalt at the top that seemed to pump Mana into the flames. Embers threw flurries of red and blue sparks from the mouth of the furnace.

"This is our blacksmithing operation," Wulfsun explained and turned to the boy with a smile. "Come along. I want you to meet the master."

Devol swallowed the numerous questions that surged within and glanced at the large Templar. "The master?"

His companion chuckled. "Aye, she's in charge of arming the order. She is an expert craftsman. Those rivets during the kinship trial? She made most of them decades ago and they still function." He leaned closer and indicated the young Magi's sword. "She's also one of the few smithies who are able to repair a majestic."

"Repair a majestic?" he asked. "I thought they repaired themselves."

"They can over time," the commander agreed. "But they can be severely damaged and even broken by certain things, typically in battle with another majestic. And as you are hopefully aware by now, that is quite a bad thing. It's not only a broken weapon but it can inflict injuries on the wielder and even death in the worst case. If such a thing were to happen, having someone who can repair a majestic is quite helpful." The Templar began to walk to the large forge. "Come along now."

Devol followed him, momentarily distracted by a couple of other human blacksmiths making repairs to armor to his left. As they approached the daemoni, a tall, lithe figure with four arms and four legs stepped from behind the forge. Ashen-gray skin was marked with what appeared to be red warpaint on his face, a line down the middle that separated into two lines that wrapped back to make circles around his large, red eyes.

"I got the exhaust going, boss," he said to the daemoni, his voice raspy yet with a pleasant cadence. "Gonna need to swap out the cobalt by tomorrow night. The shipment is coming in the morning, right?"

"Should be," the master smith replied, straightened, and stepped away from the furnace. Her medium-length gray hair was scraped into a bun, her horns sloped back and curved up, and she was not only redder than the daemoni he had seen previously, but she was far more muscular as well.

Wulfsun pounded a hand on a nearby table and grinned as she turned her head to look at him over her shoulder.

The four-armed creature waved a hand. "Hey, Macha, Rogo! How are ya?"

"Captain!" Rogo responded with a delighted shout. "Nice to see you!"

Macha turned fully, folded her arms, and nodded. "Evening Wulfsun." Her voice was cool and efficient. She looked at Devol, who bowed slightly under her gaze. "Is this your new apprentice?"

"Not quite." The huge Templer settled a hand on his shoulder as if to calm him. "He would make a good one, though. He fights like a likan."

Rogo stepped fully from behind the forge area and Devol was shocked by his size when he moved closer. He was a little shorter than Wulfsun and the daemoni but stood at least six and a half feet tall. His four knees were bent to balance him so he might have been taller than both of them at full height. He stopped a few feet away and gave them a toothy grin as he rubbed his chin with one hand. The lower two rested on his hips. "So you're the potential recruit, eh? I heard you got yourself an interesting majestic there, my new friend."

"Introduce yourself properly, Rogo," the daemoni chided. "The boy probably isn't used to seeing realmers like us yet."

"Ah, you're right, boss." He moved forward quickly and proffered a hand. When the boy took it, he placed his other three hands over their clasped ones and shook vigorously. "I'm Rogo the smithy. I'm what you humans call a melian. It's a pleasure to meet a warrior as young as yourself." He released his multiple grasps and pointed at the daemoni with two arms. "And this is Macha, the master forger in our little camp."

Macha placed her hands on the table, leaned forward, and focused on the young Magi. "So, I hear you want me to look at your sword?"

Before Devol could reply, Wulfsun intervened. "Aye, only to see if you can tell us anything about it. The boy is heading off on a mission in a couple of days so it's good to have as much information as possible, yeah?" The mention of timing surprised the boy and he raised an eyebrow.

"Wait, I am?" he asked.

The Templar looked nonplussed as the realization dawned. "Ah, right. I forgot to tell you and your mates. I should probably fill them in when we get to the dining hall." He shrugged and looked at the master smith. "Macha is one of the finest smiths I have ever known, period. On top of that, she has great knowledge of exotics and majestics, at least the known ones."

"It's hard to know about things that we don't know exist," she muttered as she turned to tend the forge.

"Not to mention that she's training me!" Rogo revealed, stooped so he was a little closer to Devol's height, and leaned closer to whisper. "My kind ain't the greatest when it comes to using Mana. Only a handful of melian every couple of decades could forge exotics and magical equipment." His smile widened as he thumped his chest with one arm. "I might even have a gift, you know? Macha says I might be able to repair majestics someday like she can. You're looking at the next legendary melian smith right here."

"You are still some time away from that declaration,

Rogo," Macha stated. It surprised Devol that she could hear him whisper over the roar of the forges and banging of metal.

Rogo looked at her with a grin. "I know, boss, but keeping the dream alive makes me work harder."

"Then be prepared for the work coming in this week," she responded. "We have more orders to fill for the party heading out at the end of the moon."

He straightened and clapped all his hands. "Right, boss! I'll go and get the choice materials and start the furnace burning!" He ran off quickly, circled the forge, and vanished into a back room.

"Well then, while he's doing that…" Macha looked at the boy. "Let me see your majestic…uh…"

"Devol," he replied. She arched an eyebrow and looked quickly at Wulfsun, who simply shrugged. "Cute name," she said and narrowed her eyes when she noticed the blade on his back. "Is that the sword?"

"Yes, ma'am." He undid the strap on his chest and handed the weapon to her. She unsheathed it and the bright glow illuminated her face. Her alabaster eyes widened as her gaze settled on the magical blade.

"This is…" She whispered, looked at Wulfsun, and returned her attention to the young Magi.

"You know about it?" Devol asked.

Her gaze shifted to the captain again, who returned it knowingly. She nodded as she sheathed the blade. "I know of it—a glowing blade with a star-like shine. But I cannot say I know much beyond that. There are a number of vague stories and notes I have come across that mention majestics like that. It's interesting to think about but not much is known." she revealed and handed it to him as she studied him. "I will have to go through the books to see if I can find out more. But I have to say that it has been a long time since I've seen someone wield a linked majestic."

"Linked?" he asked and frowned at the weapon.

"It's a majestic that has some kind of attachment to the user," Wulfsun explained. "Most are passed down or found and eventually build a bond with the wielder over time and use. But since you used it to such great effect in our bout, yours already seems to have connected to you on a much deeper level."

"And what does that mean for me?" Devol asked as he studied the sword and recalled the first time it had appeared in the Emerald Forest.

"It means it was destiny for you and it to meet," Macha told him before she shrugged and turned away. "Or dumb luck. Some Magi merely have a certain something—like class proficiency or personality—that a majestic resonates with and makes the bonding process smoother."

"But you said it yourself," the commander replied and pointed at her. "It's been a long time since you've seen one like this, right? You haven't had many chances to work on a majestic like this, have ya?"

"Which is why I've been stuck doing repairs and making simple exotics for so long," the daemoni stated and turned her focus to the weapon. "I suppose I have something to look forward to eventually." She looked at Devol, then at the sword. "The blade seems a little long for his height and he seems quite young. Humans grow more at that age, correct?"

"He will grow into it," Wulfsun assured her.

"Good to know." She placed the weapon on the table. "So tell me then, Devol. What is the power of your majestic?"

He sighed and put his palms together as he explained. "We aren't exactly sure."

"Hmm?" The daemoni paused, her expression startled. "You have no idea?"

"Well, after practicing with it during this last week, we thought it might have something to do with Mana-draining." he postulated. "When I fought Wulfsun, I was able to break through his shield because he was running low on Mana and—"

"Wait, you broke through Wulfsun's barrier?" Macha asked and her eyes widened with an impressed look as she regarded the Templar captain. "Has that been done before?"

The giant shook his head and smirked. "Interesting, ain't it?"

"Very much," she agreed, rested a hand on her chest, and tapped her fingers. "An ability that allows one to drain the Mana of others would explain that."

"Well…the thing is, we still aren't sure that is what it does," Devol continued. "When I sparred with Jazai, if I was able to get close or graze him, he would lose words in his book and his spells wouldn't have the power they usually do. In fact, he tried once to teleport or blink as he called it, and he ended up stuck on top of a tree when he wanted to teleport behind it."

"I see." She nodded. "Anything else?"

"With Asla, when she did her magical cat thing—" He made claws with his hands for emphasis. "Whenever I struck at her, she lost speed and she said she heard a ringing that distracted her."

"Heard a ringing?" the daemoni asked quickly and tapped her fingers faster in thought. "Hmm, everything else sounds like it would be affected by Mana-draining or something similar. But that ringing is an odd effect." She folded her arms and gestured to the sword with her head. "Show me then."

Devol drew it, held it up, and closed his eyes as he summoned his Anima and began to release power to the majestic.

Rogo returned with a box in his lower arms. "Hey, boss. I brought the materi—" As the blade began to charge, the light poured into it and illuminated the room with a bright glare. The melian slapped his upper hands over his eyes and surprised shouts and gasps issued from the other smiths. When he realized that he might be blinding them, the boy dimmed the light hastily and looked around with genuine concern.

Macha blinked rapidly but otherwise, showed very little reaction. "I didn't expect it to look like that," she admitted. "The bright light could be useful on its own. It is certainly an interesting majestic. I'm honestly rather excited to do some research now."

Wulfsun regarded her with a trace of suspicion. "You aren't thinking about adding anything, are ya?"

"Adding?" Devol asked and looked at the head smith. "Adding to what? The sword? I overheard Zier and Vaust talk about modifications or something."

The daemoni nodded. "I've found ways to make simple modifications to majestics," she explained. "Similar to how one would with an exotic, although it takes considerably more materials and much more skill than most are capable of." She waved a hand dismissively. "But given that we don't know what it does, it would not be smart to do so right now. But should we have a better grasp of it…" She leaned forward and smiled at the young Magi. "I would be more than happy to play with it to see what we can create." He looked away from the eager master smith and merely inclined his head in acknowledgment.

"Is it safe to look now?" the melian smith asked, his hands still over his eyes.

Macha sighed and straightened. "It's been safe," she replied and tossed him a mold of a sword when he lowered his hands, which he snatched out of the air. "Put the materials you brought with you down. Then, I need you to fetch a bag of cobalt dust and enough diament glass to make a blade of that size."

"Diament glass?" Rogo placed the box on a table and when he turned to look at her, she stared impassively at him. "Uh…right, boss!" he said and took the mold with him as he hurried to another room.

"I'll let you know what I find," she promised, turned to them, and smiled at Devol. "And you be sure to do the same."

"Yes, ma'am." he agreed with a polite bow.

Wulfsun chuckled and patted him on the back. "All right, boyo. Say your goodbyes for now. It is time to eat."

CHAPTER NINETEEN

"Rogo the smithy?" Jazai repeated after he swallowed his mouthful of potato. "Yeah, that's his real name. Melian's don't have family names or clan names like most of the other races. They use their profession as a type of marker of who they are."

"What about when they are kids?" Devol asked as he scarfed his beef and rice. "Was he Rogo the kid?"

"He would have been Rogo son of... What was his father's name?" the other boy asked as he tapped his fork on the side of his plate.

"Rogo son of Toro," Asla answered as she finished her juice. "Or Rogo son of Toro the forger. They can get somewhat wordy so their first names are usually simple."

"I see." He moved his empty bowl to the side. "By the way, Wulfsun said we'll head out on our mission in a couple of days."

"Zier said something similar." The scholar's apprentice looked at Asla. "Did Freki give you an update?"

She nodded, pierced a small piece of fish with a claw,

and raised it to her mouth. "Yes, he also told me it will be to return a package to the order."

"So a simple retrieval mission?" Devol asked and his dejection colored his tone. "Like madame Nauru said."

"Yeah, that's the long and short of it," Jazai agreed. "I'm not surprised that our first mission alone would be something so simple."

"I wonder why they haven't given us the specifics." He picked his cup of water up. "I would think it would be important for us to know what we're looking for and all that before we set off, right?"

"It could be they don't know the specifics themselves," Asla pointed out and swallowed the piece of fish. "Freki said that we might meet someone to recover it."

"And can't they use the portals?" Devol asked. "That seems faster and safer."

"They might not be a member of the Templars," the young scholar reasoned as he began to eat a soft yellow dessert cake. "We have partners who help the order and some alliances with brokers and guilds will send those looking for us to certain anchor points. But only the most trusted among them have the ability to open the portal or even know where some of the anchors that lead here are. Otherwise, even if you find one of the anchors, a Templar will come to meet you if you try to access it."

"Oh." He frowned as he recalled the day he had opened the portal. "I wasn't a member of the Templars so how did I get through?"

Asla glanced at him. "You mentioned that you had opened it but that you used your majestic to do so, correct?"

"Yeah," he confirmed. "Now that I think about it, both Mr. Lebatt and Wulfsun seemed surprised at that."

"Maybe that's simply another facet of your majestic," Jazai suggested. "It's starting to sound like a real multi-tool kinda deal. I wish you had more control over it."

Asla frowned and her ears twitched. "No kidding."

Devol chuckled but he did agree with them. His majestic seemed far more useful and fascinating than he had given it credit for since he first received it, but he still had no idea what it did. A weapon you could not wield properly was not the most dependable.

While the trainees continued to chat, their mentors, Zier, Wulfsun, Freki, and Vaust, were seated at another table across the dining hall and discussed the mission.

"Well...I understand the logic," Freki conceded, although his scowl clearly showed his hesitation. "But this could be far more than they can handle right now."

"The grand mistress agrees," Vaust stated and sipped from his gourd, frowned, and shook it. He grimaced when he realized very little of its contents were left. He sighed, placed it on the table, and looked at the wolf wildkin. "Which is why I'll shadow them."

"You will?" Zier seemed surprised. "I would have thought you would be on another mission by then."

"This is my mission," the mori replied. "Technically, it would be much too dangerous for them. But we currently do not believe anyone knows that the item is out in the open yet. Sending three younglings to retrieve it would raise less suspicion, but we cannot be sure that won't change between then and now so I will be on standby and observe them."

"Who got in touch with us?" Freki asked.

"A hunter's guild in the Britana Kingdom," Vaust revealed. "Or I should say the Hunter's Guild of Britana."

"That means Henry's boys and girls, correct?" Wulfsun asked and received a nod in reply. "Huh, why not get it to us directly? They are in good standing with us. I know the Britana anchor point is a little out of the way but—"

"The grand mistress asked the same thing," the mori interjected. "And it would be one of the reasons I am going. They didn't only find one item. There was another but the team sent to retrieve it never returned."

This caused the jaws of his comrades to clench around the entire table. "Any more information?" Zier asked.

"Only that the search party never found them. And a couple of other individuals in the guild have gone missing," Vaust explained. "They cannot rule out that they are followed or watched. Even if they did use the portal to get here, they could be attacked before that happened or the enemy could use a spell or majestic to keep the portal open and thus allow whoever is interested in that item to enter."

"And we have so many in storage—not that it would be easy for them to steal in the abyss," Wulfsun grumbled and ran a hand through his wild mane. "Damn. It feels like I'm hearing more tales of people looking for those cursed things than merely stumbling upon them now."

"Should we tell them?" Freki asked with a hasty glance at Zier. "I've only mentioned them to Asla as I didn't want to frighten her, but does Jazai know?"

"I'm sure he has some idea of what they are, given his father's work," the scholar replied and sipped his wine. "Although he has been reticent about whether he knows much about them or not, I'm almost certain it means he at least knows of them. I have told him to keep any rumors or specifics of his father's work to himself. He is cheeky but he wouldn't cause a fire he couldn't put out."

"They will be instructed to keep the box closed and secured," Vaust assured them. "And as I said, I will be there to make sure everything goes well. Think of this less as a dire mission and more like a test similar to what Devol recently went through." He scooted his chair back far enough to place his heels casually on the table. "After all, they are gifted students, but what good are those gifts if they don't get a chance to use them?"

Freki looked down and sighed. "What good are those gifts if they are killed?" he responded grimly and looked up to see the concern on the faces of his comrades.

"Come now, Freki," Wulfsun chided. "You've been training Asla for a few months now. Not only that, you've seen them working together over the past week and they aren't pushovers."

The wildkin nodded slowly "I know, but…"

"I, for one, am excited to see what my apprentice accomplishes on his own," Zier admitted and surprised the others. "What? Jazai is intelligent and can be a help when he bothers to apply that intellect. But after working with him all this time, I know that unless something drastic changes in his demeanor, the path of the scholar will not be his first choice. If anything, he may take a path similar to his father, something I think Ekon is aware of. So this will be an interesting trial for him."

"And Vaust will be there," Wulfsun stated and hoisted his stein. "You have confidence in your comrade, right?"

"Keep it down, would you?" Freki asked and gestured at his ears before he nodded. "Of course I do. It's only… It can be hard to send them out like that when you've grown attached." He bit his lip. "I've known Asla since she was a child and hated the fact that I wasn't there to help her when she needed it. If I was, maybe she wouldn't be here at all."

"You cannot continue to dwell on that," Vaust stated and surprised the wildkin. "She is coming into her own now and even before, has she ever done something she didn't wish to? I am sure that if she had an issue, the grand mistress would have been happy to find another place for her to grow. But Asla remained here—with you and to find her path. This is her taking another step and if you care for her, you will see her as a sister-in-arms, not as a child to shelter."

Zier chuckled as he finished his wine. "I would never have thought I'd hear something so profound from you, Vaust."

"Hey, the kids are leaving," Wulfsun told them as the trio left their plates and glasses at the cleaning area and departed. "It looks like they are headed toward the scholar spire."

"Perhaps they are going to end their night with a session of studying," Zier suggested.

The mori chuckled. "Were you ever a child?"

With a sigh of annoyance, the dryad filled his glass again with the remains of the bottle on the table. "Yes, a very studious one, thank you."

"Hey, up here!" Jazai called over his shoulder as he opened the hatch to the spire roof. The three youngsters scrambled through and Devol caught sight of the unobscured night sky above.

"Wow, it's so clear up here."

"Peaceful too," the apprentice scholar agreed. "I come here to get away from it all—specifically Zier when he gets cranky."

Asla sat quickly and stared at the stars. Devol noticed that the lights of the night gave her an ethereal glow, which made her seem rather enchanting although he also saw a look of concern on her face. "Is something wrong, Asla?"

She shrugged and frowned slightly. "I couldn't hear what the older Templars were talking about, but from Freki's tone... Well, I don't think he expects us to succeed."

"The folly of youth is what Zier would call it." Jazai sighed as he leaned on the brass railings around the edge of the roof. "It can't be that bad. If it was important, they wouldn't send us if they didn't think we could do it."

"That doesn't sound much better," she mumbled. "Either we're running a pointless errand or it is some kind of test."

"Well, of course." Devol's statement drew odd looks from the other two. "It seemed obvious to me that this was more of a test than a real mission. They haven't exactly been subtle about it."

"Really?" the other boy asked. "I didn't catch that."

"I'm sure the mission is real," he assured them. "But they put us together and made us train. I think they want to see what we can accomplish on our own." He held a hand out, the palm down. "And I want us to promise each other that we will make it through. I've seen you two in action now, and I'm sure we could go on solo missions and do well. Together, this should be no problem."

Jazai chuckled and stepped closer with his arms folded. "Zier would call you too optimistic." He unfolded them and placed his hand on top of his friend's. "But I don't agree with him on much anyway."

Asla placed her hand on top of the apprentice's and surprised her companions. She wore a look of fierce determination on her face. "You are right, Devol. Even if they believe we can't succeed, we should show them they are wrong."

"Exactly." He nodded and smiled at his teammates. "This'll be the first official mission ever given to me by someone besides my mom, but I don't think those count. I'm glad I'll be working with you at my side."

"Same," Jazai said and grinned at them.

The wildkin did the same. "I'm excited once again. Let's do our best."

Their promise to each other sealed, they spent another hour talking and looking at the stars before they wandered to their quarters to sleep. They would train for one more day before it was time to depart on their first mission for the Templar Order.

It was a mission that would change their reality over the course of their journey, although they did not know it that night.

CHAPTER TWENTY

"Man, I forgot how cold it is out here!" Jazai grumbled as he drew his jacket closer. "Where's Asla? We need to get this show on the road."

"Calm yourself, Jazai," Zier ordered sharply. Although he did a better job of bundling his garment around him for warmth than the young scholar, he was also rather chilled by the outside air. "We are still waiting for the grand mistress as well."

"It looks like you won't have to wait long," the apprentice said and gestured to the bridge. "Here they are."

Devol and the others looked to where Asla, Freki, and Nauru strode out of the entrance to the castle and hurried to join them. The young Magi saw that Vaust was not with them. As the group huddled together, the two boys noticed that Asla carried a rather large backpack. "You do know we'll only be gone for a couple of days at most, right?" Jazai managed to restrain a chuckle at the fact that her pack of supplies was almost as tall as her.

"Freki insisted." She sighed. The wolf wildkin wore a

concerned and perhaps even melancholy expression on his face. He must have been sad that his trainee was leaving his side for a while and it was cute in a way.

"Good morning, everyone." Nauru greeted them with a small bow that all in attendance reciprocated. "Are you ready, young Magi?"

"Yes, ma'am," Devol stated and stood tall. "Tell us what we need to do."

"That would be helpful for completing the mission." Jazai snickered and Zier nudged him in the back in annoyance.

"I certainly agree." Nauru allowed herself a small smile and cleared her throat to draw the group's attention as she took a small card from her robes. "These are the instructions for your contact. You are to meet in the town of Rouxwoods."

"Rouxwoods?" Devol asked as he sheathed his majestic and took the card. "That village is near the border of Renaissance and the Kingdom of Britana."

"Do we have a portal near there?" the young scholar asked.

"No, but it shouldn't be more than a day and a half's travel from Fairwind, which is the closest anchor we have available," she told them. "You can head through the forest toward the King's Fall Mountains. From there, you can go around or through the mountains and from that point, you should have a straight route to the town."

Devol nodded as he slid the strap of the sword's sheath to his back. "I am very familiar with the Monleans' territory. I should be able to get us there, no problem."

"Then we'll rely on you," Jazai said quickly. "I'm terrible with directions."

"Isn't your father a traveler?" Asla asked. "Did he not teach you anything?"

"That would imply he listens to an instruction other than when it benefits him," Zier snarked and earned an eye-roll from his apprentice.

The young swordsman looked around the group again. "Hey, I noticed Mr. Lebatt isn't here."

The grand mistress nodded. "He had to depart earlier on a different mission."

"Oh, I see." He was more than a little disappointed. "I was hoping to thank him before he left for getting me here and the training."

"You'll see him again, lad," Wulfsun promised and placed a hand on his shoulder. "Everyone here comes and goes but this is our home. He'll be back. You can tell him then."

He smiled. "Right."

"Are you ready to depart?" Nauru asked. The three young adventurers looked at one another before they nodded to her. "Very good. Let me open the portal for you." The group moved to the anchor point and she held her hand out. Immediately, the rock began to glow before a large portal erupted in front of them.

"That's not how Mr. Lebatt opened it before," he remarked.

She chuckled. "It's one of the perks of being the grand mistress," she stated and darted him a questioning look. "And I heard that it isn't how you opened it either."

Devol grinned and rubbed the back of his head a little sheepishly. "Well, you do have a point."

"Let's get going," Jazai ordered and waved over his shoulder as he stepped through. Asla turned and bowed before she followed him.

"Bye, everyone!" Devol yelled as he hurried to catch up. "We'll be back soon."

As soon as he stepped through, the gate closed. The older Templars took a moment after they left to stand idle. It had been quite some time since they had seen a group of adventurers as young as these leave on a Templar mission and for them, it was inspiring.

"Man, feel that sea breeze!" Jazai shouted as he stretched his arms wide with enthusiasm. "I've been cooped up in that castle for so long, I almost forgot what the outer wilds feel like."

"Fish?" Asla asked and sniffed the air. "There's fish in that village."

"Yeah, it's a fishing village," Devol told her. "This is where Mr. Lebatt and I came from. We should get some when the mission is over. They have many great restaurants."

"So which way should we go, Devol?" the scholar asked as he circled the rock formation to look at the fields beyond. "Past the forests, right?"

"Through the forest to the northwest," he clarified and pointed over the fields. "We should reach the mountains in a few hours and be past those by nightfall. If all goes well, we should get to Rouxwoods by tomorrow afternoon."

"All right, sounds good." Jazai smirked and began to glow blue before he vanished, a now-familiar sign that he was using his blink cantrip. "See if you can keep up!" he shouted from about a hundred yards away.

"Wouldn't it be less Mana-intensive to simply use Vis?" Devol asked as the other boy blinked farther away.

"He's showing off," Asla muttered as she adjusted the straps on her back. "Besides, do you think he could keep up with us only using Vis?"

"I would have slowed so he could." That drew a giggle from her before she crouched.

"Come on. Let's get going." With that, she pounced and landed at the bottom of the hill before she repeated the action to catch up to Jazai.

Devol charged his Mana and hurried to join his teammates. Vaust, who was seated behind one of the rocks and hiding his Mana, smiled in amusement. It appeared that their mission had officially begun.

CHAPTER TWENTY-ONE

"According to the card, we'll make contact by the evening of the twenty-first, and the call sign is…Caw-caw?" Devol read aloud.

"Like a bird call?" Asla seemed unimpressed. "That doesn't exactly seem inconspicuous."

"Do you think they may be a bird wildkin?" he asked.

She shrugged as she leapt off a large tree branch. "Possibly, but most guilds aren't multi-racial. If this was a wildkin guild, I would think they'd have mentioned it."

"All the card says is that the carrier's name is Zeke and the guild is the Hunters of Britana." He slid the card into his pants pocket. "That's the main hunters' guild of the kingdom. I'm surprised they reached out to the Templars for something like this."

"I am too, honestly," Asla admitted. "I wonder what we are collecting and why the guild wouldn't want to keep it for themselves or sell it."

"Some rare item that belongs to the Templars?" he suggested.

The wildkin shook her head. "I'm sure there are many of those around as the order is quite old, but if that were the case, I don't think anyone is that gracious, at least to us."

Devol recalled Wulfsun mentioning the Templars' fall from grace. There was still much he did not know about it, but it appeared it had traveled much farther than he had imagined if people weren't even willing to do the right thing and return their treasures.

"Hey Jazai!" he shouted, caught the diviner's attention, and almost made him fall out of the sky.

The boy blinked and reappeared as he landed neatly and his teammates caught up to him. They maintained a quick pace but continued to run along the ground. "What do you need?" he asked.

"We're trying to work out what we're retrieving," the swordsman explained. "We know it's some kind of box. But what do you think is inside?"

"Beats me," he confessed. "I don't think they would send us out here for a simple supply run. It might merely be an artifact or something that needs study. Although if that were the case, Zier would probably have been more excited about the mission."

"Hunter guilds don't typically have a scholar division. At best, it's usually a small research team," Asla stated. "If they did find something of interest that they couldn't identify… No, even in that case, I think they would hand it to their kingdom's academics before they gave it to the Templars."

"Zier and the other scholars specialize in many different subjects," Jazai pointed out. "Including areas that aren't typically studied by most modern academics and Magi. So if it is a case where they couldn't learn what it was, they probably had little choice other than to hand it to us." The diviner's face contorted in confusion. "Well, no. That brings me back to the fact that Zier would have been more eager to get his hands on it."

"Was he not?" Devol asked.

The boy shook his head. "No, he was more...tepid, I guess."

"That sounds about normal for him," Asla replied.

Jazai chuckled. "Finally, someone else gets it. Most of the other scholars have been away for the last couple of weeks. I miss Wadia. She could at least take a joke."

Devol leapt upward and saw the mountains in the distance. He landed and caught up with the other two. "The mountains are coming up. We should be there in no time."

"Very well then." The other boy held a hand up, his thumb pressed to his middle finger. "Meet you there." He snapped his fingers and blinked away in a blue glow as his two teammates charged their Mana and quickened their pace.

When they arrived at the edge of the forest only about half a mile from the foot of the mountain, they paused to discuss their options as they stared at the massive red-and-gray bulwark in their path. "So are we headed through or around?" Jazai asked. Devol noticed that he was breathing a little more heavily than before although he was impressed that for all his teleporting, his Mana only seemed to be reduced by a small amount.

"I'm curious," Asla began and caught the attention of her companions as she pointed to the mountain. "It is called King's Fall Mountain, correct? Why is that? Did a king fall off it?"

The boys chuckled and the diviner shook his head. "That would make a better story than the real one."

"It used to be called something else," Devol said and tapped his chin as he tried to recall the details. "Red Ravine or something like that? Because of the red stones along the path. But a few hundred years ago, the Monleans king was ambushed in the mountains during a Britana invasion. It is said that he was able to hold off most of the attackers while he ordered his followers to retreat as they had a more important mission to undertake. Legend has it he was such a powerful Magi that he managed to rout the attacking army himself but died in the process."

"Yeah, King Piero." The other boy nodded. "I think they wanted to name the mountains after him but over the centuries, a couple of other kings met their ends in these mountains and not as heroically. The range earned the morbid name as a result. I hear both Monlean's kings and visiting royalty don't cross it to this day."

"That's true," he agreed. "But King Jeauxn doesn't leave the castle much anyway. I think the only time I've seen him in person was during the thousand-year celebration of Monleans when I was six years old."

Asla looked at the mountains again. "I get an ill feeling looking at them," she said and dragged her gaze away. "We are not kings but perhaps it is best that we take a path around?"

"It'll be a little longer but most likely safer," Devol agreed. "I'm not sure if the mountains are cursed or anything, but there are reports of bandit activity in the area. My father would often have to send teams out to search or scare them away, but they always seem to be replaced or return after a time."

"Is it worth merchants traveling through, then?" Jazai asked.

"Well, most can't move as fast as we can," he pointed out. "I have heard that they are building a teleport network between merchant and supply channels, but it's still in the beginning stages."

"It's something to look forward to and it would make these missions way easier." The other boy adjusted his pack and looked around. "All right, Devol. Which way?"

"Let's go left," he said. "The forest stretches to the side of the mountain for a fair distance so we'll still have some cover."

"Sounds good to me." Jazai lifted a hand to snap his fingers but Asla reached out and stopped him.

"Run with us," she said. "Conserve Mana. It is a long trek."

Devol studied her curiously. The seriousness in her tone seemed more like a warning than a simple suggestion. The other boy gave her a brief questioning look before he lowered his hand and nodded. "All right, I'll keep up. Let's move."

The three set off again. Vaust had watched them from within the cover of the forest and was pleased to see that

Asla's instincts were as sharp as ever. There was something there, although it did not appear to be anything he should be too concerned about, even for them. They should be safe henceforth. He stepped into a clearing, continued to shadow the trainees on their journey, and made sure to hide his Mana along the way.

"We're almost out of the forest," Devol announced. "There should be nothing but fields. I think the next town beyond the mountains is Granvy, but we'll be able to go farther than that, so we should think about camping for the—"

Asla held an arm to stop him out and her ear twitched. Jazai stopped of his own accord, took his book out quickly, and opened it. "I have eleven names," he stated quietly and peered into the trees around them.

"We're being followed," the wildkin noted and her gaze darted in all directions. "Or trapped, rather. They are wearing thieves' oil. I could hardly discern their scent."

"Bandits?" Devol asked and slid his hand to his majestic. Before he could draw it, however, dozens of arrows whistled through the trees toward them.

Jazai moved quickly between Devol and Asla, held his arms out, and pointed to either side. "Shield!" he yelled and two large circular shields made of Mana formed in the directions in which the young Magi pointed. They were barely in time to block the projectiles, which dropped harmlessly when he dispersed the magical barriers.

"Got some Magi in our midst, eh?" a rough voice commented. Devol drew his sword and held it in front of him as a group of men in dark-brown jerkins and pants walked out of the forest and surrounded them. Some were armed with bows or crossbows and others with swords or bludgeoning weapons on their hips or back.

Two more of these bandits stepped onto the road, followed by a much taller man with an unkempt beard and dark eyes. He was dressed in a black coat and pants with a red bandana tied around his arm and wore an iron helm with metal gloves and bracers. They must have been enchanted because they neither clanged nor shuffled as he walked.

He studied them with amusement. "You seem quite young. Sorry about the attack. We felt considerable Mana coming from ya. Can't be too careful in these parts."

"He's the leader," Jazai stated as he peeked at his tome. "His name is Jett and he has an exotic but I can't read it clearly right now. The Mana of all these other bandits is getting in the way."

"Should we be worried about them?" Asla asked and slid her pack off slowly.

The diviner shook his head. "Nah, not at all. A couple of them have more Mana than your average academy graduate, but they know nothing about Anima like the big guy does. He probably didn't teach them so he could keep them in line."

"What are ya scheming over there?" Jett asked with a grin that revealed large, yellowed teeth. "No need to be making any grand plans, children. Drop your supplies and those pretty items of yours and we'll leave you be." He placed a hand over his heart. "My promise."

"I'll take the ones on the right," Jazai said and slid his gaze to the four bandits on his side.

"Then I'll take the four on the left," Asla replied and let her pack fall as she glared openly at the group. At least one winced and looked at the others.

"I'll take him and his guards," Devol stated, drew his sword, and prepared himself to attack.

"Focus on getting rid of his buddies first," the other boy recommended. "Under normal circumstances, I'd say you could defeat the leader easily, but we don't know what his exotic is capable of so keep your guard up."

"Got it. Be quick and safe," he stated as they all prepared to attack.

Jett began to reach into his coat. "Don't go doing anything foolish now."

"Go!" Devol shouted and the trio separated to attack the bandits.

Vaust scowled where he lay prone behind a tree stump. This certainly was not the plan but it would be a good warm-up and a chance to see how they worked in the field. He peered over his hiding place and watched the fight, paying particular attention to Devol and his light-bladed majestic. It was time to see what he could do with it.

CHAPTER TWENTY-TWO

Jazai was the first to lure his group away from the road. He blinked quickly behind one of the four bandits and, in a display of ingenuity or simply a desire for expediency, he thunked him on the head with his magic-imbued tome. The man fell and when the other three focused their attention on the young diviner, he led them deeper into the woods.

The wildkin pounced on her targets much faster than any of them expected and caught them all unprepared. She drove one onto his back when she leapt into his chest and delivered a heavy kick before she landed on top of him. In the same motion, she slashed the legs of two other bandits before the fourth attempted to swing his mace to crush her head. Alsa rolled to the side and the mace almost pounded into the fallen bandit's chest before its wielder managed to stop it. She scurried into the woods with both the injured and uninjured brigands in pursuit.

Devol decided the best way to draw Jett's bodyguards would be to feint an assault on their leader. He surged into a mock attack and as expected, the two men intercepted him. With his sword held ready in both hands, he slid along the path as both guards swung their weapons in aggressive arcs. He lifted his blade to catch theirs and the two struggled against him.

"What the hell?" one of them protested. "How is this kid so strong?"

His comrade directed a vicious kick at the young Magi, who strengthened his limb with Mana seconds before the bandit's boot struck his knee. The impact made the man cry out in surprise and he almost buckled from the pain. "My foot!" he yelled. "My toes are broken."

"Hey—don't back off, idiot!" his comrade yelled. "He's going to—"

The boy did not let him finish and instead, shoved him back and broke their stalemate as he thrust the pommel of his majestic into the guard's chest. The force of the blow dented the light armor he wore under his jacket and he hacked painfully and spat a glob of something vile before he stumbled back and collapsed.

"You little bastard!" the man's comrade roared, steadied himself, and attempted another wild swipe with his weapon. Devol intercepted the strike, blocked it with ease, and used his strengthened leg to deliver a powerful kick to his opponent's jaw. The ruffian staggered and flailed to regain his balance before he landed heavily on his companion.

Surprisingly, the bandit leader laughed raucously as he shook his head and clapped. "Well I'll be— You're something else, kid!" he remarked, his tone impressed, and slid his hand into his coat. "I underestimated you and your little friends. I usually have a good eye for easy targets but guess I was way off the mark this time."

"Will you fight too?" Devol asked and observed the man as he rummaged in his jacket.

"Well, I have to save face now," Jett stated. and withdrew a small hammer. "This is about pride, not merely plunder."

Jazai had told the young Magi that the leader had an exotic, and the boy's gaze studied the hammer. The one-handed weapon with a head that was no more than six or seven inches wide and a few inches tall was a little disappointing and he wondered if it was truly his exotic or merely a ploy.

The brigand twirled the hammer for a moment. "Nice sword. What is that?" he studied the light-blade as a thief might a precious jewel he intended to steal. "Some sturdy glass, I suppose, although it's nothing I've seen before. My boys have truesilver blades, so it wasn't only you strengthening your sword with Mana that kept it intact. I wonder how much I can get for something like that. It's a collector's item, no doubt. I might keep it for myself."

"My majestic sought me out," Devol stated and pointed it at the bandit leader. "And I have only recently acquired it. I won't give it up."

"A majestic?" Jett chuckled. "Either way, that sounds like a pompous way to say, 'you can pry it out of my cold, dead hands.'" He held his hammer up and a dull red glow now surrounded it. "I can oblige you there, boy."

His eyes widened. He had his answer. The hammer was indeed his opponent's exotic and it was much more than it appeared to be. He decided to not give the man any advantage he might gain with more time to prepare himself and surged into motion. Jett merely laughed wildly.

"Where'd he go? Did anyone see him?" one of the bandits shouted as they thrust through the forest in search of Jazai.

"Over here!" the diviner shouted. The group was bewildered but followed the voice hurriedly to a small clearing, where their quarry stood in the open, reading his book. "Let's see… Both James and Kane have short fuses. Vick and Vince are brothers who attack together."

"What the hell?" Vick demanded indignantly. "How does he know our names?"

"Must be a trick!" Kane reasoned and brandished his mace. "We beat the kid and worry about the rest later."

"Did you know that Vince has been seeing your girl, Vick?" Jazai asked and caught both of the bandits' attention. "Lola in Sherbrook? Yeah, they've had a few flings. I guess brothers do share everything."

"Is that true, Vince?" Vick demanded, turned immediately, and pointed his sword at his brother. "Well, is it?"

"He's only trying to get in your head, man!" Vince said and tried to calm him as he held his sword up defensively. "Don't let him get to you."

"I'm not sure what I have to worry about with Kane and James," the boy remarked when he flipped a page. "It says here you think you're the worst fighters among your group. Both of you are worried that the boss will toss you out on your ass sooner or later, and that's the best outcome."

A NEW LIGHT

"Shut up!" they yelled almost in unison as they lunged toward him. He closed the book and waited for them to strike. He might not have been an up-close fighter like Devol or Asla, but even he could see how sloppy the two were and slid easily between them as they attempted to land their blows at the same time. His ploy worked and their weapons clashed noisily against each other.

Jazai placed his hands on the back of their heads. "Shock!" Electricity coursed through his palms and into the bandits, who yelled in pain before they fell at his feet. He shook his hands and felt them tingle. "Huh. I need to work on that one," he muttered as he turned toward the forest. Vick and Vince now brawled openly with one another.

For a moment, he wondered if he should simply let them keep themselves occupied, but he decided to be on the safe side. He pointed at them with his index and little finger. "Missile." Two orbs of blue Mana formed in front of his fingers and streaked unerringly into the heads of the bandit brothers to render them unconscious and end their little spat. The diviner grinned and departed.

"Holly!" a bandit shouted in an attempt to locate his comrades. "Xav! Did you find her?"

"I don't hear anything." His partner grimaced. "Only birds and insects. How far did they go?"

"Maybe she got them?" the first man reasoned and tightened his hold nervously on his mace.

"No way. That scrawny little—" His partner's words

ended in a sudden shout and a sound that suggested he'd thunked into a tree trunk.

He spun hastily. The other man lay in a crumpled heap and Asla stood over him. "Son of a—" He acted reflexively and pushed into a charge as he raised his mace. The wildkin turned, formed a claw with her hand, and lashed out even though he was several yards away.

His mace suddenly felt considerably lighter and he gaped at it in astonishment. The weapon had been cut into three pieces and most of it was now on the forest floor. Before he could even utter a word, she darted behind him, struck the back of his neck in one swift motion with the side of her hand, and felled him instantly.

She watched for a moment to see if he recovered but once she was sure he was as incapacitated as the other three bandits, she began to run toward the road. The wildkin wondered how Devol and Jazai had fared but she heard a loud impact, something that caused the forest to shake. She increased her pace even more. It sounded like it had come from the main road, which meant Devol was in trouble.

When Jazai blinked into view on the road, he was immediately shoved to the ground as something large streaked overhead. "What was that?" he asked in surprise as Devol helped him up and they both retreated a short distance. The bandit leader held a massive hammer—almost comically big in comparison to the large man—but he wielded it with intent to kill, which made it even more threatening.

"It looks like he can increase the size and length of it as he pleases," the young swordsman informed him and held his blade up. "It's been quite tricky to get close."

"I can imagine. It's only an exotic, though, so you should be able to guard against it easily with a majestic."

"It won't break the blade," he agreed and pulled his sleeve up to reveal a bruised arm. "But I still feel the hit. It tossed me into a tree a minute ago."

"Yeah, that would be a problem," Jazai conceded and held his hands out. "I'll see if I can get you an opening, although it would probably be easier if Asla was—"

The wildkin launched out of the forest, leapt onto the leader's back, and sank her claws into his armor.

"You too?" Jett roared as he struggled to dislodge her. "Are all my men incompetent?" He was able to catch hold of her hair and yanked her off him. She struck with her claws and left scratch marks on his chest plate but little more. "You have to do more than whiff me, girlie!" He spat into the dust.

Asla landed and bounded away to join her two teammates. "Good timing," the young diviner remarked.

"He has an Anima," she told them. "Otherwise, that strike would have wounded him."

"Devol needs an opening," Jazai stated. "Let us get it for him."

"All right." She nodded, bared her teeth, and surged forward with him close behind.

Devol began to prime his majestic with Mana and the light flowed quickly into his blade. Asla lashed out and her claws scored the leader's armor as he swung his weapon at her. The hammer had enlarged enough to strike almost her whole body in one blow, but she was able to contort herself enough that it narrowly missed her and whistled overhead. She landed, jumped onto the hammer, and vaulted off to strike the man's helm.

The diviner moved close enough that he was only a few yards away and pointed at the brigand. "Chains!" he shouted. Immediately, links made of Mana slid around the arms and chest of their target and held him in place for a moment while Asla circled for another strike.

Jett responded with an angry shout and his Mana flared. He broke the chains, snatched the wildkin in mid-air, and hurled her into the dirt, then raised his hammer to flatten her.

As he prepared to swing his hammer, a bright light filled his vision and the young swordsman raced forward, prepared to sink his majestic into his chest. The leader shrank his hammer as he closed in, which allowed him to change the arc of his swing toward the young Magi. When his weapon met the sword, a blast of light and wave of force exploded from the clash.

The majestic grew brighter and Devol pushed his blade forward. A second vivid explosion catapulted Jett off his feet and he hurtled along the forest path, his hammer following. He was finally stopped over a hundred yards away when he careened into a group of trees. Dazed, he struggled for a moment to stand but before he could get to his feet, his hammer drove into his chest and thrust him deeper into the forest.

The trio looked on wide-eyed. Jazai and Asla turned to Devol. "Well..." the boy began and an amused grin snuck onto his face. "I don't think that counts as Mana draining, do you?"

The only response his teammates had was to shake their heads.

Vaust was equally amused and excited. It had been a treat to watch the three handle their foes so deftly, and seeing Devol's majestic in action was an impressive sight. He realized, however, any theory they currently had notwithstanding, that what it could do remained a mystery. Still, he would have to remember this moment as it would make a great story to tell the others once they finished their mission.

CHAPTER TWENTY-THREE

After their run-in with the bandits, they searched their unconscious bodies and helped themselves to anything that seemed useful. Even Jett was only knocked out cold, much to their surprise, and they conceded that for all his nasty behavior, the man was certainly a worthy opponent if a somewhat broken one at that moment. They all agreed to not take the weapons as they were cumbersome and would slow their journey.

With the procured supplies shared between them, the boys discussed taking the brigand leader's exotic, which would certainly be of real benefit to the Templars—and prevent its use against unsuspecting travelers.

Before they could agree on it, a loud growl and a flash of orange light ended their debate and they turned as one. A furious Asla clawed the hammer viciously and destroyed it. They watched her in silence. While they had to admit that this may not have been the plan they would have gone with, it was a fair compromise.

The three continued until nightfall but were unable to

find a cave or shelter nearby. The skies were clear, however, and no sign of impending rain meant they could easily build themselves a campfire and settle around it for the night. They found a river a short distance away, where they were able to refill their canteens and freshen up.

Dinner was made from rabbits Asla had hunted followed by bread and various jams they had brought with them from the castle. Thereafter, they simply stretched beside the campfire, stared at the stars, and took a moment to rest.

"You know, Devol," Jazai began and turned on his side to look at the young swordsman. "You've been rather quiet since we started to make camp."

He shifted under his blanket and nodded. "I guess I have, huh? Sorry, I've been thinking about the last fight."

The diviner snickered as he flipped onto his back to look at the sky again. "You obsessing about your mistakes or something like that? I know you fighting types always seem to go on and on about things like that. We defeated them all in a few minutes. Nothing to—"

"No, it isn't that," he interjected. "When I looked at the leader's body, he was banged up good."

"Well, yeah." The diviner chuckled. "You threw him a hundred yards and his hammer pounded into his chest. I have to admit I was surprised to see he was still breathing after that."

Devol tensed slightly before he sighed heavily. "I was too—and relieved, to be honest."

His teammates focused on him. "Were you worried you killed him?" the other boy asked.

He nodded. "I've killed beasts and creatures. But another human?"

Jazai regarded him with a thoughtful expression. "You are fairly young so I guess you've never had a fight end that way, eh?"

The young swordsman shook his head. "No, I have not." He rolled his eyes at his friend. "Have you?"

"Not me, no," the boy responded and looked away as a memory surfaced. "But when I was about ten, I was traveling with my father and I saw him kill a couple of guys." He sighed when he recalled the incident. "We were ambushed on a road to Luxor or someplace like that by bandits very similar to those we fought. He dealt with most of them himself. I got a couple down too but two had exotics. They got the jump on my father and he… His instincts took over. He attacked them with a powerful cantrip. It wasn't graphic or anything, but I knew they were dead even before they landed."

"Did it…disturb you?" Devol asked, his full attention on the diviner.

Jazai shrugged. "Not disturbed, that's too harsh—maybe unsettled?" He sounded uncertain and frowned as he tried to find the right words. "I remember feeling numb and taken aback. It was my first time seeing someone who was alive not seconds before suddenly gone. But at the same time, I realized what my father had to do in his line of work—and what he was capable of doing also hit me. I suddenly thought, 'this is how it is,' and it shocked me as much as the dead men did." He turned his hand palm-up in a show of indifference. "He was quite apologetic that night that I had to see it, but he also used it as a moment to teach me what could be expected of me should I choose to walk the same path."

"And did that worry you?" Asla asked as she turned to join the conversation.

He responded with another shrug before he rolled onto his back again and placed his hands behind his head. "I already knew about it on some level, even then. But seeing it happen is a very different thing. I guess it put it in perspective. I've had years to think about it since then and I'm prepared to kill if need be, but I'm sure it won't be easy when it happens." He glanced at the other boy. "Your pops is a guard captain, right? I'm sure he's had to deal with some terrible people in that fashion."

Devol nodded and cast his mind back. "I know he has, but he's never discussed it with me. He was even responsible for a few executions while I was growing up but I've never had to see it." He considered it and thought about the bandit leader's body. "I know that if I become a guardsman or a Templar or anything like that, I'll have to get used to it. I guess I'm not that great at thinking ahead."

"I've come to that conclusion," Asla interjected and although her tone didn't contain malice or sound chiding, it still stung a little.

He continued as if she hadn't spoken. "I thought this was a simple retrieval mission. I should have expected that we could run into complications like bandits. It is a wonder I did not run into so much as a peddler on my way to the Templar Order, I suppose. Even during the fight, I thought I could handle them without much trouble, but when I was pushed too far in the end and my majestic's power came out…" He extended his hand to trace the sheath of his sword. "It could have ended differently, I guess."

Jazai mumbled an agreement but wasn't sure what to say. He had found peace with the idea of having to maim or kill others over the years, but Devol seemed quite vexed about it at the moment. He didn't feel right to simply tell him to buck up and deal with it, but it could end in tragedy for him if he pursued any profession that might demand that from him and he was not prepared for it.

More immediately, it could cause issues with their mission if they encountered another complication like the bandits. He looked at Asla to see if she had any words of wisdom or comfort, but she stared off into the distance.

"Do you see that bush?" she asked after a moment and pointed directly ahead. The boys sat quickly to peer at a rather large bush with many brown-red nubs along its branches. "Those seeds-like lumps are special. They are bloodflowers that have yet to bloom."

"Bloodflowers?" Devol asked. "I'm not sure I'm familiar with them."

She nodded her understanding. "They aren't particularly common in the Monleans kingdom. Most consider them to be an ill omen. It is said that bloodflowers only bloom when someone is near who is either about to experience death or is quite familiar with it." She brought her knees to her chest.

"I'm not sure if you've seen the gardens we keep in the castle," she continued, "but we have bloodflowers there, both blossomed and not. I pass them almost every day in the morning." She bit her lip. "I am not sure how much I believe in many of these tales, but this one has always stayed with me. Blossomed bloodflowers are indeed beautiful, but that story always runs through my mind when I see them. I find some solace in that."

"You do?" the young swordsman asked. "How so?"

The wildkin looked at him. "I plan to assist the Templars, grow with them, and see them restored to their former glory as thanks for what they have done for me. And I know that I too will one day have to kill both monsters and villains as many of them have. Seeing those beautiful flowers and thinking of that story reminds me that even when we must do something we prefer not to—or even in tragedy—something beautiful can come of it."

He was struck by her words and even Jazai's eyes widened before he smiled and closed them as he lay back and shifted to make himself comfortable. It appeared that she did indeed have some wise words to say.

Devol took one of her hands and she looked at him in surprise. He returned her look with one of calm and gratitude. "I do understand what you mean, Asla. Thank you."

Her eyelids closed for a moment and she squeezed his hand softly and nodded. "You are welcome." She withdrew her hand gently and they said nothing more. It was already quite late and they needed to rest so they could reach their destination by early afternoon on the morrow.

His fears had not abated but they did not haunt him further that night. Thankfully, he was able to sleep more comfortably than he had expected to.

CHAPTER TWENTY-FOUR

"We're almost there!" Devol called as he bounded down the hillside. "You can already see the red trees."

"They are hard to miss," Jazai told him before he blinked away from his friend, who laughed. Asla bounded past them both as they approached a large archway that welcomed travelers to Rouxwoods.

It was a quaint little village nestled deep in a wood of the perpetually red-leaved trees from which the forest and town took its name. Red-and-white cobbled roads stretched from the gates into the town center, where it split into several directions. The town bustled with villagers and passersby and the houses all seemed to be made with the dark timber from the trees—an amusing detail Devol noticed as they walked under the swirling arches that were built in front of many of the buildings where the slanted roofs met.

"We made it," Asla said smugly as she looked at all the people with frank interest. "It wasn't a long trip at all."

"Well, not for us." Jazai chuckled and his gaze paused at

one of the establishments. "Hey, this courier we're supposed to meet—he will contact us, right?"

Devol took out the card Nauru had given them. "Yeah. I'm not sure how exactly, but we have to wait for him. He's traveling from farther away."

"Then we might as well get something to eat." The diviner pointed his thumb at an inn a short distance ahead. "We can also see how much rooms will be if we have to stay the night."

The other two looked at one another and nodded together in agreement with the older Magi. "Sounds good," the young swordsman said.

Their friend smirked and cracked his knuckles. "All right. Let me haggle for the rooms. It's one of my specialties."

"Damn conmen," Jazai grumbled and sipped his spiced juice.

"It's not like it was our money," Asla told him and swirled a cup of berry juice. "We took that from the bandits."

"Still, we could have kept more of it." He sighed. "I wouldn't have thought a place like this would have such a bustling tourist economy."

"It is very pretty," Devol pointed out. "And it's also something of a waypoint for merchants and travelers since it's so close to the border of Britana."

"Still, a whole shard for a couple of rooms?" The scholar huffed and took a swig like his drink contained alcohol with which to drown his woes. "I was hoping I could lower it to three splints. It would have saved us two, at least."

"I'm sure you have other specialties that are of use, Jazai," the wildkin responded.

"Like what?" Devol asked and earned only a shrug from her as the scholar glared at them both.

A female server stopped at their table. "Your food is ready," she announced and put a plate of fish and rice in front of Asla. Grilled chicken with mashed potatoes and gravy followed for Jazai and slices of steak and seasoned vegetables for Devol. They thanked her as she replaced their empty breadbasket and began to dig into their meals.

"So, any idea when we're supposed to meet this courier?" Asla asked as she began to cut into her fish with a knife and fork. It amused the young swordsman to notice that she was not that proficient, given that she normally used her claws.

He considered the question. "Well, if he's coming from the capital, he has a far greater distance to travel than we did," he reasoned as he speared a piece of broccoli with his fork. "I don't know if he was using any portals, but we would have to wait more than a day for him to arrive."

"I guess we'll get some use out of those rooms," Jazai muttered as he took another sip of his juice.

"But if he began earlier than we did, he should arrive soon, yes?" she asked.

Devol nodded. "Assuming he can move as fast or faster than we can, it shouldn't be a difficult trek, merely a long one."

"How is he supposed to find us?" Jazai stirred the

mashed potatoes on his plate with his fork. "Or how do we find him?

He shrugged and swallowed the vegetables he had been chewing as he patted his left pants pocket. "The card doesn't specify but the signal word is 'caw-caw.'"

"Oh right, the bird's call," the diviner mumbled as he cut into his chicken. "That won't be suspicious at all."

"We discussed that it could be an avian wildkin," Asla reminded them. "It might not be likely but I did notice some wildkin in town."

Devol nodded and recalled their features. "I saw a verta wildkin in the merchant row who looked like a deer, so maybe people around here are accustomed to wildkin."

"Most in Monleans and Britana are," she confirmed. "The homina wildkin kingdom is in Monleans lands, and the verta kingdom island is off the coast of Britana in the Pendragon Ocean, so they are more common in these parts."

"I don't remember seeing that many growing up," he admitted. "There was Mrs. Rena—another guard captain who worked with my father—and a few others in the city, I think, but most were traveling merchants."

"Many wildkin are nomadic," she informed him. "At least in youth and when out of the kingdoms. I suppose that would make me something of a special case."

"I'm glad you are," Devol said with a smile. Jazai flinched and stopped in mid-chew as his gaze drifted to him. Although it hadn't been intentional, he might have stepped on a sore spot. "Otherwise, we probably would never have met. I think we've gotten along great so far."

The diviner looked at Asla, who wore a perplexed look

for a moment before she smiled. "I suppose there are benefits to my situation. I am lucky, all things considered." Jazai drew a quick breath of relief and continued to eat his meal.

"What do you mean you are cuttin' me off?" A loud, belligerent shout stilled the conversation in the dining area. The group looked at the bar, where a tall man in slightly tarnished armor was on his feet and yelled at the barkeep. "I'm fine! I've had a long spell of travelin' and simply want to relax. You're turning profit away, old man."

"You're redder in the face than the leaves of the trees, pal," the other man chided. "I can't have you collapsing outside the establishment—or plastered while carrying that ax of yours."

"He has an exotic," Jazai noted and gestured to the man's waist. Devol narrowed his eyes and studied the one-handed, double-bladed ax, and he noticed a rune carved into the flat side of each blade and an enchanted pommel.

"I said I'm fine!" the man roared and slapped his hands on the bar. The barkeep folded his arms and inclined his head toward the door. A few men in the dining area stood in case the aggressive drunk tried anything. Doors from the kitchen opened and a few of the larger staff members walked out. The inebriated patron noticed their presence and looked over his shoulder before he grunted and stormed away. "Fine! I'll find another bar that respects my cobalt." He all but spat the words as he shoved the inn's main door open and slammed it behind him.

Those customers who had stood now sat again and continued to eat, while the staff returned to their duties. A couple headed to the bar to check on the older man as the three friends returned to their meal.

"That was a very nice exotic," Devol mentioned. "But his armor wasn't well-kept. And if he spends money on drinks and overlooks something like that, my guess is that he didn't buy it."

"It could be an heirloom," Jazai suggested with a shrug as he finished one of the chicken breasts. "Although if you're implying he stole it or won it from someone, those also seem likely. They aren't as precious as they used to be, after all."

"Finished," Asla declared and slid her plate away with a contented sigh. Jazai and Devol stared down at the clean plate with amusement and surprise respectively.

"You were much hungrier than you let on," the swordsman mused.

"I finished cutting the fish while everyone was distracted," she explained and tapped her pointed nails together. "It made it a much faster process."

"You can simply enjoy a meal now and then." Jazai chuckled. "It's not like we're going anywhere until that courier arr—"

Shouts and a series of loud noises from outside the inn startled those in attendance. Devol looked at his teammates. The other boy was about to take another spoonful of mashed potatoes but he sighed and placed the spoon on his plate. "You want to check it out?" he asked. His friend nodded. "Bored or worried?"

"A little of both, I suppose," the young swordsman admitted.

The diviner frowned and glanced at Asla, who rubbed her claws together. She met his gaze and shrugged and he stood with a sigh. "Fine, but I swear to the heavens if my food is cold when I get back, I'm taking some of yours."

"You don't have to come," Devol said as he pushed from his seat and headed toward the door with the others close behind.

Jazai grinned cheekily. "Ah, guess I'm a little bored too."

As they hurried out to see what all the commotion was about, a figure watched them idly. He had listened to the various conversations around the inn while he waited for a certain group to wander past. With a smile, he ran a hand through his violet hair. It seemed he had found his target.

CHAPTER TWENTY-FIVE

When Devol stepped outside, a crowd of people huddled in a circle in the town's square and a shattered cart with spilled jugs of ale and wine stood nearby. He and his friends pushed through as someone cried out and something landed with a loud clang. For a moment, he was afraid someone had been killed, but his fears were assuaged when he reached the center. Two men in uniforms with a red crest on their chests and arms signaling that they were city patrol sprawled on the road but they were still breathing.

"Damn guards," a drunk, bitter voice mumbled. The warrior from the inn breathed heavily and stood over the guards with his ax in hand. "My day has been bad enough. Don't need you to make it worse." He turned and focused on the crowd as if he had only now noticed them. His irate gaze became an angry glare as he spun completely and realized he was surrounded by curious onlookers. "What are you staring at, huh? Get the hell out of here unless you wanna end up like these two."

That drew some concerned yelps and gasps but others in the crowd looked like they did indeed want to challenge the drunkard. Devol beat them to it. He was the first to move but took only a single step forward before a hand grasped his arm.

When he looked over his shoulder, Jazai regarded him with a questioning look. "Are you sure?" he asked, mainly to check before his friend involved himself in a street brawl. The swordsman nodded and the other boy returned it and released him. He moved quickly in front of the warrior.

"Hmm?" The man muttered and glowered at the young Magi. Now that he was only a few feet in front of him, the full size of this man surprised him. He was not as tall as Wulfsun, but only by a few inches. His muscles showed that he was at least familiar with combat and training and the exotic ax was also a sign that violence wasn't uncommon for him, but he already had proof of that now.

The warrior bent forward and his hand slipped off his knee before he caught himself, propped himself a little more securely, and peered into the boy's eyes. "What do you want, kid?" He scowled. "Think ya are gonna be a hero? I ain't here to start trouble. Those guards came after me for nothin'."

Devol pointed behind him to the destroyed cart. "Was that you?" he asked and the man raised an eyebrow quizzically. "I saw you at the inn. You wanted more to drink. My guess is you saw an opportunity to get ale and broke the cart—on purpose or accidentally, it doesn't matter. I would assume that would count as disorderly conduct and theft."

At the quiet challenge, the stern visage became even

more aggressive and the man clenched his teeth. His breath reeked of alcohol, heavy and almost suffocating. So far, however, that was the only intimidating thing about him.

"So what? You wanna play guardsman?" The drunk growled in annoyance, straightened to his full height, and rolled his shoulders. "Didn't work out for them two, did it?"

"I want you to apologize," the boy announced and folded his arms. "You've hurt two men and scared people in this town. You are a traveler, right? That makes this worse. People live here and—"

"Shut yer trap, kid!" the warrior demanded and tossed his ax onto the ground, where it cut through and sank into the cobblestone. "Like I'll take a lecture from some brat. Yeah, I am a traveler—a mercenary. And all I wanted was a drink. I think I deserve a little hospitality." He raised his hands in front of him and formed them into fists that began to shake in anger. "And if you and these other gnats don't get out of my face, I'll do more than scare ya." He gritted his teeth and his muscles became engorged and grew from their already stocky girth to almost double in size. "See this? I can use my Mana to enhance my strength, and I could probably already snap your tweedy little neck without it."

"That's called Vis," he corrected. And not proper Vis, either. It enhanced the capabilities of the body but the whole point was that the Mana augmented the user's physical form. He merely injected it into his muscles, and while it might have given him a small boost in strength and power similar to the innkeeper in Bluebell, it provided nothing else. He might as well have worn a suit of clay. "And you don't have an Anima."

His opponent lowered his arms and tried to stand straight, but a slight hunch in his posture ruined his efforts somewhat. The boy looked at him and waited, amused by the way he craned his neck, which made it appear that a shadow was cast over his eyes. "Vis? Anima? The hell is that?" The warrior grunted dismissively.

Devol looked at the ax. Exotics were relatively easy to use but someone not skilled in Mana arts would not get long or even effective use from them. He now thought that his drunken opponent had very likely stolen it without knowing what it was.

When he looked up, the warrior held his fist close to his face again. "Spare me another speech, brat. I'll give you one last chance to get the hell away from here. If you want to face me as a warrior, I will treat you like one."

He met the man's heated gaze and nodded. "All right, then do so and we'll make this quick."

The anger faded momentarily to show confusion and surprise before a grim smile formed on the warrior's lips. "Wanna be a man, then?" he asked and reached his arm back. "You ain't ready for something like that."

Devol held one finger up. "One thing before we start," he said and the aggressive drunk paused briefly. "I don't want to cause more of a commotion than you already have. So we will make this simple." He looked at the man's enlarged biceps. "You seem proud of your muscles. So on the count of three, we will each throw a punch. The one to knock the other down is the winner." He began to summon his Anima as he said the last few words.

His adversary responded with a howled laugh. "Are ya kidding me, boy? I've got almost twice the reach you do, and that's only the start of it!" His laughter continued as he shook his head. "I guess I can give you points for guts. Well, this was your call. Yer about to feel the punch of a real warrior."

With a small nod, he drew one arm back and placed his fist against his other palm to hold it in position. "Very well, on the count of three. One…two…"

"I ain't waitin'!" the man bellowed and swung his fist toward his young adversary's face. Devol's Anima flared quickly to life but he was careful to control it and use only enough to protect himself. The crowd hollered and gasped as the punch landed and the drunk smiled when it connected. A second later, his expression changed to one of shock when he realized that the young Magi was unmoved. "What the hells?" He scowled as he moved his fist away from the boy, who now stared at him with surprising calm.

"Three." Devol finished the count, allowed his Anima to surge, and launched a charged fist into the warrior's gut. His adversary uttered a pained shout as saliva spattered from his mouth. His feet lifted and he careened down the street, made a clumsy landing, and skidded along the cobblestones before he came to a stop in front of a group of guards who ran toward the town center.

The crowd stood in silent shock for a few moments and the boy let his Anima fade. As he composed himself, the spectators began to clap for him along with nods and shouts of approval to congratulate him on his victory. He waved a hand sheepishly to them in thanks as Jazai and

Asla stepped beside him. The diviner clapped him on the shoulder. "Nice work, man. You've gotten the hang of Anima quickly."

"Thanks. That week of training helped. I would probably have summoned too much without proper control. He would have known something was up even without knowing anything about Anima."

"Or you might have killed him," his friend pointed out "That was also possible."

"It is a little sad," Asla said as three of the guards dragged the warrior out of the street. "If he was speaking the truth, being able to survive this long as a mercenary without proper Mana training shows that he at least has good instincts and some discipline. What a waste."

"If we're done here," Jazai began and stretched before he pointed at the inn. "Let's go finish our meals before they get cold."

"You there!" Devol turned as a guard ran toward them. "Are you the one who fought that ruffian?"

"Me?" he asked and pointed to himself. "I am."

"Ah, come on guardsman!" a man shouted from the crowd. "Don't tell me you're gonna bring him in for that. He stopped him from causing more of a ruckus."

"No, no, nothing like that," the guard stated as he stopped in front of the three youngsters. "I need a report, and the guardsmen who initially confronted him are... well..." He and the young swordsman glanced to where another of his comrades walked up to the two the drunk warrior had knocked unconscious. "Probably not in the right headspace at the moment. I need to ask a couple of quick questions."

"Oh, all right." He nodded and gestured to Jazai and Asla. "It's all right guys. I'll be back soon."

"Works for me." The young diviner turned to stroll casually into the inn.

Asla fretted for a moment before she inclined her head in agreement and followed the other boy inside. "I'll make sure they bring more bread for you."

"Sounds good!" he called to her before he turned to talk to the guard. The other two men were escorted away for treatment as the crowd began to disperse and return to their activities. The man asked his questions quickly and seemed rather surprised that a young boy was able to hurl a large man like that away with one punch. Fortunately, he seemed more knowledgeable about the applications of Mana than the warrior so it was not too much of a stretch for him. He thanked him for his assistance but stated that the next time something like that happened, to summon the guards instead. They did not want civilians to potentially get hurt.

Devol nodded and waved as he left. Two guardsmen approached the ax and studied it cautiously. They probably needed to confiscate it given that it had been used in a crime.

He had taken a couple of steps toward the inn to join his friends when he felt an odd sensation like a mist enveloping him. He recalled a similar, albeit heavier feeling before with Vaust. This was Anima. Hastily, he looked over his shoulder and across the town center and his gaze settled on a figure that seemed to stare directly at him. He couldn't make out many details from this far away other than purple-colored hair.

The figure slid into an alley and he hesitated as he considered calling the others, then changed his mind. He didn't know who this person was. Perhaps it was the carrier? They did not call the password, though, so maybe it was too busy in the town center and they didn't want to draw attention to themselves.

Instinctively, he reactivated his Anima and the heavy feeling dispersed as soon as his was summoned. This did not feel quite as strong as Vaust's, but perhaps the stranger was deliberately hiding it. Well, there was a direct way to find out. He marched toward the alley and while the claustrophobic feeling from before was gone, he could not shake an ill sensation.

His hand hovered close to his blade. This mission might not be so simple after all.

CHAPTER TWENTY-SIX

"Excuse me?" Devol called as he entered the alley. It was shadowed but the afternoon sun allowed sufficient light and he could see no one within. "Is someone here?" He took a few more tentative steps and looked around for signs of movement. The thoroughfare was as straight as an arrow. There were some skinny crevices, perhaps, but nothing for anyone to hide behind and he moved forward.

As he reached the halfway point, he felt nauseous and his hand moved from the grip of his sword to his head. He steadied himself and breathed deeply. His stomach felt like it was in knots. It could be the food, he reasoned, but he had been fine a moment before.

"A wonderful display back there," a charming, light voice proclaimed playfully. When he looked behind him, his gaze settled on a tall, lithe man. The stranger wore an ornate jacket of fine materials—white with purple trimming a darker color than his violet locks. His hair seemed to have a life of its own at odds with his tidy appearance. It swept fairly neatly over his head and curved toward his neck before the ends stuck out from his head in sharp points.

His grin was wide and he wore a simple black eyepatch over his right eye, this one more form-fitting than Wulfsun's with violet embroidery along the edges. The one good eye looked welcoming, but it put the boy on guard rather than giving him ease. "Someone as young as you has already begun to learn the ways of Anima? I was beginning to think your generation was becoming too reliant on exotics and novelties to be of much use as Magi."

"Who are you?" Devol tried to remain standing as he fought the headache that seemed to be growing worse. "Wait, were you staring at me before? How did you get behind me?"

"That's a simple trick for someone such as myself," the man answered and placed a hand on his shoulder from behind him. The boy whipped around and staggered back as the stranger chuckled. "Sorry, I suppose that is rude of me. I'm a Magi merely traveling the land and looking for work. I can get bored rather easily, so when I run into other Magi of notable skill, I have to have a little fun when I can."

He stared at the odd Magi, a little concerned about the sensation that the walls shifted or wobbled around him like he had come down with something that left him feeling decidedly unwell. "I see. But you still haven't introduced yourself."

While the man was eccentric, he did not appear to be overly menacing or dangerous at present, even if the sight of him left him with an uneasy feeling.

"You are quite right." The violet-hued stranger stood

with his legs together and made a deep, theatrical bow. "My name is Koli and as I said, I am a wandering Magi." He straightened and grinned disarmingly. "And who might you be, my young friend?"

"I'm Devol," he responded. "I'm…well, I suppose I don't have a profession yet but I'm in training."

"Is that so? Training for what? I can't help but notice that lovely sword of yours." Koli pointed at the majestic. Strangely, each of his fingernails were sharpened to a fine point. "It looks nothing like any blade I've seen. Is it some type of exotic? A family heirloom perhaps?"

"Yeah, an heirloom," he lied and decided it was better to not give away that it was a majestic in case the man knew what those were. "Something crafted for my father before I was born. He wanted to give me a proper blade when I started to take my practice seriously."

"Aw, that's heart-warming." The man chuckled and folded his arms. "So tell me little Magi, what brings you to Rouxwoods?"

"I'm…running an errand for my father," he said. "I was having a meal when the commotion broke out. I saw the drunk warrior and decided it was best for me to handle him before he got out of control and that it would be good training to see how I fared against him."

"Well, you'll certainly need more powerful sparring partners in the future. He was no trouble at all, it seemed." The strange Magi laughed and took a couple of steps forward. Devol felt the nausea return in force and the alley seemed to spin around him. "Perhaps," he muttered as he leaned forward, "I could help you with that."

Devol wanted to respond with "maybe another time,"

but his mouth felt suddenly dry. He was too dizzy and simply shook his head as he rested against the wall and slid down slowly. "What is… I feel so lightheaded…"

"Hmm?" Koli remarked. "Feeling a little under the weather, my friend? We can't have that. We're in an alley!" He bent closer and his smile widened and became a little devious as he stretched a hand toward the young man. "Even in homely little towns such as this, many a terrible person can still be wandering about."

"Hey, Devol!" Jazai called. "Where are you, man?"

Koli grasped the young swordsman's hand and helped him to his feet. "Is that your friend?" he asked as he brushed a trace of dirt off his shoulder. "It seems I've kept you for far too long." He bowed again and smiled. "It was a pleasure to meet you, little Devol. I hope you become a great Magi one day." With that, he began to walk away as the diviner stepped into view, saw Devol in the alley, and jogged quickly to him. He passed the odd man, who didn't look at him as he turned left into the street.

"Hey, Devol," Jazai began and studied him with concern. "You all right? You're sweating hard."

"Yeah, I'm…" He drew in in a deep breath. "I'm fine." It wasn't exactly a lie because although he still felt a little dizzy, it certainly wasn't as bad as it had been a minute before. He shook his head and slapped his cheeks a few times. "I felt a little dizzy there for a while. I think I'm getting over it, though."

"That's good. We still have to complete the mission and it's harder to do that with you sick." Jazai helped him up. "So, what took you so long? Did you spend all this time chatting to that lady?"

He looked curiously at the scholar. "Lady? I guess he looked a little feminine but that was a man."

"You think?" The diviner grinned and shook his head. "The breasts are usually a giveaway."

Baffled, he looked at the entrance to the ally, then at his friend. "The what?"

Vaust watched the two young Magi exit the alleyway, debating with one another. He held Myazma in his hand under the cloak and had been prepared to strike should the being have gotten any closer. Something was off about the stranger who had approached Devol. He saw her dance around the boy as if he could not see or feel her before she introduced herself to him. From his vantage point, he couldn't even get a proper description. It was like her features were muddled. He clambered off the roof and stalked after the stranger. Whether she was working with the enemy or merely a random thief was something he had to find out. Because whatever she was, she was most certainly not a simple traveler.

He kept his distance and drew his hood down to obscure his visage. It was unlikely that these villagers would be surprised to see a realmer, but mori were still a rather rare sight in this realm. Some of the more superstitious did not hold them in high regard, so it was better that he did not cause a scene. He sipped casually from his gourd as he continued to follow the woman, who seemed to be studying something she had taken out of her pocket.

The Templar looked ahead and realized that they were

headed to the edges of town. His quarry veered through the people on the street as if she intended to turn left into what appeared to be a less busy road. He would look for an opportunity to confront her there—an alley or empty building—and would rather take the risk that he was wrong than leave this woman to simply wander about.

The stranger turned and Vaust used a small burst of Mana to sprint forward quickly and try to keep her in his sights. When he turned the corner, however, she was gone.

How did she escape? His Mana flowed into his eyes and he located the trace remains of a violet-colored Mana only a few paces away. He extended his hand so he could get a feel of it, and he felt a disconnect between it and the user. This was some type of teleportation over a long distance. It had probably been accomplished with a curio or trinket. Outside of blinking, teleportation was not something a Magi could do so quickly on their own.

Vaust placed his kama into the sheath on the back of his waist and debated his next step. This seemed a good indicator that it would not be as simple a mission for him as he'd expected.

CHAPTER TWENTY-SEVEN

When Koli reappeared, he was in the mouth of a cave a few miles outside of Rouxwoods. He walked calmly inside and heard heavy, savage breathing from within. "Salvo?" he called. "Are you still here, my friend?"

"Koli?" a voice responded with a chuckle and a fist-sized flame appeared deeper within. "Finally. I was beginning to get bored here."

"You could have participated," he pointed out as he walked into the spartan cave that contained only some bedrolls and the packs they had brought with them—aside from their pet in the cage. "It may be a small town but there are many people there we need to look into."

"Hey now, someone has to make sure the big guy stays," Salvo countered and held the flame near his face to reveal a toothy grin against his tanned skin and short-cropped white hair. "And remember who got us the information in the first place, eh? I say I've been pulling my weight."

"I'm not here to guilt-trip you," he said, leaned against

the wall, and folded his arms. "But I was bored too, and lonely. I could have used the company."

Salvo approached his partner and studied him. "That dull, huh? Well, maybe if I could see you in your female form, I would be more inclined."

Koli shrugged. "I have no control over that. The rune on my neck creates the illusion and you interpret what it shows you."

The man rolled his eyes. "You keep saying that—like I would choose to see a guy over a babe." He cast his flame to the side, where it landed on a stack of firewood, ignited it, and illuminated the cave. "So I take it you weren't able to find anything out today?"

"If that were the case, I wouldn't have come back," he stated with an amused chuckle and held a card up. "I ran into an interesting group in the square and one of them had this on him."

He threw the card at his partner, who snatched it out of the air and studied it. "Call sign is caw-caw? What the hell is this?"

"It appears to be instructions for a meeting," he replied. "It says they will meet by the evening of the twenty-first, which would be tonight."

"Are you sure these are our guys?" Salvo asked and examined the card again. "So what are we looking at? A team of Templars?"

"A team, yes," he conceded. "But if they are Templars… well, they are rather young."

"So recruits or something?" his partner asked with a frown. "Is this some kind of a joke? Why would they send brats to fetch it?"

"Brats," said thoughtfully. "Perhaps that is quite apt, Salvo. From what I saw, they were mostly teenagers."

"A group of kids?" The man balked. "This ain't gonna be fun at all." He hissed through his teeth as he stretched his neck and muttered. After a moment, he stopped and turned slowly with his eyes narrowed. "Wait, you said mostly?"

"Indeed I did," Koli confirmed. "While I was preparing to head back, I was followed by another Magi, this one quite skilled. I almost didn't detect him for a brief time. He hides his Mana well but I could feel a disturbance in my area and my powers were being blocked," he revealed. "I don't know if he is their leader or a third party, but he is quite powerful and either way, he will probably be a not inconsiderable hindrance."

"Is he strong?" Salvo asked and excitement crept into his voice. "Tell me he is."

"I didn't fight him so I couldn't tell you that." The other man's face fell with undisguised disappointment. "Oh, don't be like that. I said he was powerful and good at controlling his Mana too. But that does not necessarily mean he is a good fighter. You would be disappointed if I said he was and turned out to be wrong."

"Yeah, yeah. Fine." Salvo grimaced in irritation and looked at the card again before he slid it into his pocket. "So these might be our guys. But we still don't know where they will meet."

"I can take a guess," Koli said and held a finger up. "Just before I ported here, I saw an artifice in the sky."

"An artifice?" His partner frowned, then shrugged. "One

of those little mechanical things? It could be something the guards use."

"It was an exotic artifice," he clarified with a smile. "And it was in the shape of a bird."

Realization dawned on the man's face and he drew the card out and looked at it again. His toothy grin returned. "Well, caw-caw then. Did you see where it came from?"

"The forest on the west side of the village." Koli pushed away from the wall and walked to the cage. "I could trace the user of the artifice. They'll have to use Mana to control their device, after all. But it now seems like a good opportunity to test your boss' little project, don't you think?"

Salvo's grin faltered as he joined him to look into the cage. "Well…I guess so. He did want us to do that," he mumbled hesitantly. "Eh, but do you think we should let the big guy out? It'll cause a commotion."

"And you won't?" Koli asked, amused. "It's not like you care all that much about subtlety."

The man rolled his shoulders and shrugged. "You got me there, I guess. I'll get the door." As he reached for the lock, the cage began to rattle and the occupant uttered a hungry, enraged roar. Birds took wing frantically outside the cave, startled by the beast within.

"Maybe we should double-check that the runes are working," his partner said cautiously and took several steps back.

Koli laughed. "I think that would be smart of you."

"Jazai, Devol," Asla called as she ran up to them. "There you are."

"Hey, Asla." The diviner pointed to Devol. "I found our buddy. He got stuck in an alley with some lady."

"Lady?" the wildkin asked and looked at the other boy. "Alley?"

"I'm telling you he wasn't a lady!" Devol repeated. "He was clearly a man."

"Slender body and long violet hair that went down to her waist," his friend recalled. "Are we talking about the same person?"

"To her waist?" Devol questioned. "He had long violet hair but it kind of spikes away from his neck. If it were straighter, it would fall to maybe the middle of his back." He sighed and waved dismissively. "Whatever. It doesn't matter. Sorry for holding you two up."

"It's all good," Jazai assured him. "I finished my meal, at least."

"Speaking of which..." Asla handed the swordsman something wrapped in cloth. "Here. I brought it for you since you didn't get to finish."

He opened the parcel to find a sandwich inside, made from the inn's bread and the rest of his meal. "Oh, thanks Asla!" he said happily and began to scarf it with enthusiasm. As his teammates watched him, a bird cried loudly above them. All three looked up as it continued to call over the town square.

"Man, that is loud," Jazai grumbled and put his hands over his ears. "I thought birdsong was supposed to be pleasant."

"It's not birdsong," Asla stated and studied it with a frown of concentration. "It's a message."

"Hmm?" Devol swallowed a mouthful. "A message?"

"Remember the call sign?" she prodded.

"Caw-caw?" Jazai said quickly. "Wait, the bird is our carrier?"

"No, the owner is," she replied. "And that's not a bird—not a real one anyway."

The two boys narrowed their eyes at the large avian that seemed to look directly at them. It appeared to nod and spread its wings that looked almost segmented. It banked into a turn and headed toward the forest.

"I hope you can run and eat, Devol," Asla said as she began to pursue it.

"I'm more used to it than she probably thinks," he told Jazai as he took another bite and they hurried behind her through the village and into the woods.

They ran along the ground for a while, but when they reached a safe distance from the settlement and away from curious eyes, they began to leap up through the trees to get a better view of the bird as they traveled deeper and deeper into the woods.

"These red leaves are so pretty," Asla noted as she pushed forward through the various hues of red and orange that adorned the trees.

"Ah, that hit the spot," Devol said merrily as he patted his hands to get rid of any crumbs. "I was worried that I had lost my appetite."

Jazai shook his head. "I would think eating and running so quickly would make you sick."

"You know, I think it should too," he agreed. "But it has never been a problem for me."

"The bird is circling," Asla informed them and pointed. "Over there."

It flew around a patch of land a few hundred yards ahead. The friends nodded to one another as they dropped from the branches and onto the forest floor as they approached, looking for the owner. The avian swooped from overhead, passed them, and landed on the waiting arm of a figure in deep brown leathers with a blue tunic and cowl.

"Are you the carrier?" Devol asked.

"It's one of the things I do," the man stated and regarded the three of them curiously. "Among many things. I suppose I could be a carrier for you, but I wouldn't know that without knowing who you are first."

He nodded and pointed to himself. "Oh, well I'm Dev—"

Jazai held a hand out to interrupt him. "That's not what he means, Devol. He's looking for proof that we're here for the box."

The young swordsman nodded. "Right, let me find the card." He began to search through his pockets but it wasn't there. Confused, he frowned and tried to think where he might have dropped it.

"Even in the storms, the light will break through," the diviner stated. The stranger nodded and relaxed. The other two glanced at their teammate. "It's a passcode," he explained. "We have several different ones depending on who we're working with. Zier makes me learn all of them when they change."

"So, new Templar recruits, eh?" the man chuckled as the bird—which appeared to be much like a falcon if it weren't for the odd movements and box-like head—scuttled up his arm and onto his shoulder. "You're very young, I have to say."

"It isn't something they usually do," Asla stated. "Send young trainees, that is, without at least one experienced Templar. I guess they had their reasons, though."

"I suppose," the man conceded and lowered his cowl. He appeared to be in his mid-forties with black hair tied into a bun, a handlebar mustache, and deep-set gray eyes. "Nice to meet you. My name is Zeke of the Britana Hunter's Guild." He gave them a nod and confident smile. "Today, I am a carrier, and I think I have a package here for you three."

CHAPTER TWENTY-EIGHT

Zeke patted his artificial bird and it launched from his shoulder and flew to a tree behind him as he walked to a small green sack nearby. He picked it up and returned as he unwound the knot on the top. "I have to admit, this was a first for me," he stated as he slid the bag open and revealed a locked black box within. "Normally, we try to give these a wide berth, but it basically fell into our lap."

"So what is it?" Devol asked as he took the item. Almost immediately, he felt a powerful burst of dread and his hands began to shake.

"Devol?" Asla asked as she stepped forward hastily to place her hand on his. "What is wr—" When she touched it, her tail went stiff and her eyes widened as she looked at it.

A firm hand settled on their shoulders. "Take a deep breath," Jazai instructed. "It ain't gonna harm you, not as long as it stays in there. Relax." The two responded with quick nods and tried to steady themselves with deep breaths as they brought their Anima up.

"So you know what it is?" Zeke asked him.

The apprentice shrugged. "I can guess—something I tried to do ever since we got the mission. But seeing their reaction and that hint of twisted Magic? I'm fairly sure."

"So your leaders didn't tell you?" the man asked and he shook his head. "Well then, I guess it isn't my place to fill you in. I merely ran it here." He returned to his original position and picked his large backpack up. "Sorry to toss my job onto you, but I have other messages and items I need to get to their recipients much farther from here. My advice is to get that back to your order as quickly as yo—"

The carrier's mechanical bird began to caw loudly and urgently. Zeke took a monocle out of his jacket pocket. "What in the hell is it squawking about?" he muttered as he placed the eyewear on. His body stiffened and he gasped in surprise. "Get out of here!" he ordered and turned as his bird flew skyward and dived sharply toward something deeper into the forest. "Hurry! I don't think I can hold it off for long."

"What's going on?" Devol asked and snapped back to the present as he tied the box to his belt. "If it is an enemy, we can help."

"It isn't that simple," the man warned. "This may be beyond the four of us combined." At a loud crack, he staggered and dropped to his knees. His monocle fell and shattered. The three rushed forward as he clutched his arms, and fresh scratch marks were visible on his hands.

"He must have had a link to his bird to control it," Jazai muttered. "His exotic was wounded so some of that damage reflects onto him like a majestic."

"It wasn't merely wounded," Zeke stated, his voice cold and angry. He stood slowly and unhooked a pair of hatchets from his belt. "It was destroyed. My artifact once took a full-force hit from an exotic morning star and simply shook it off— What the hell am I giving you the details for. Get away!" A loud, angry roar issued from the tree line. "That monster is here."

A beast took hold of two trees outside the clearing, split them apart, and tossed Zeke's mechanical bird at his feet. Devol took a step back, awed and terrified by the creature before him. It looked humanoid—or at least was at some point—and had dark-gray skin with blotches of white around its arms and waist. The monster was massive, easily nine feet tall or more, with a wave of stringy black hair.

Its arms seemed to be bigger than his body, with fists that looked like they could crack his chest with a single blow. But the mask on its face drew his immediate attention. It looked like it was modeled after the demons he had heard about in scary stories shared by other children in his youth. The black background was broken by a wide grin of white or silver-painted teeth, and pure white eyes stared angrily at them. He was unsure if they were its own eyes or the mask's. Traces of red paint or some smooth material underlined the sockets and curved around the top to give the appearance of horns.

"That's..." Jazai began and paused to gather his words as his eyes widened and he balled his fists. "That's a malefic."

Devol looked at his teammates, who were both in shock. Before he could ask what that was, Zeke cried, "Goliath!" The two hatchets in his hands grew to the size of battle-axes as he summoned his Anima. It was the color of the open sky and surrounded him and the weapons. He roared and charged as the boy reached for his sword.

He was given a quick demonstration of how futile joining this fight would be. As the man hurled one of the axes at the terror, he leapt upward as high as he could to try to sink the other blade into its head. The monster merely growled as the thrown weapon struck its chest and sank home, but no blood followed. It seemed indifferent to both the blade and the injury and simply ignored them as it extended a long limb and snatched Zeke before he could land.

The beast's hand almost encircled the carrier's entire torso. He still attempted to attack the monster's head but it responded by headbutting the ax as it descended and shattered the blade. The man cried out in pain his captor squeezed relentlessly, and his metal chest plate bent under the strain.

Zeke was thrown onto the forest floor and blood spurted from his mouth as the monster raised a leg. Devol wanted to rush forward to try to distract it, but before he could move more than a step, the creature stamped its foot down. Bones crushed and broke and after another burst of blood, the man was no more.

"We should have taken his advice," Jazai stated and his voice cracked slightly. "We need to go!"

"But…" Asla began and her slight frame trembled. "Can we even outrun it?"

Both boys felt a new twinge of fear. She was the fastest among the three and had the best instincts for battle and reading an opponent. If she doubted they could flee, it was almost assured that they could not.

A NEW LIGHT

Devol drew his sword and held it out in front of him. "Even if we could, we would simply lead it to the village or get lost deeper in the forest," he surmised. "I don't want my last actions to be flight, especially if it is pointless."

Although his teammates did not completely snap out of their shock, his words did reach them. Jazai held his tome up as Asla hunkered in a battle-ready stance. Both would fight alongside him for however long they could last.

The monster looked at them after it ground its foot into Zeke's corpse again. It stepped forward and the young swordsman noticed how little its body moved—like it was not even breathing. Furiously, it pounded its chest before it crouched and prepared to attack them. They waited anxiously but instead, it slumped and uttered a gurgling noise. The three were confused but none let their guard down. About a dozen shapes glowed purple around its neck—no doubt runes of some kind.

"Now, now, let's not get too hasty," a familiar voice sang. The group spun toward the trees from which two figures emerged, one with snowy white shaved hair, a long dark coat, and red-lensed glasses. The other was very familiar.

"You!" Devol shouted and pointed to the second figure. "You're the man from the alley—Koli!"

"I'm so glad you remembered," the newcomer said with a smile and a bow. "I suppose it has only been a short time since then but I would be more saddened if you had forgotten so soon."

"So that's the kid you ran into?" the other man asked. "They are simply a group of brats, huh? But they all got majestics." He smiled, slid his hand into the left sleeve of his jacket, and removed a wand made of dark-black wood that coiled around a red jewel at the top. "This could be a very productive day."

"Calm yourself, Salvo," Koli ordered and frowned at his partner. "We are here to test the ghoul, not indulge ourselves."

"I think we've already seen what it can do." His partner chuckled and pointed at Zeke's corpse with his wand. "I don't know if he was a great Magi or fighter or anything, but he was a member of the Britana Hunter's Guild and the big guy killed him in minutes without a scratch."

The violet-hair man sighed and pointed at the monster's chest, where Zeke's other ax was still implanted. "I would say that qualifies as more than a scratch."

"Oh, yeah." Salvo sighed. "Ah well, still no harm done. Why do you need to dodge when you can shrug a beating off, right?"

Koli frowned at his partner before he rolled his eyes. "That's one way of looking at it, I suppose." He focused on the three friends. "Now on to you as you can see we've called our little pet off." He gestured toward the monster. "But that can change in an instant if we would like it to. While I can't speak for my partner, I would rather spare you today."

"Do what?" Jazai questioned.

"Yeah, Koli," Salvo stated irritably. "We should take their majestics. Why do you want to leave them be?"

The man scanned the three and tapped a finger on his chin before he focused on Devol and licked his lips. "They have potential but they aren't quite ripe yet."

They were somewhat unnerved by Koli's longing,

devious stare, and his partner shook his head. "That junk again? How many times has that paid off? How many good fights have you had by letting someone live to come back for you?"

"Exactly twice out of roughly fifty-seven times," the violet-haired man responded and his smile widened. "And both those times—even a single fight, to be honest—makes the possibility worth it."

Salvo twirled his wand in his hand. "Damn, you are freaky, but whatever. We still need that box."

"Quite right." Koli nodded and ran one hand through his violet hair as he pointed at the box now attached to Devol's belt. "My young friend, I'll be happy to let you and your teammates leave here unscathed if you simply hand the box over with the contents inside." He shifted his hand to indicate the monster. "Otherwise..." He flipped his hand and pressed his middle finger and thumb against one another. "Well, I think you can guess that much."

"Take the box and run," the young swordsman instructed his teammates. "I'll keep them at bay."

"Don't be a fool!" Jazai hissed his exasperation. "I won't leave you and besides, you wouldn't last long enough for it to matter."

As much as he wanted to refute that, he had to admit his friend was right. He might be able to hold the beast off for a minute or two, and that was assuming Koli and Salvo did not jump in.

"And..." Asla began and clenched her teeth. "And it is our mission to bring the box back. I would rather die fighting to protect it than return in disgrace."

The boys looked at her, surprised by the fierce determination that grew in her eyes. Jazai sighed and nodded. "I guess we're committed, and we all know how this will probably end, huh?" His friends simply nodded as they once again positioned themselves in preparation to fight. The diviner held his free hand up and ran through cantrips in his mind. "Well, all right then."

Salvo looked at the three young Magi who stood ready for battle, then at Koli, who smiled in genuine delight. "Marvelous," the man remarked as he prepared to free the monster.

"Whatever." His partner walked to a standing tree and leaned against it with his arms folded. "It works out for me. We get some new majestics and our box. Make it quick so we can get out of here."

"That's not up to me," Koli remarked as he snapped his fingers and the runes around the monster's neck faded. "It is up to him."

CHAPTER TWENTY-NINE

The beast roared to life. It hammered its fists into the ground before it launched itself high, its target the trio of young Magi below.

"Scatter!" Devol shouted, and they raced out of the way in different directions as the giant landed. He was almost upended by the shockwave of the impact. It swung an arm toward Asla, who was able to leap over it, but the massive arm battered two trees behind her, destroyed them, and scattered splinters and dust around her to blind her briefly. It reared in preparation for another strike.

A moment before it swung, Jazai blinked next to her, caught hold of her shirt, and blinked away before the massive fist connected. They appeared near their friend and the diviner scrambled to his feet and pointed at their adversary. "Chains!" he shouted and deep-blue chains of Mana wound around the titan's arms and neck in an attempt to keep it in check.

From behind them, Salvo laughed loudly. "Is that all you got?"

The monster uttered a belligerent growl, flexed its muscles, and snapped the restraints.

"What the hell?" the boy muttered. "I don't sense an Anima from it. How did it break my cantrip?"

"I'll say it is a safe bet that it isn't normal," the swordsman responded and prepared to strike when the monster made another assault. The expected attack did not come, however. The giant sagged, its knuckles dug into the dirt and grass, and it began to twitch.

"What did you do?" The question was asked by Devol and Salvo at the same time. The young diviner shook his head. He hadn't done anything but use the chains cantrip, and Koli didn't respond. He simply narrowed his eyes at the creature. The giant took a rather shaky step forward and its skin had become noticeably paler. Its bulging muscles began to shrink and wither along with its entire body. Finally, it fell and the two groups stared at a large black wound in its back. A figure in a black cloak holding a kama stood behind it.

"Mr. Lebatt!" Devol shouted when he recognized him.

"Vaust?" Jazai asked and gaped at the mark on the giant's back that spread rapidly along its entire body. "What are you doing here?"

"I believe that gentleman was the one who was tailing me earlier." Koli bit his lip. "It appears he is affiliated with the children."

"Yeah, I could have guessed," Salvo grumbled and pushed away from the tree. "Well, now we have to retrieve the mask and the box."

"It won't be an issue. I'll take care of it," his partner offered.

"Fine, then I'll take care of the new guy and the brats," he stated, which drew a chuckle from Koli.

"Quite confident, aren't you?" He patted his violet hair before he placed his hands in his pants pocket and approached the slain giant.

"Hurry up," his partner instructed and smiled as he spun the wand in his hand. "I get to play now."

Vaust saw the violet-haired man approach and pointed his kama at him. "Halt, or I'll kill you as well."

"I have no doubt," the man said with an easy smile and stopped only a few yards away from the mori. "You have made short work of our pet. I'm impressed."

"Why are you here?" the Templar asked and let his Anima seep through the area as a warning sign to the two thieves.

"It was requested of us," Koli answered. "I cannot divulge by who."

"Perhaps not right now," he retorted and revealed an air of menace and command that Devol had not seen in him before. "But I can make you talk. I merely wonder how many appendages it will take."

"Oh, that is quite violent of you." The man closed his eyes for a moment and violet Mana covered his form. "I must say, I approve."

Vaust leapt at him with his kama raised to arc in almost a blur at his adversary. He covered the distance in less than a second and to Devol, it felt like it was almost instant. Before the kama struck its target, however, Koli vanished in a flash of violet light. He reappeared beside the monster, which had now almost melted into bone and viscera. He reached down hastily and took the mask it had once worn before he turned and looked at the young swordsman.

"Devol!" Vaust called and Asla and Jazai prepared to fight. Instead of attacking, the man disappeared again, blinked behind him, and yanked the box from his belt. He spun and swung his sword. It seemed clear that it would connect with his arm and that the thief was too close to jump back. But in a moment, what had seemed so clear had suddenly changed. Koli was now several inches away without stepping back at all. Devol could not believe his eyes as the blade passed in front of the Magi's tunic. Stunned, he looked at his opponent, who gave a self-satisfied smile before he blinked back to the trees outside of the clearing.

"You are going nowhere!" Vaust yelled and prepared to leap after him. Before he could move, a large circle of fire caged him in, followed by rows of flame that formed above him. The Templar looked at Salvo, who pointed his wand and grinned at him.

"That's my line, buddy." The man laughed. "You and I will have some fun. Get out of here, Koli!" he shouted to his partner, who placed two fingers against his forehead to salute him in thanks and raced through the trees.

Devol grimaced, determined to not let him take the box. He ran after him and jumped into the trees as Salvo pointed his wand in his direction and launched a large fireball at him from the tip of his wand. Calmly, the boy leaned closer to slash the fiery projectile with his blade. With a single swipe, the orb was halved, then snuffed out, and he continued with his pursuit and left his attacker standing with a look of surprise on his face.

The man formed two more fireballs as Jazai and Asla followed their friend and he launched them both at the youngsters. She maneuvered easily around them while her teammate blinked to the ground and immediately into the tree. Both projectiles struck nearby trees and set them alight.

"Damn, I guess they aren't such easy pickings," the fire mage muttered and glowered at Vaust. "Ah, whatever. Consider that a warm-up. Heh, I'll be on my game now."

"Release me," the mori ordered and brandished Myazma, "and I'll make this quick."

Salvo frowned and shook his head. "You noble and devout types always have the same lines." He pointed his wand at the cage of fire again. "Survive this and you might provide a good fight." The flames began to increase in size as the cage retracted slowly around the Templar. It seemed his adversary intended to burn him alive while he was trapped inside.

He simply raised his weapon and cut into the fire in front of him, which vanished in a fog of darkness that traveled through the connected flames. The fire mage stared in surprise before his eager smile returned. "I had a feeling that was it, looking at what you did to the big guy," he stated and tapped his wand against his shoulder. "Your majestic has corrosive power or something like that, right? You turned our giant pet ghoul into mush so it has to be something like that. I didn't expect it to work on flames, though."

Vaust walked forward and pointed at Salvo. "Immolation." The man barely had time to raise an eyebrow before his suit was set aflame. He uttered a surprised yell and patted frantically at the flames that engulfed him. In mere minutes, he sagged to the ground.

But, as quickly as he fell, he stood and twirled his wand in his fingers and the flames vanished. The mori stopped in his tracks as his opponent raised a finger and wagged it sideways. "Was that supposed to be just desserts or something? You see me throwing flames and think that a simple fire cantrip is gonna work on me? My clothes aren't even singed." He ran a hand down his jacket to prove his point and held his wand up "This isn't merely an exotic, buddy. It's a majestic like yours. I call her Kapre." A large orb of fire formed above his head before it split into a dozen smaller ones. "And she doesn't like you." He flicked the wand toward Vaust and a hail of fireballs streaked at the mori, who simply stared at them while Myazma emitted its black fog.

Koli leapt off a tree branch before he blinked to another tree in the opposite direction. He had to admit, the boy was faster than he gave him credit for—not enough that he could catch up but certainly fast enough to keep the chase interesting. He had slid the mask into his tunic and held onto the box. While he knew he should have used his marble to return to base by now, this was too much fun. If Salvo's boss had an issue…well, he couldn't use a marble with an enemy so close. They could potentially track it.

"Missile!" a voice shouted ahead of him. He looked around to see the book-boy pointing at him. Several glowing orbs launched from his palm. Well, he hadn't expected him to cut him off. He must have been too preoccupied with the other young Magi. Jazai fired five Mana missiles at him and he barreled into them. They curved around him and shocked the apprentice, who had expected his attack to deliver some injury at least.

With a smile, he removed several small blades from his belt and threw them at the diviner. The boy blinked out of the way of the blades, which wasn't an issue. He wasn't the one he was interested in.

"Link!" Jazai shouted, and Koli felt something drag him back.

He craned his neck to look over his shoulder. A line of blue Mana connected to his back. He followed it to the boy, who hauled on the line and prevented him from moving forward. "You are crafty. I respect that," he conceded as he grasped the link and his Anima flared. "But you don't seem to think of the repercussions of your cantrips." He yanked hard and dragged his young opponent out of the tree toward him. When he came within striking range, he delivered a punch to his face that catapulted him into the forest. He raised his hand and severed the link with a chop before the diviner could drag him back with him.

As he turned to continue his run, he felt a sudden flare of Mana coming closer. Instinctively, he ducked and several small trees were scored with what looked like claw marks. He straightened and Asla landed on her hands on the ground and tucked her legs in to kick him. She was amazingly fast, he had to give her that as he brought an arm up to block the kick and infused it with Mana. The wildkin drove into him and knocked him back, and he slid deeper into the forest before he finally came to a stop on the road.

Koli checked his arm. It had been a powerful kick but left no more than a slightly pink bruise. He looked around and realized he had been knocked off-course. Before he could gain his bearings, he heard a rustle and looked up. Devol plunged toward him, his blade pointed at his head. He smiled. Well, it appeared he would have to fight for a while. This was certainly not the worst outcome.

It was a pity, though. Maybe in a few years, the boy would have made a great adversary. It looked like he would have to find another prospect after today, although perhaps he would last at least a few minutes.

CHAPTER THIRTY

As Devol landed, his blade struck nothing but the earth below. He looked up to where Koli stood only a few inches away from him. The man lifted a hand and swung the back of his palm across his head, almost dislodged his sword, and hurled him several yards away. He flipped himself in midair and stopped himself with his hand. Asla bounded out of the forest to attempt a kill-strike. Their adversary simply lowered his head and her claws swiped through empty space and scored the bark of the trees. She bounced off one of the trunks for a second strike.

The man looked at her and made no effort to defend himself as her claws lunged at his eye. Impossibly, they stopped barely short of a strike and Devol couldn't believe it. He had been so certain she would land a sure hit. Koli snatched her arm, spun her, and flung her at the young swordsman. He caught her and both stumbled back a couple of feet as their friend appeared next to them. "He's strong," he muttered.

"No kidding," Jazai mumbled, holding his cheek. "And I didn't say this before but come on, man. That's a she!"

"What?" He looked at Koli in confusion. "It's a man with spiky violet hair, isn't it?"

"I see a man as well, Jazai," Asla confirmed and the other boy raised an eyebrow as he examined their adversary. "But I do not see the spiky hair either, Devol. I see long hair that hangs down his back."

Devol stared at Koli and tried to discern the truth. "Some type of illusion?"

The man smirked and nodded. "People tend to see what they want to but it is more literal in my case." He used his free hand to point to the back of his neck. "I have a rune—had it since I was a child, actually. It casts a simple illusion that alters my appearance enough that my visage always looks slightly different to each person."

"I see you as a woman," the diviner told him. "They see you as a man. That doesn't sound like a slight difference."

"My power increases the effectiveness of the illusion," Koli explained. He tossed the box behind him and rolled his shoulders. "Or, I should say, the power of my malefic."

Jazai tensed, as did Asla. "Malefic?" Devol repeated and glanced at the other boy. "When we saw that mask, you said the same thing."

The scholar nodded slowly and his jaw tightened. "I can't give you the entire explanation, not when we need to focus. But they are extremely dangerous and work similarly to a majestic." He held a hand up. "I don't know what his power is, but it seems to protect him from almost anything. Watch. Missile!" He launched five orbs at Koli. They circled him for a moment before each attempted to strike from a different angle. The man did not move, but each orb slid around his body. Two impacted with the road while three redirected and headed at the team. Asla jumped out and slashed with her claw to send a Mana-infused strike through the missiles that destroyed them.

"I was controlling those missiles before they attacked," Jazai stated. "They should all have hit, but they veered around him."

"I saw." Devol nodded. "Is it another illusion? Maybe a power that lets him control the Magic of others?"

"No, he has been able to do that even against physical attacks," Asla reminded him.

"You are thinking about this too hard," Koli all but purred. "Here, allow me to show you." He pulled his eyepatch off and the team gasped. His other eye had been replaced by some type of dark orb that shifted between hues of violet, purple, blue, and white at a rapid pace. Something that resembled an iris was in the center, but more elongated and diamond-shaped. He pointed to the unnatural eye. "This is my malefic, known as Madman's Eye," he explained with a hint of mirth. "It allows me to distort space around me."

"Distort space?" The swordsman frowned and considered his missed attacks. "I see."

"Why would you tell us that outright?" Jazai demanded. "That's putting you at a major disadvantage."

Their adversary laughed. "Thank you for your concern but I think I'll be fine." He stared at them for a moment, enjoying their discomfort. "You see, my malefic gets stronger when it can see the target or area I wish to distort."

"He doesn't feel any stronger," Asla noted before she looked down and realized she had an orange glow around her. "My Mana—" She gasped as she backed away.

"It responded automatically to mine increasing to shield against you," Koli explained and pointed two fingers at the two boys. "As did yours."

Devol saw a silver glow around him, while Jazai's was a deep-blue. His sword began to glow brighter.

"It's a good thing too," the man noted. "A strong Anima is one of the few things that protects one from my power. If you did not have one…well, I could simply snap your neck in an instant."

He held his blade up. "Why are you telling us all this?"

The man shrugged casually. "Well, I suppose that in my line of work, people not knowing my identity is quite useful. I don't often get the chance to have a good fight and fully sate my bloodlust," he explained with a grin that grew more deviant by the moment. "I see promise in you three and I want to have a little fun, so I'll give myself a handicap as it were."

"You think this is fun? You take lives for pleasure?" the young swordsman demanded.

"For work as well," Koli added and glanced at the trees. "I am an assassin, after all. It's what I'm supposed to do. Still, I hope you can amuse me, at least for a while. But I don't think a sneak attack is very sporting."

"Sneak?" Jazai looked confused but his eyes widened when he realized Asla was missing.

She bounded out of the woods and the orange Mana around her took the form of a large, feral tiger. Both arms extended to rake her claws at him but he looked calmly at her as a small smile pulled at the corners of his mouth. In the next moment, the wildkin flipped and fell face-down. She tried to pick herself up but seemed to be held in place on all fours. "There's a good kitty," the man whispered

"Asla!" her friends shouted and Devol lifted his sword, ready to attack.

"This is exciting," the strange Magi said thoughtfully. "Her Anima is keeping her alive against my malefic's power, but how long will it last? If she runs out...well, I hope she is quite flexible." He glanced at a fallen tree and it elevated sharply and broke apart to create several spears that pointed toward the boys. "Now, satisfy me."

Vaust leapt back as a whip of flame ignited in the place where he'd stood and a small pillar of fire flared. He spun Myazma and released the dark fog to snuff out some of the flames. Salvo had not held back and had cast his fire in different shapes and forms and with abandon. He strolled casually through them as the mori weaved and dodged around the fiery pits and attacks.

"Man, this forest went up fast," the man stated when he noticed the many burning trees around them. "The village has probably noticed by now. I wonder if they can put it out?"

The Templar saw his chance and sneaked the fog around several of the flames outside of his adversary's line of sight. He needed to strike him with his weapon to ensure the kill, but infecting him with the fog would deplete his Mana and break his control briefly, which would provide an opening. The fog surged toward the fire Magi, who noticed it when it was only a few feet away.

Quickly, he flipped his wand and tapped it against his jacket, which set it aflame. The fog met the garment and began to snuff the flames rapidly while he slid the jacket off and moved away from the fog. "Clever bastard." He grinned at the Mori. "You're wilier than I gave you credit for. And even amongst all this fire, you don't look like you are breaking a sweat. Is that a mori peculiarity?"

Vaust made no response and simply recalled the fog to the kama as he approached his opponent. "If this is your only trick, I've had my fill."

"I have a specialty," Salvo retorted. "But more than one trick—take a look." He held the wand skyward. The flames launched from the trees and they elevated above the two men, where they formed into a multitude of fireballs in different sizes. "My majestic allows me to control fire, not merely create it," he explained. The mori made a hasty count of the orbs—fifty-five in all and some were rather sizeable. This much pyro could potentially burn the entire forest down. "Doing something like this with Mana alone would be too much for me, but throwing a few of these orbs around to spread the fire makes this much easier."

He closed his eyes and rested Myazma against his shoulder "It is indeed impressive," he admitted. "A pity you use it for simple mercenary work."

The man's grin faltered. "This is more than turning in a bounty, mori. I'm doing a mission for someone, same as your brats."

"And who might that be?"

"It won't matter to you in a minute," Salvo stated and

his grin returned. "Besides, even if I do use it to get rich, it's better than what my master was doing—simply studying the damn thing all the time."

"That is your master's majestic?" Vaust asked.

"Former master. It's a little hard to teach when you're dead. But it doesn't matter. I had more of a knack for it than he ever did. He once said it took him seven years to master it. Then he spent over a decade studying it. I could use Kapre the first time I picked her up, almost like she wanted me to wield her."

"So, I take it you never progressed very far in your training?"

Salvo began to twirl his wand in the air. "I got the gist, you could say. Natural talent beats book smarts any day."

"I see." The Templar held Myazma out to his side. "And you may be right in some circumstances. But in our world, you strive to learn all you can or you will never evolve." The black fog consumed the majestic before it spread around him.

"Wait, what are you—" The man felt intense pressure and a feeling of terror overcame him.

"I'm going to show you something your master never had the chance to," Vaust said, his voice eerily calm as the fog began to fade.

His adversary's eyes widened and he gestured hastily with his wand to launch the hail of fireballs at the mori. An explosion of darkness turned the projectiles to ash and any remaining flames extinguished while all the plant life around Vaust withered instantly and died.

CHAPTER THIRTY-ONE

Koli could no longer feel Salvo's presence. Had he died? No, his Mana had vanished all at once instead of gradually so he must have used the marble to teleport out of the forest. He could still sense the mori's Mana very keenly. In fact, it was stronger and had grown to the point where it was almost sickening. He heard a grunt and looked at where Asla strained against the warped area she was contained in. Distracted by the possible fate of his partner, he had almost slipped. It would be bad form to have this battle end due to their negligence. A better option would be that Devol finally attacked.

A hasty glance at the swordsman confirmed that he'd had the same thought and was now only several feet away. The boy began to swing his blade—valiant but foolish, of course. He began to shift the space in front of the blade enough for it to swing harmlessly to his side, which would leave his young opponent wide open.

The light in the blade flared and it corrected its trajectory to remain on a direct course toward him. He was surprised and the young Magi seemed a little shocked too, although it was mostly masked by his anger. Unfortunately, he could not move if he continued to hold the girl in place. He needed to concentrate to keep her there, but it looked like that was no longer an option.

Regretfully, he released his hold on the wildkin and jumped back. The blade sliced along his chest and when he landed, he checked his tunic. It appeared that it had narrowly missed the flesh although it had certainly cut the tunic rather cleanly. But as he raised his fingers, he felt a warm substance on them and he scowled at the blood that stained their tips. Small droplets of it seeped through the garment along his sternum.

He looked at Devol, who was helping the girl up, and smiled. While he was unsure if this was his skill alone or something to do with the majestic he wielded, it appeared that his intuition was quite right. The boy would make a wonderful plaything in the future.

For now, however, he needed to complete the mission. He'd had his fun, but with the real Templar approaching, he could not guarantee the retrieval of the box. While he might be able to defeat the mori, the younglings could easily escape with the box. If they found an anchor point… well, all would be lost. He turned to snatch the prize but before he could, it sparkled with blue light, elevated sharply, and hurtled to Jazai, who smiled cunningly at the thief.

Koli frowned slightly. "You are becoming annoying."

"I pride myself on that," the diviner retorted and pointed three fingers at him. "Bolt." Three Mana arrows formed and launched at his adversary much faster than his missiles had. The man's Anima surged and a wave of his arm simply knocked the projectiles away.

His malefic flashed and the earth began to shift around the young apprentice. The ground burst open and threatened to swallow him while the trees behind him fell and almost crushed him. The boy was able to blink away but had to use far more Mana than usual to break through the assault.

In turn, this left a clear image of where he would reappear for a skilled Magi such as Koli was. He drew three small knives from his belt and flung them at his opponent as he manifested. Jazai's eyes widened as they were too close for him to dodge, but before they struck, they were intercepted by Asla and fell harmlessly at his feet.

"Asla!" he called and the wildkin gasped as her Mana flickered around her. She released it as she toppled.

Well, that was two, but where was Devol? Koli turned as an immense light broke through the trees. The boy surged out and his blade glowed brighter than it had before. He focused on the young swordsman and attempted to trap him in the same distorted cage he had used with Asla. As his opponent pushed forward and increased his speed, light poured out of the blade. Surprised, he reacted by distorting the space around him.

When the weapon impacted with him, the sword unleashed a surge of light that enveloped him and continued to streak through the forest behind them. It tore through it and obliterated anything in its path for more than a hundred yards.

Devol could feel his Anima depleting from the strike. What had just happened?

When the assassin reappeared, his clothes were torn and various wounds were visible along the top of his arms. He stood motionless for a moment before the shock of the assault subsided. The two combatants stood in silence and stared at one another in a moment of mutual surprise. But the older Magi's stunned expression turned to one of happiness, almost like he was looking at the swordsman with pride in his eyes. At least that is what it appeared to be before he delivered a solid kick across the boy's chin and hurled him away as he produced a small black marble.

"Truly magnificent," he whispered, broke the marble, and vanished.

"He teleported," Jazai muttered and glowered at the area where the thief had stood. "Far, far away. I can't even track him."

"Devol!" Asla called and jogged to the swordsman, who pushed himself into a seated position. "Are you all right?"

He rubbed his chin ruefully. "It hurts but I'll be fine," he stated as she helped him up. "Thank you. That could have been much worse. My Anima was weak but so was his."

"No doubt." Jazai snickered and shook his head as he turned the box in his hand. "What was that? It looked like you launched some kind of holy fire from your sword." He pointed to the section of forest that had been caught in the light's path. Everything but the dirt had been obliterated along it. "Well… maybe 'holy' isn't the right word. Unless flora can be sinners."

"I don't know," Devol admitted and studied his blade warily. "I simply…I wanted to stop him."

"Killing her is a way to do that." Jazai laughed, flipped the box, and caught it. "Yes, I know it's an illusion and the thief's gender is male, but when it looks like a girl and acts like a girl…" He shrugged. "My brain has a hard time seeing him as anything but a girl."

"You think we'll run into him again?" Asla questioned and clutched her left arm to try to dull the pain.

"It's a possibility," the diviner reasoned. "Or at least someone from the order will. If they are after the malefic, they'll be back eventually."

"Asla, Jazai, Devol!" Vaust called and the three friends looked down the road as the mori appeared almost out of nowhere. "Are you all right?"

"Yes, sir." Devol nodded and pointed to the other boy. "We retrieved the box but the thief got away with the mask."

"You did?" The Templar seemed rather surprised. "That is…quite impressive. I thought she would be too fast for you to catch up."

"He was," Asla admitted. "Even for me. If he'd wanted to, he could have easily outrun us."

"It turns out she had a thing for fighting." Jazai sighed, tapped his cheek, and flinched. "The only reason she stopped is that she wanted to fight."

"And you took the bait?" Vaust demanded in annoyance. "You may be gifted and have majestics, but even you had to know you were outmatched."

"Oh, we were well aware of that," the young diviner responded and handed the box to him. "But I think I speak for all of us in saying that it was more stubborn pride than sense."

"It was Devol who finally forced him to flee," Asla noted

and gestured at the destroyed forest behind them. "His sword did that."

The Templar observed the damage and looked at the blade. "I see. Interesting." He looked the boy in the eyes. "You must have wanted to defeat her very badly."

He grimaced. "I did, but I would think that is normal in a life or death situation."

Vaust chuckled. "Sure enough, but there is a difference in wanting to win and simply not wanting to die." He frowned at the young Magi. "But I think you're confused. That was a woman."

"Nope." The diviner shook his head and grinned. "We'll explain later but trust me, she seems to be a he." His grin broadened when the Templar stared at him in bewilderment. "So, Vaust," Jazai began and pointed to his head. "What's going on with your hair?"

His two friends frowned when they noticed several dark streaks in the mori's silver hair. "It is nothing to worry about," he said and ran his hand through his locks. "It happens sometimes. For now, let us return to the village. I think we all need some rest."

Devol nodded, took Asla's arm, and put it over his shoulder. "Oh yeah. Without a doubt."

When they had returned, the town was in a tizzy. The residents had watched the fire blaze and then suddenly go out, and guards who went to investigate the incident said that a large section of the forest was now completely dead.

"A mori?" a surprised villager called. Vaust turned and

nodded politely. His hood was completely gone now, so he could not hide it at this point.

"Excuse me, you four!" a guard shouted and caught the group's attention. A small team approached. "You were seen coming out of the forest. Did you see what happened in there?"

Vaust held a hand out to stop the other three from speaking. "Indeed. We came across two evil Magi who were after this." He raised the box. "We dealt with them, but they used their powers openly. I'm sorry it caused such devastation to your beautiful forest."

"No kidding," a guard muttered before their leader shushed them.

"Do you have any descriptions?" the captain asked.

"One wielded a wand that produced and controlled fire," the mori began. "He called himself Salvo, had white hair, and wore a black jacket, boots, trousers, and sunglasses with red-tinted lenses. The other was a woman who—"

"It wasn't a woman," Devol interjected and drew the attention of the guards and another confused frown from the Templar. "Well, he appears to be a woman to some people, but his name is Koli and some type of illusion changes his appearance a little depending on who sees him. And he had a malefic."

"A malefic?" the guard shouted and Vaust twitched slightly. "Someone with a malefic was here?"

"Yes, sir." The young swordsman nodded. "But he has gone now. He teleported away."

"Far away," Jazai added.

The guard captain frowned and focused on the

Templar. "A malefic? If you were able to take on someone like that…" He looked at the box, then at the mori again. "Are you here on Templar work?" Vaust nodded and tucked the box behind him. "I see. All right, boys, let's continue the investigation and try to restore the peace."

The guards left them, but as they headed to the inn, they could hear some of them complain that they had let them off too easy. Their leader responded with things like, "Doesn't matter," and, "Nothing we can do anyway. Can't touch them." But one of the more irate comments from one of the men caught Devol's attention.

"Templars always bring curses with them."

CHAPTER THIRTY-TWO

Vaust hissed as he placed a large cloth soaked with some kind of wine-colored liquid over the burnt skin on his shoulder. Asla had finished applying ointment onto her feet and studied her bruised shoulder with a frown. Fortunately, Koli's knives had grazed rather than stabbed, but the injury was still surprisingly tender. Jazai currently nursed a bump on the back of his head that the Templar had given him after he mentioned that he couldn't tell what the difference was between burnt skin and normal skin on the mori.

"Is something bothering you, Devol?" the older man asked as he bound the cloth in place with a bandage. "You've seemed rather quiet since we returned."

"He could simply be tired," Asla interjected grumpily.

"It's not that," the boy admitted and slumped on one of the beds. "Well, I suppose I am, but I overheard the guards bickering when we left them. One of them said something that got to me."

"And what was that?" Vaust asked. "If it was a generic

insult, don't mind it. Many guards are rather foul-mouthed in this realm—at least that has been my experience."

"It was, but it wasn't about me. It was about you," he replied.

"Something to do with the evil mori?" The Templar chuckled and stretched his arm. "You should have been around a couple of hundred years ago. Almost everyone believed those rumors. In fact, much of your superstitious lore comes from early run-ins with mori before the realms were widely known—"

"It was more about the Templars," he said quickly. "They said Templars always bring curses with them."

Vaust tensed slightly, Asla looked away, and Jazai merely shrugged and flopped onto his back on the other bed. "If you stick around, you'll get used to that." The apprentice yawned. "Or simply lie. I mostly tell people I'm a busboy in a brothel. I get fewer angry looks that way."

The mori sighed as he took a red silk shirt out of his pack and put it on. "He is right—a smartass but a correct one."

"It balances things," the diviner quipped.

Devol recalled his first day at the order. "I remember Wulfsun telling me that the Templar had a dark past. It seems my life in Monleans was rather sheltered."

Vaust regarded him curiously. "What makes you say that?"

He sighed and gestured with a mixture of frustration and impatience. "All these things I'm unaware of. Like the malefic Koli wielded. Jazai and Asla knew what it was. Even the guards seemed to understand that it's important."

"Most try to suppress the knowledge of those objects,"

Asla pointed out. "It would not be too surprising for you to not know of them."

"Still, things get out," Jazai countered. "They may not exactly be taught about in most academies and schools, but malefic were a big deal several centuries ago. That information doesn't disappear as long as someone knows about it."

"And there are quite a few who know," Vaust muttered and sat beside the young swordsman. "Wulfsun is better at things like this than I am, but I'll give you the summary. You deserve that much after today."

Devol turned to examine the mori. He was still learning how to read him but even with what little he did know, he showed signs of remorse and sorrow.

"The malefics are based on majestics. You could probably tell that much," the Templar began and glanced at his kama where it rested against his bag. "Majestics weren't invented—not in the way we usually think of such things. There are many legends that try to reveal where they come from."

"Some say they were divine weapons of the Astrals, if you believe in them," Jazai interjected. "Others say they were a physical manifestation of the Mana or souls of legendary Magi, while some claim they were legendary weapons that became majestic over time after completing great tasks—like many heroes you hear about in stories." Vaust cast the apprentice an irritated look but the boy simply shrugged and shifted a little to get more comfortable. "Hey, I've heard this spiel from both my pops and Zier enough times to make it a paragraph rather than a two-hour lecture. I thought I'd help."

The mori relaxed and chuckled. "Fair enough. But no one is able to say for certain which of these tales, if any, are true. You would perhaps find scholars and archeologists who swear up and down that they could, but that's pride speaking."

"You have them in your realm as well, correct?" Devol asked.

Vaust nodded. "Indeed, all realms have majestics and their stories of what they are and where they came from. But your realm is rather unique, not only for having a plethora of them in comparison but quite a number of suitable wielders. Majestics are typically more hallowed in other realms and often with elaborate legends to the effect that those who can wield them are destined for greatness." He chuckled darkly. "We mori found out rather quickly that greatness is a personally defined term."

"I'm getting more familiar with majestics," Devol noted. "But what does this have to do with the malefics?"

The Templar sighed again and grimaced. "Right. I suppose I'm delaying. As I said, majestics cannot be made. Over the centuries, we have found ways to modify and even repair them but no one has been able to successfully make a weapon or object that compares to a majestic, although some good has come from trying."

"Like the exotics," he ventured.

"Correct," Vaust agreed. "But the idea of creating a majestic is something I'm sure a great number of people have been fascinated with ever since they learned about them all that time ago. That included a large number of Templars roughly five hundred and forty years ago, and they came the closest to success."

A NEW LIGHT

Asla perched on top of a dresser at the window of the room and gazed out as the mori continued his explanation.

"These Templars were able to craft magical weapons and items that could indeed match a majestic in power, but they were not equal. Majestics can only be wielded by certain people for various reasons, but malefics can be wielded by anyone regardless of their skill or power."

"Truly?" Devol asked. "But then they succeeded, in a way. They are more powerful if more people can use them."

"It's true that people don't like being left out of things," Jazai commented. "But sometimes, that is for the best."

Vaust straightened and pointed at the blade. "Tell me, Devol, even if your sword wasn't a majestic, would you hand it to a child?"

The boy studied the weapon where it glimmered faintly in its sheath. "I started training young, but I'm guessing you mean would I hand a deadly weapon to someone inexperienced?"

"Correct." The mori nodded. "Malefics also draw their power from their host exactly as a majestic does, but the user is nothing more than a supply of Mana to power the malefic. An inexperienced person may wield one for no more than a few minutes before dying, and even those who survive are...changed."

"A majestic's power is a focus, one that reveals the inner soul of the user. It calls you to power," Asla said as if quoting the lines of a book. "A malefic's power is like wine, sweet but corrupting. It tempts you to power." She looked at the others and the moonlight illuminated her eyes. "That is how madame Nauru once described it to me."

Vaust nodded again. "And some have given more than they could truly afford. Malefics not only take your Mana and potentially your life, but you must make a pact with one to use it at all."

"A pact?" Devol asked. "They can speak?"

"Not like you or I," the Templar corrected. "But in a sense, yes. It is like they plant ideas or thoughts in your mind. Every malefic has its own desires or needs." He ran a finger down his face. "I have heard about that mask before. It is referred to as the Demon Mask in common tongue and grants monstrous power to the wearer as you saw, but the price demanded is your sanity. In time, you become nothing more than a furious demon, wanting nothing more than to destroy."

Devol bit his lip, confused as to why would anyone make that trade. "If these malefics were so powerful, how have they not been used in wars, or—" He stopped himself as the mori gave him a grim look. "They have been, I guess."

"Almost since their very creation," Vaust confirmed. "The Templars tried to destroy them, but those who had made the malefics broke away from the order and created their own known as the Council of Numen. They believed that they had set a course for themselves to surpass the Astrals. The Templars fought in what is known as the Malefic War, which lasted over forty years and eventually destroyed the council. That would be the first part of what would lead to our current less than illustrious standing." He looked mournfully at the ceiling. "The second would be that they tried to hide their wrongdoing."

"But it wasn't the order's fault," the boy reasoned. "The

bad ones left, right? The Templars even fought them, so they shouldn't be held accountable."

"Some agree," the mori conceded. "And perhaps that is how they should have explained it back then. I could not tell you what they were thinking as this occurred about two centuries before I was born. But they tried to hide the evidence and burned many of the notes and sketches the malefic creators had left there. It is a pity as we could have used those nowadays, and they might have told us how we could destroy them."

"They can't be destroyed?" Devol questioned. The Templar pointed at Jazai, who rolled his eyes.

"Now he wants to tag me in." The apprentice chuckled but seemed pleased. "So majestics are an extension of their user. The wielder strives to bond and grow with their weapon and in the process, unlocks more power and the true nature of their majestic. But a malefic…" He extended an open hand and closed it slowly.

"It binds itself to its user—almost like a leech in a way," he continued. "Unless the wielder is powerful enough to wield it properly, it takes continually from them—Mana, sanity, and strength. The one real weakness of majestics is also their strength—their connection to their user. Malefic are…maybe not autonomous, but that connection is absent most of the time. If a majestic's user is killed while a strong connection is present, it can break or even lose its power. But a malefic, unless it is with a user who has found a way to truly subjugate it—you know, make the malefic their tool instead of vice versa—well, it simply keeps going."

"We've had some majestics that could destroy a malefic," Vaust added. "But even then, it wasn't safe. Their power runs deep, and when you destroy a malefic or majestic, that power erupts before it vanishes and can cause havoc before departing, which has cost us some brave Templars." He gestured to the box. "Which is why we hide them in a vault within the order that has a unique anchor point to a forgotten, desolate realm we simply know of as the abyss. We keep the recovered malefic there in a cavern that was discovered during a reconnaissance mission through that realm many years ago."

"If you do all this," Devol said thoughtfully, "why are there people who seem so suspicious of you?"

"Keeping secrets...well, it's a hard thing to do," the Templar admitted. "And even hints of one can breed rumors much worse than the secrets. On top of that, even after the Malefic War, the council had followers who escaped to spin the tale to the Templars themselves that they had created the malefics under orders from the grand master at the time and that their council was just and trying to stop their heresy."

He uttered another wicked, coarse laugh as he shook his head. "I don't think there are many who believe that now, but the damage was done. Malefics have wrought much pain and suffering over the centuries and their creation did stem from the order so over time, much of the anger and sorrow has been directed toward the Templars. But that is why we continue to move forward. Many in the order itself believe we need to make atonement, and we will continue our pledge until there is no order left, should it come to that."

Devol considered the explanation for a moment and

looked at his hands, then at his sword. "So stopping the malefics... That is the Templar's true duty?"

"We are Templars. We stop the wicked," Vaust stated. "And the malefics are an embodiment of that."

He nodded, stood, and looked directly into the mori's eyes. "Mr. Lebatt, I've made a decision."

CHAPTER THIRTY-THREE

"Well done, young Magi," Nauru said approvingly as Devol handed the box to the grand mistress. "I trust everything went well?"

He pressed his lips together and looked at his teammates, both of whom were unsure how to respond—much to the amusement of Vaust, who stepped forward in their place. "There were some complications, madame."

"I would suspect so," she said dryly, "given that you are with them instead of simply following them."

"Wait, he was tailing us the whole time?" Jazai whispered to the other two. "I never caught him. Did you guys feel anything?"

"Not at all," the young swordsman stated.

"I never felt him or saw him," Asla confirmed. "He is quite proficient at sneakiness."

"I can fill you in," the mori offered and sipped from his gourd. "I think the younglings should probably get a little rest now."

"Of course," the grand mistress said with a slight nod. "It was their first mission alone."

"Not alone if he was following us," Devol muttered.

"Honestly, when I think about what could have happened, I'm not as annoyed as I thought I'd be," Jazai told him.

"Same with me." Asla nodded.

"I am sure your mentors would love to see you again so feel free to take the day for yourselves," Nauru said with a soft smile and bowed to them. "Thank you for your help."

The three mirrored her gesture and each said a variation of, "You're welcome," as they stood and departed the room, talking excitedly with one another.

"What is your evaluation?" the Templar leader asked, her tone still playful and genuinely curious despite the more clinical question.

"They did far better than we could have hoped," Vaust admitted. "I did have to step in, but the box was briefly lost after the carrier was killed and they retrieved it."

"The carrier was killed?" She frowned as she looked at the plethora of flowers on the ceiling of her room. "I need to contact the hunter's guild, then, to tell them their comrade will not return."

"Don't worry about it. I'll take care of it," Vaust promised and folded his arms. "I think he had some other deliveries, but they were incinerated in the fight."

"I see you were pushed quite far," Nauru noted and toyed with her hair as she looked at him. "What happened?"

He grimaced as he recalled the fight. "It appears we

have new enemies—ones who seek the malefics themselves. They wore no insignia and didn't claim allegiance with any guild or council we are aware of. The man I fought did say they were working for someone but would not name names."

"I see. We should be mindful," she said, her voice calm. "It seems your opponent must have been powerful."

"It was more the location," the mori stated slightly defensively. "He wielded a majestic that conjured and manipulated fire, something of an advantage in the woods. But that also meant there was no one around, which allowed me to—" He traced the black lines in his hair. "Well, you know. Hopefully, they do not remain for much longer. I can't say I care for the look."

"You must not hate it too much." She chuckled. "You are one of the few who can truly harmonize with their majestic. It would reflect that if you wished it to."

Vaust simply shrugged as he crossed the room to sit on one of the larger chairs. "It might merely be something left from Myazma's previous wielder. It seems disrespectful to try to take it out."

"Well, that's very charming of you," Nauru said as she descended the stairs to her bed. "You said new enemies. What were the others?"

"One was a giant—some kind of golem I think," he explained as he began to unstrap his boots. "He referred to it as a ghoul and it appeared to be made of flesh."

"Blood Magic?" Her demeanor shifted to one of concern at the description.

"Potentially," he conceded reluctantly. "If it was, it was

quite advanced. More likely a majestic or malefic power." He ran a hand over his face. "It wore the Demon Mask."

"A golem?" She scowled, baffled by the revelation. "That is rather concerning."

"I very much agree." Vaust snorted as he took his boots off. "That is the only confirmed kill I have out of the mess. The last one was the fire mage's partner, who stole the box and the kids recovered it. I assume she is an assassin of some kind—although 'she' might be relative. Both the young diviner and I saw a woman, whereas Asla and Devon are adamant that she was a he. I suspect that Devol's majestic enables him to see the true form more clearly, which means 'he' is probably more appropriate although my mind constantly reminds me of what I saw, so it's somewhat confusing. From what they told me, she—he—told them that he has a rune that alters his appearance. On top of that, he also had a malefic."

"And they fought him?" Nauru's eyes widened in amazement.

"I believe the thief was holding back," he said thoughtfully. "It seems he regards fights as a sporting encounter. I couldn't get a good look at him in action, but he was able to detect me and shake me off. This isn't some run-of-the mill ruffian." He glanced at her. "Devol told me he has the Madman's Eye."

Nauru's eyes narrowed. "It seems logical, then, that he killed the count in the Britana Kingdom."

"And twenty-three of his men." Vaust reminded her. "The count was going increasingly mad so he was using it. Given that one of the prerequisites is to replace one of your eyes with it, I doubt he gave it up willingly."

"The count might not have been able to fully control the eye, but he had used it for over a decade so he was skilled." The grand mistress shook her head. "The assassin had no other malefic or majestic?"

"He didn't even have a spare exotic from what I could see. I suppose he might have had something before he acquired the eye but he doesn't seem to have it on him now."

"I'll have Wulfsun talk to Devol and see if he can get any more details." Nauru looked at the wall as if she were looking at someone through it. "Tell me, what do you think of the boy?"

Vaust leaned back and looked at the flowers. "He's earnest, certainly skilled with a sword, and adept at Mana arts."

"You know what I am asking." Nauru showed the first hint of annoyance. "Do you believe he is *his* son?"

"Of course," he stated calmly. "Why else would he have the other half of Chroma? And it's not like he would be able to use it otherwise."

"And in the field...did it resonate?" She turned to him, her gaze intent.

"It did some rather impressive things if that is what you are asking." He shrugged and continued. "He certainly doesn't have a hold of it yet—not like its power is easy to define. In fact, it might be worse if we try to explain it to him."

"I am aware of that." She sighed. "To think he did so much to try to keep him away from this life."

"That did not go as well as he probably hoped," Vaust

said thoughtfully. "It is not in our hands, though. He told me last night that he has decided to become a Templar."

Her eyes widened. "He did?"

The mori nodded and pointed in the direction in which the training area would be. "He's probably telling Wulfsun right now and asking if he'll be his mentor. He wanted to get everything in place before he asked you." He watched her curiously. "I told him I couldn't think of any reason why you would deny him entry, especially after such a good performance on the mission."

Nauru looked away with a sigh. "Do you think he'll be upset?"

"He never said anything to us about stopping his son should he find his way here," Vaust pointed out. "Only that he wanted him to have a choice."

"True." Nauru nodded, thinking back. "I don't think I've seen him in almost ten years. I don't know where he is or if he's even in this realm right now."

"We'll have to get a message to him," the mori said quietly. "I'm sure he'll want to know about this development. But he may still keep to himself. Ever since he went on his quest, he's mostly been a loner."

"Do you think Devol will find out?" she asked.

"I think everyone seems to be on the same page about keeping it quiet. I don't know about his parents—or the people who he thinks are his parents. They may be compelled to tell him the truth given this development."

"Most likely. It would be better to hear it from them than from us." She sighed, pushed to a seated position, and ran her hands over the dark-blue sheets. "Although I may be a little hesitant, I do feel a sense of joy."

A NEW LIGHT

"Oh?" he murmured. "About what?"

"We have three young recruits now," she said. "Jazai may whine but if he truly did not like it here, he would go to be with his father. Asla arrived due to unfortunate circumstances, but I have seen her come back to life slowly, especially during her week training with the other two. And now we have the son of the astral wanderer." She laughed softly. "I respect our order and care for everyone here, but it has been a while since we've had a new light for our path."

He smiled and nodded as he closed his eyes. "Agreed. Hopefully, they don't get into too much trouble."

"Yes, about that," Nauru began and looked at him with a twinkle of an idea in her eyes. "Given what happened during the mission, I would say it probably scales up to a red- or black-marked mission, wouldn't you agree?"

The mori's eyes jerked open and he straightened quickly and leaned closer to her. "Wait, what are you suggesting?"

"Well, they certainly are remarkable young Magi," she said calmly. "I believe that if they could succeed on a couple more missions like that, red at worst, that would qualify them, no?"

"Qualify?" he asked before realization struck and he pushed out of the chair. "Wait, you don't mean…"

"Why not? It is up to them, but I think they would do well in the Oblivion Trials."

Vaust's face wrinkled as he scowled in frustration. "How are you this insane and our leader?"

Nauru laughed. "That doesn't sound like a nice thing to say to your leader at all."

The two began to converse, the mori more heatedly as the night stretched on. Above them, amongst the garden of flowers in the grand mistress' bedroom, a small cluster of bloodflowers began to bloom.

BLOODFLOWERS BLOOM

The story continues with Bloodflowers Bloom, available at Amazon and through Kindle Unlimited.

Claim your copy today!

AUTHOR NOTES - MICHAEL ANDERLE
MARCH 25, 2021

Thank you for reading through this story to the author notes in back!

For those who know nothing about me, here is the 'introductory message' (I'll add more after this part).

A Bit About Me

I wrote my first book *Death Becomes Her* (*The Kurtherian Gambit*) in September/October of 2015 and released it November 2, 2015. I wrote and released the next two books that same month and had three released by the end of November 2015.

So, just at five years ago.

Since then, I've written, collaborated, concepted, and/or created hundreds more in all sorts of genres.

My most successful genre is still my first, Paranormal Sci-Fi, followed quickly by Urban Fantasy. I have multiple pen names I produce under.

Some because I can be a bit crude in my humor at times

or raw in my cynicism (Michael Todd). I have one I share with Martha Carr (Judith Berens, and another (not disclosed) that we use as a marketing test pen name.

In general, I just love to tell stories, and with success comes the opportunity to mix two things I love in my life.

Business and stories.

I've wanted to be an entrepreneur since I was a teenager. I was a very *unsuccessful* entrepreneur (I tried many times) until my publishing company LMBPN signed one author in 2015.

Me.

I was the president of the company, and I was the first author published. Funny how it worked out that way.

It was late 2016 before we had additional authors join me for publishing. Now we have a few dozen authors, a few hundred audiobooks by LMBPN published, a few hundred more licensed by six audio companies, and about a thousand titles in our company.

It's been a busy five years.

This series.

So, this story came out of 'the other guy' and I talking about different types of stories that are popular in Asia, and their interpretations here in the United States. For example, we spoke about manga, wuxia, and anime.

From there we spoke about the types of characters and stories we enjoyed in those genres.

So, here you are. This is the first book of a trilogy and we hope you like it.

If you do please review this book to help us know if we should continue or allow these characters a rest!

We look forward to your thoughts and wish you a great week or weekend!

Ad Aeternitatem,

Michael Anderle

BOOKS BY D'ARTAGNAN REY

<u>The Astral Wanderer</u>
A New Light (Book One)
Bloodflowers Bloom (Coming soon)
The Oblivion Trials (Coming soon)

BOOKS BY MICHAEL ANDERLE

Sign up for the LMBPN email list to be notified of new releases and special deals!

https://lmbpn.com/email/

For a complete list of books by Michael Anderle, please visit:

www.lmbpn.com/ma-books/

CONNECT WITH MICHAEL

Connect with Michael Anderle

Website: http://lmbpn.com

Email List: http://lmbpn.com/email/

Social Media:

https://www.facebook.com/LMBPNPublishing

https://twitter.com/MichaelAnderle

https://www.instagram.com/lmbpn_publishing/

https://www.bookbub.com/authors/michael-anderle

www.ingramcontent.com/pod-product-compliance
Lightning Source LLC
LaVergne TN
LVHW041620060526
838200LV00040B/1369